The Legend of Texas Gold

A Historical Fiction Novel
Based on the
Remarkable Life
of Karl Steinheimer

By John Kelley Jr.

ISBN: 979-8-9959993-1-7
Printed in the United States of America
First Edition

For My Kids –

May the timeless message be your
inheritance of the heart …

Adapt. Stay positive.

Love is always the answer.

You have what it takes!

Love, Dad

"For where your treasure is, there your heart will be also."
— Matthew 6:21

A Note From The Author—

As the saying goes, *I wasn't born in Texas, but I got here as soon as I could!*

My family moved to Dallas in 1969, when I was seven years old. Like so many before me, I fell under the spell of the Lone Star State—vast horizons, fearless past, stories that seem to resonate for generations. That fascination stayed with me, deepened over time, and even led me to teach seventh-grade Texas history for a few years.

Yet, it was not until my fifty-sixth year in Texas that I first encountered the name Karl Steinheimer—and the legend of his gold. I came upon it by accident, turning the pages of a book filled with scattered curiosities. There, in a few lines, was the outline of a life that refused to be forgotten:

A boy leaving Hamburg at eleven... A whispered connection to Jean Lafitte... A love found, then lost... A fortune made in Mexico... A rumor, overheard in a cantina, that she still lived—unmarried in St. Louis... A journey begun, but never completed... A deathbed letter... And somewhere in Texas, a buried fortune.

The details were fragmentary, almost reluctant. But the story lingered. I found myself wondering about the spaces between those facts—the choices, the hardships, the love that endured. It seemed to me a story not only about gold, but about what we carry, and what we leave behind.

This book is my imagining of what might have happened.

Like many who hear such legends, you may feel the quiet pull of possibility—the thought that *you* might be the one to find the buried treasure. Please be reminded that treasure hunting on private land is, of course, against the law.

The richest treasures, we all learn eventually, are not buried in the earth. They are carried forward—heart to heart—across generations.

Thanks for reading!   *Warmest regards, J.K.*

San Gabriel River Valley
Central Texas, Circa 1839

Prologue

Central Texas, 1839

The ground was harder than it looked. The ground in Texas is always hard.

Karl Steinheimer drove the shovel down again, metal striking hard earth with a dull crack that echoed past three slow-moving rivers. He paused, breathing through his teeth, and wiped the sweat from his brow with the back of his hand. Dust clung to his skin, mixing with blood from a cut along his knuckles.

He decided the hole was deep enough. He stood for a moment, listening. Wind moved through the tall grass in slow waves. The three men with him were silent. There was no obvious sign they had been followed. Still, Karl turned in a slow circle, scanning the horizon. Life had taught him that silence could hide truth.

At last, Karl turned and motioned for the men to drag the two chests closer. The wood on both chests was scarred from travel, iron bands worn but unbroken. He ran his hands along the top of the first chest. He didn't need to open it. He knew what lay inside—gold coins stamped with foreign kings, silver bars earned through an unwavering ability to adapt. Enough currency to change a man's life. He hoped his life would be the one to change.

Karl exhaled slowly as the other men helped him lower the crates one at a time. He was searching his feelings, hoping that burying the treasure would bring relief. Instead, it simply brought back childhood memories.

"This time," he said to himself, "nothing is taking it from me. I will find my way back." He lingered at the edge, looking down, before grabbing a shovel.

The three other men followed Karl's lead. Dirt fell fast at first, then slower as the hole filled. Each shovelful covered the past—layer by layer, choice by choice. When the last of the earth was packed flat, he stepped back and studied the ground.

The exact spot would remain unmarked. A giant oak tree with an iron spike, forty paces away, would be the marker.

Karl turned away, then stopped. A lifetime of memories washed in front of him. He pictured himself as a boy standing on a distant shore with his hands buried in the sand, certain that the precious shells he hid would still be there when he returned. Then, he saw himself as a young man burying treasure for Jean Lafitte in the banks near Barataria.

Karl let out a breath that almost became a laugh. "I was a foolish boy," he said quietly. "I hope I am not a foolish man."

The wind carried the words away. He looked once more at the tamped soil. This time, he thought to himself, the treasure will stay buried and I will return with the love of my life to enjoy the fruits of my labor.

Karl and his three remaining travel companions mounted their horses and began the journey north, each man certain that they would be back soon for the life-altering riches.

Chapter 1

Hamburg, Germany 1806

Karl Steinheimer stood barefoot on a dock piling along the River Elbe, arms stretched wide for balance, imagining the swell beneath him was open sea. No one watching would have guessed where that balance would lead. The wind pressed against his chest as if testing him. He leaned into it, refusing to step back.

"Careful," his brother Johann called from below. "You'll fall."

Karl grinned without turning. "Pirates don't fall."

"Pirates hang," Johann replied calmly. "Usually in public."

Karl jumped down, landing hard in the sand beside his older brother. Johann brushed charcoal dust from his fingers and looked down at his sketchbook. A swan rose from the paper with wings extended and neck arched toward some invisible horizon.

Karl briefly glanced at the sketch. "You draw it the same every time," he said.

"It's leaving," Johann replied.

"Does everything have to leave?" Karl asked. Johann looked at him then, gray eyes steady and said, "Some things are meant to leave."

Karl picked up a willow switch and practiced his sword fighting, each stroke more playful than fierce. He flicked the switch, knocking Johann's sketchbook into the sand. Johann lunged for it. Karl blocked him with a shove. For a heartbeat Johann bowed up, a sign that he might take a swing. Then he glanced at Karl's solid frame and thought better. He retrieved his book, brushed the sand from it, and said, "You won't always be the strongest."

Karl smirked triumphantly, a younger brother flexing his might, but only for a brief moment before an uneasy feeling emerged. He tried to make amends. "You draw it the same every time," he said, softer now. "Maybe it doesn't want to leave."

Johann brushed the sand away carefully. "That's how I see it." Karl crouched beside him, his bravado draining. He reached out without thinking and used the edge of his sleeve to clear sand from the paper. The drawing was not ruined, only blurred.

"You always make them look free," Karl said, after a pause. He kept his eyes on the page so Johann wouldn't see his sincerity. "Mine would look like they were falling." Johann glanced at him, surprised. The tension lifted. Karl straightened abruptly, as if embarrassed by his own admission, and reached into his pocket. He tossed a smooth white shell into Johann's lap. "For your swan," he said. "It needs a sea."

Karl—eleven now, sturdy as a deck beam—threw himself into his beach kingdom with unthinking devotion. He built towering sandcastles with deep chambers where he buried shells he deemed precious, always marking the spot with a stick. He called the shells his treasure, though the only true value they ever bought him was wonder.

Karl watched in silence as the tide crept back in to wash away his towers and carry his hidden treasures back to the sea. When the last tower crumbled, he knelt down to plan the next one. Karl Steinheimer never liked losing treasure.

Johann, two years older, moved differently, slipping into spaces rather than filling them. Their father Matthias Steinheimer, a harbor carpenter, possessed the same sturdy build as Karl, his hands shaped by rope and timber from years of working aboard the great sailing vessels that passed through Hamburg's port. Papa looked at Karl with a gleam of recognition of his own youth.

Despite his rough-hewn exterior, Papa was gentle with Mama and his boys. His hands were callused from rope and timber, yet he touched Mama's cheek as if afraid she might bruise. When the boys were little, he would often lift Karl onto his shoulders and pull Johann close beneath his coat, humming sailor tunes that exalted salt and pine pitch.

Papa said a man's work was not just earning coin. A real man showed his children how to labor without complaint and how to care for a woman without shame. "Strength isn't loud," he'd say, tapping Karl's chest with one broad finger. "If a man must shout that he's in charge, then he isn't." Papa always returned home from work with a laugh ready for his boys and a kiss ready for his wife. It seemed a kind of magic to Karl, that a man could be steel in the world and still turn soft at his own kitchen table.

Matthias often worked aboard foreign vessels—ships bound for London, Boston, even New Orleans. He claimed ships had no true homeland. Ships, he said, drifted to wherever money flowed. Karl listened with wide eyes, imagination soaring.

One night Matthias returned home with a lanky Englishman named Thomas Brackett, whose accent slid from Portsmouth to the Caribbean depending on the story he told. Brackett was boatswain aboard the *Mary Ellen*, a Boston brig that ran cotton and hides up the Atlantic coast. Mama insisted he stay for supper. German politeness could not be outdone even by the sea.

Brackett sat at their rough-cut table, cap in hand, as Mama ladled out steaming barley stew. Papa asked simple questions about weather and ports, but Brackett's replies carried the world with them. He spoke of fog choking the Thames until ships felt their way upriver by bell. He mentioned cocoa-dark harbors in the Indies where mosquitoes sang and sailors swore they could feel gold in the air.

Karl ate slowly, his spoon suspended half the time as his mind chased Brackett's words from one corner of the globe to the next. Thomas noticed and grinned.

"Your boy's got a sailor's ears," he said to Papa. "Never misses a word of a good yarn. That's the first sign, mark me."

Papa chuckled, though his eyes veered toward Mama, who pretended not to hear.

After supper they moved to the stove for warmth. Brackett described tar boiling on decks, cannon lashed tight against a rising swell, and the way a ship leaned into the wind like a horse that knew the road home.

Karl drank in every breath as if it were nectar. He'd never seen the horizon from the deck of a ship, but he could almost feel the planks shifting beneath his feet.

When Brackett finally stood to leave, Matthias clapped him on the back. Karl followed them to the door, half-hoping the Englishman would offer him a berth on the spot. Instead Brackett only winked and said, "Mind your letters, lad. The sea takes fools quick and scholars slower."

Then he vanished into the cold Hamburg night, leaving Karl staring after him, thinking not of school or chores, but of faraway ports with names that tasted wonderful on the tongue. He had wanted to ask the man about pirates, but never got the chance with Mama in the room.

Karl lingered by the window until Mama's voice broke his stare. "Enough, my dear," she said. "The night will not bring another ship to our door." He did not move for a moment, eyes still turned toward the dark.

Later, when Karl had gone to bed, Mama sat at the table with her knitting. The needles clicked, slow and thoughtful, while Papa drank his coffee in silence.

"He listens too hard," she said at last.

Papa exhaled. "He's a boy. Boys listen to stories."

Mama set her knitting aside. "Stories are harmless. The sea is not."

Papa waved a hand, half-dismissive. "Plenty of lads dream of the sea. Most stay put."

Mama didn't argue further, but her gaze drifted toward the boys' closed bedroom door. She recognized the look on Karl's face tonight, the hunger for somewhere else.

Before putting out the lamp, Mama whispered a small prayer that her youngest son would keep his feet on solid earth, and that the wind and salt would pass him by. In the dark of his room, Karl lay awake, imagining a ship's wake glowing like a comet in the night.

To her lasting credit, Karolina, Mama to the boys, was tireless in her encouragement of both her husband and her sons. She saw to it that two truths were woven into the fabric of their days: honest work gave a man dignity, and gratitude was a discipline, not a feeling.

Papa taught hard work by simply living his life. Mama took the lead on the counting of blessings until the boys absorbed it as routine.

On evenings when Matthias returned late and the sea wind knocked at the door, the boys would complain that other families ate meat twice a week or wore boots without patches. Mama would set tin bowls of stew before them—thin, yes, but warm—and tap gently on the table with her spoon.

"List them," she would say.

"List what?" Karl would grumble, even though he knew her meaning.

"Blessings," she replied, matter-of-fact. "Three. No sighing."

So the boys would comply, Johann reluctantly, Karl with rolled eyes.

"Papa came home," Johann might offer. "Mama's stew didn't burn," Karl would add resignedly, which always won him a raised eyebrow. "And we have a roof that keeps out most of the rain," Mama would finish.

It became a quiet ritual, so familiar the boys barely noticed when it anchored their moods after hard days. Mama believed blessings counted aloud settled a restless spirit. In a neighborhood bordering the docks, restless spirits were abundant.

Karolina was not physically imposing like her husband, yet she possessed a presence that filled a room more effectively than strength. She was slim with a quiet grace that made neighbors describe her as "delicate," though anyone who watched her manage a household knew better.

Papa worked six days a week. Sundays found the Steinheimers in Mama's refuge, St. Catherine's Church, built in 1256 A.D., its spire rising heavenward and providing solace and hope for the harbor community. Mama believed its walls held answers strong enough to shape boys into good men. Her life's ambition was simple and unwavering. Her sons would grow to know God and walk uprightly in the world.

For Karl, Sundays stirred a particular disquiet. He would sit between Mama and Johann, stiff in his wool coat, watching dust float in stained-glass light. Karl listened. He even tried to care the way Mama wished. But his mind betrayed him with images of pirates and gold and sleek ships and Papa swinging a sword while shouting orders. Each image glowed with color, while the sermons felt gray and distant.

After service, Mama regularly marched the boys past the scripture posted on the vestibule board. "Store not up treasures on earth where moth and rust destroy," she would say. Karl nodded dutifully, but could not help wondering if maybe treasures beneath the sand, hidden from moths and rust, were of a different category entirely.

After supper, Papa often entertained the boys with rambunctious stories, tales that grew larger than sermons in Karl's mind. Casting a long shadow across the kitchen wall, Papa would raise a pretend sword and declare, "I am Klaus Störtebeker, the great pirate of the Baltic Sea. Give me your loot or you shall meet the business end of Old Betsy!" The boys laughed and cheered. Mama smiled too, though she worried that pirates and pulpits were poor companions.

Mama preferred Martin Luther's teaching that forgiveness could never be bought. She believed renewal was delivered through repentance. She wanted her sons to be filled with the fruits of the spirit—love, joy, peace, patience, kindness, goodness, faith, gentleness, self-control.

Goodness, she felt, carried many of the others along with it.

Karl tried to make sense of goodness while his thoughts chased adventure. When Mama taught that faith was stronger than steel, Karl believed her. When Papa described Störtebeker felling ten men in a single clash, Karl felt the thrill in his blood.

Karl would kneel by the family Bible and trace the verse Mama kept open: *For the love of money is a root of all kinds of evils...* Even then, he could not quite banish visions of glittering bracelets stretched around city walls or golden masts gleaming in moonlight.

Naturally, the wonder of adventure sometimes splintered, with Mama's words threatening to swallow Karl's dreams. One weekday afternoon, the boys were sent for bread, a regular errand for the brothers. Karl balanced along the harbor pilings, imagining himself crossing a swaying gangplank to join a crew. Suddenly, a drunk sailor cursed and smashed a bottle against the dock, wobbling Karl and his dream. Was this the real face of adventure? Men staggering, bleeding, and shouting?

Before Karl could retreat, another figure stepped from the shadows—a tall, wiry man with sun-baked skin. He caught the drunken sailor by the shoulder, murmured a few quiet words, and sent him staggering toward the tavern.

The stranger turned to the boys and smiled.

"Name's Nathaniel Harwood," he said, tipping his battered hat. "Friend of our friend here, though I prefer my afternoons sober." His voice carried the ease of someone used to being listened to. "You boys look like you've got the sea in your bones already."

Karl hesitated only a second. "Is he a pirate?" he blurted, pointing after the drunken sailor. Johann stiffened. "Karl—"

Harwood smiled wider. "No," he said. "Just a fool with too much rum and not enough sense." He studied Karl for a moment. "Why? Are you hoping to meet a pirate?"

Karl didn't answer right away. Then, quieter—"Are you a pirate?"

Johann shot him a look.

Harwood chuckled, low and amused. "That depends on who's asking." He crouched slightly, bringing himself closer to Karl's height. "There are men who call anyone a pirate if he takes what they think belongs to them."

Karl leaned in. "So you know pirates?"

Harwood's gaze moved toward the harbor, where the masts swayed against the gray sky. "I've known men who fly no flag," he said. "Men who don't ask permission. Men who take gold from places it was never meant to stay." He looked back at Karl. "Some call them pirates. Some call them something else."

Karl felt something spark in his chest.

"Do you want to know what the sea is really like?" Harwood asked.

Karl nodded before Johann could speak. "There are ports," Harwood said, his voice lowering, "where gold slips quietly from the pockets of kings into the hands of men brave enough to take it. Chests unlocked at midnight. Coins clinking in dark warehouses. Guards asleep while fortunes change hands."

Karl's imagination leapt. He could almost feel the weight of coins in his hands—the cold certainty of them. Not shells. Not pretend.

Johann kept his gaze steady, studying Harwood as if he were a merchant with hidden terms. "Sounds like trouble," he muttered.

Harwood caught it and smiled. "Trouble? Maybe. Or maybe the world is just waiting for boys like you to learn how it works." His eyes returned to Karl. "One day, you might even join men like that—if you've the stomach for it."

He straightened, dusting his hands. "Gold," he said softly, "has a way of slipping through the fingers of men who are too afraid to reach."

The words settled deep. For a fleeting moment, Karl imagined walking home with something heavy in his pockets. Something real. Something that might make Mama stop counting. His pulse quickened.

Nathaniel Harwood tipped his hat and turned, disappearing into the maze of warehouses and masts.

Karl stood still, listening. The harbor sounded different now. Louder. Alive.

Johann tugged his sleeve. "Come on," he said. "Let's get the bread before Mama worries." Karl followed, but not before glancing once more toward where Harwood had vanished. His mind was still at sea, imagining following the wiry stranger he had just met into storms and distant ports. Would he ever be brave enough?

Mama's steady counsel and the seductive legend of Störtebeker drew against one another inside him, their opposing forces breeding a storm. He adored Mama and wanted her approval. He sensed, even at age eleven, that goodness and greatness did not always follow the same path. He hoped, as boys do, that the world might someday allow him both.

That night, beneath a thin blanket, Karl tried to pray as Mama instructed. He asked God if adventure was wicked or simply misunderstood. Could a boy be both good and daring? Could he please Mama and chase budding dreams? No answer came, but the questions lingered.

Johann heard Karl whispering and said with a giggle, "You'd make a terrible pirate."

"Why do you say that?" Karl asked.

"You would miss us too much," Johann replied. "You would beg to come back home."

Karl smiled. Maybe Johann was right. But that didn't mean he couldn't dream.

Karl reached beneath his pillow and drew out two smooth shells he'd pocketed from the beach, his secret "gold." He liked knowing exactly where they were hidden. He pressed the shells into his palm as if testing the weight of treasure.

Somewhere beyond the dark, ships were rising and falling with the tide. He felt the pull. It was stronger than a wish. He wondered if such longings were planted by God Himself, set deep in the hearts of boys meant to explore.

He did not yet know how far that call would carry him… but he could hear it.

Chapter 2

Karl stood at Mama's elbow, staring at the lone dark loaf the baker slid toward them. Mama no longer allowed the boys to buy bread unaccompanied. She needed to make certain her family received fair value for their hard-earned coin. "Price went up again," the man said without apology.

War did not arrive in Hamburg with drums and bayonets. It crept in through bakery doors. The shelves were thin, the loaves smaller than yesterday, and Mama's coins looked tiny against the counter's worn wood.

Mama counted her copper once, twice, three times. A crease formed between her brows. "That's all we have," she whispered. The baker hesitated, then pushed the loaf closer. Karl saw Mama's fingers tremble as she paid, and saw how quickly her eyes darted in hope that he hadn't noticed.

Out on the street, Johann pretended to be absorbed in sketching gulls along the pier, but even he couldn't ignore the shouting between sailors and merchants, voices cracking over food and survival.

The advance of war continued, eventually kicking down Hamburg's door and ripping through Karl's childhood fantasies with reckless speed. Mama's cherished idealism wore thin, too, threads loosening one by one.

By 1806 men spoke Napoleon's name like a storm overhead. The British owned the sea. The French owned everything else. Karl only understood that fewer ships meant fewer coins, and fewer coins meant Mama counting twice.

Rumors multiplied, first as whispers, then as headlines. Prussia was mobilizing and Hamburg would not remain untouched. Mama's prayers grew more frequent. Papa began listening instead of talking at supper. Karl caught himself doing the same, waiting for words from Papa that never came.

At the docks, sailors spoke in low tones. Even the most optimistic shopkeepers admitted that Napoleon's reach had grown too large to ignore. Karl absorbed the way grown men glanced over their shoulders, the way Mama folded her hands too tightly, the way Papa's face flattened when the topic of military service surfaced.

Matthias had never been one to stand idle when principles were at stake. Napoleon's rise stirred something fierce in him—disdain for the little French emperor who treated German lands as prizes to be rearranged at his pleasure.

Papa returned one afternoon with a quiet resolve about him. He had signed his name at the mustering office to enlist with the Prussian forces. Voluntarily.

Boldness, some called it. Recklessness, others whispered.

Papa had tired of living with an unknown future tied to the decisions of others. He thought a man should choose his own destiny.

Mama stood in the doorway, dish towel in hand, staring as though she could somehow erase the ink of his signature. She pleaded with him to leave such matters to kings and generals. She clung to his sleeve, eyes wet with fear that war would swallow the Steinheimers as it had swallowed so many families already.

Beneath the immediate fear of war lived another fear that haunted Mama's mind but she never voiced aloud. Would she be enough for the boys if Papa did not return? She sensed she could keep them clean and fed, teach them verses and manners, but would that make them men? Who would sharpen them, correct them, steady them? The thought alone emptied the color from her face.

"The boys need their father," she whispered to Papa.

Papa set his cap on the peg and exhaled slowly. "They need to know their father stood for something when it mattered," he said. "I won't have them believe a tyrant gets to choose their future." Johann looked away, uncertain of this version of Papa. Karl seemed to understand that Papa had crossed a threshold. Men sometimes cross thresholds without permission. Or applause.

Weeks later, Papa's battalion, destined to reinforce the Prussian Army, was scheduled to depart Hamburg in early October and travel by way of the River Elbe, then continue toward the River Saale by barge. Rumor suggested the French were gathering near Jena. No one knew for certain, news moved slower than fear, and every dockworker had an opinion.

Though the boys had begun to outgrow bedtime stories, on the night before Papa's departure, they requested a complete retelling of the Klaus Störtebeker saga. Papa obliged, partly to amuse them, partly to stiffen his own courage.

"To your knees, you cowardly Frenchmen!" he began, dancing with an imaginary sword. "You have met the mighty Steinheimer, descendant of Störtebeker, and now your demise is certain! I have inherited Störtebeker's courage and ability, and I shall surely defeat you!"

Johann and Karl beamed, and a twinkle appeared in Papa's eye. The look on Mama's face was revealing. The future had dimmed.

Papa continued with unbridled animation. "I will garner the same wealth as Störtebeker," he declared. "I too will build masts of gold!"

Legend has it that the masts of Störtebeker's ships were filled with precious minerals—gold, silver, and copper. Karl dreamed of the life he might lead if he possessed unlimited treasure. Treasure was always safer when it found a new location.

Mama held her tongue and forced slight optimism on her face. On some level she understood that men were created for adventure, even if adventure sometimes resembled fantasy.

"I will be revered by men and loved by women!" Papa boasted. Mama shot him a glance that suggested he tone down the part about women.

"Papa, tell us the end of the story!" Karl pleaded.

Papa hesitated briefly. The outcome was grim, but one more retelling seemed harmless, perhaps even fitting.

"After a great battle in which his men were outnumbered ten to one, Störtebeker was captured," Papa continued. He described how the grand pirate was convicted of piracy in Hamburg and sentenced to death by beheading alongside seventy-three of his men. Mama cringed.

Papa quoted Störtebeker: "My crimes are petty compared to what our senate does, but I am willing to bargain. Spare my life and I shall give the city a solid gold bracelet so long that it will encircle Hamburg!" The senate declined, figuring they would claim the gold without negotiation.

With death imminent, Störtebeker made a second offer. "Execute me first," he said, "and any man I walk past must be freed." The senate saw no harm. How far could a headless man walk?

The next day Störtebeker met his demise. Then, against all sense, rose and walked past eleven men before a stunned sentry tripped him. The boys cheered at the thought of the fearless pirate sparing his comrades.

Conversely, war left no space for grand stories. Papa's departure came the next morning, before the sun had fully lifted over the river. The family walked together to the docks, the cobblestones damp beneath their feet. No one seemed sure what to say. Words felt either too small or too large for the hour.

At the pier Papa crouched so he was level with Karl and Johann. The wind tugged at his hair while sailors shouted orders up the wharf. "You're wondering why your Papa must go," he said, not judging, just knowing.

Karl's throat burned, but he said nothing. Papa rested a hand on Karl's shoulder, another on Johann's. "Sometimes a man has to make choices that don't feel kind," he said softly. "I have to make sure you boys have a future worth growing into."

He looked toward the ship, toward the stacks of powder. "Sometimes a man has to fight. When the war is done, the men who fought will have something to show for it. A man can't just stand still and hope the world is gentle. Because it's not."

Johann clung to his coat. Karl finally found his voice. "But why you?"

Papa smiled, and brushed Karl's hair off his forehead. "Because I'm strong enough to go, and because I love you enough to make the hard choice. If I stay, we get by. If I go, maybe you have a better life. I'm leaving because I want what's best for you."

Papa kissed Johann's crown, pressed his forehead briefly to Karl's, and then turned before any of them could see the tears he refused to let fall.

Soldiers were gathering their packs, adjusting straps and shifting their weight as they prepared to board. Karl spotted Papa's canvas bag on the cobblestones and, without asking, bent to lift it. He wrapped both hands around the straps and heaved. The bag barely budged. A flush crawled up his neck as he tried again, teeth clenched, shoulders tensed.

Papa stepped in with a quiet smile and lifted it with one arm. "Not yet," he said, as though the failure were merely a matter of timing rather than strength. The words stung. Not yet meant someday. But someday suddenly felt worlds away.

Karl wanted to say he would manage it soon, that he would grow, that Papa could count on him. He said nothing. He hated that strength was always measured in what a man could carry.

When it was his time to board, Papa knelt in front of Karl and placed a rough hand on his shoulder. "Take care of Mama," he said, not as a suggestion, but a duty. Karl couldn't speak. He did not know how to take care of anyone. He couldn't even help Papa lift his bag. He nodded anyway.

Papa rose, but Karl didn't let the moment pass. His hand lingered on Papa's sleeve, fingers tightening as if courage might be squeezed from cloth. "Papa," he said, the word catching in his throat. "What if I can't?" Papa studied him, not as a boy to be instructed, but as a son standing on uncertain ground. Karl pressed on, the truth tumbling out. "Everything is changing. I don't know who I'm meant to be without you here."

Papa's mouth softened in recognition. He glanced toward the waiting barges, the world already moving on without them. Then he looked down at Karl.

"Neither do I," he said. "War has a way of rearranging the world." He set both hands on Karl's shoulders now, steady and warm. "You do two things. You adapt. And you stay positive."

Karl frowned slightly, as if testing the weight of the words. "Adapt," Papa repeated, tapping Karl's chest. "Because standing still will break you.

And stay positive," he added, quieter now, "because despair is a luxury no one can afford."

The whistle blew. Papa drew him into a brief, fierce embrace. "This is our new reality, son," he said against Karl's hair. "We'll both meet it the same way." Karl stepped back, the phrase settling deep—*adapt, stay positive*—a compass handed over without a map.

Johann stood with his sketchbook clutched to his chest, eyes wide and dry. He didn't cry, not because he was brave, but because the meaning had not yet settled in him.

"Do you have your promise with you?" Karl asked immediately before Papa boarded. Papa slid a folded piece of paper from his pocket, just enough to confirm it was still there. He saw three signatures, Johann's cramped handwriting, Karl's uneven one, and his own deliberate script. "I promise I will return," the boys had written in large letters above the signatures.

The boys made two copies of the promise, one for them to keep and one for Papa to take. All three of them had signed both copies. The night they had signed the promise, Papa had kissed their foreheads and swore he would return. A foolish oath for any man in uniform, yet Papa knew there was no other answer he could have given while the boys watched him with the kind of faith that made lying feel like love.

Papa had told Mama the boys needed to know their father was not afraid. Now he prayed they would never see him shaking like this. He walked onto the barge. He did not wave. He faced forward as the barge pushed off, shoulders square to whatever waited downriver. Karl calmed himself by imagining this is how Störtebeker departed on voyages. Face forward. Shoulders square.

The walk home was mostly silent, each of them measuring the morning—and mourning—in their own way. Karl did not feel brave, but he did not feel as small as he once had. Somewhere between the docks and the front door, childhood loosened its grip.

Mama steeled herself enough to break the silence. "Now is a good time to count our blessings. This time, I'll go first. I am thankful for you boys and for the love of Papa. He is a strong, capable man. I look forward to his embrace when he returns."

The moment sailed past Johann, who declared, "I am thankful I have another book with blank pages. I can't wait to fill them up."

Karl understood better. "I am thankful for Mama," he said. "She is the best and wisest Mama in the world. I know we are in good hands until Papa returns."

"And I'm thankful we are descendants of Störtebeker," Karl added. "Papa's fighting skills will amaze the French. They'll flee for Paris by Monday!"

Mama allowed a small smile. "It hasn't been proven that we are related to Störtebeker," she said, though for once she seemed willing to believe in pirate lineage. She wanted Papa to have every advantage possible.

Suddenly, Karl stopped. The reality of what just transpired tightened his chest. For a moment he saw it all at once: Papa alone on a battlefield among strangers, the family sitting at the table with three bowls instead of four. The fear came quick and sharp. He bent forward, hands braced on his knees. Johann turned back to stand beside him.

Karl did not look up. He stared at the cobblestones. He could feel a spiral. What-ifs stacking on top of each other like crates ready to fall.

No. He couldn't let it happen.

He straightened carefully and did what Mama had trained them to do when their thoughts ran ahead of truth. He named what was certain. The church spire still rose high into the sky. The river moved as it always had.

Papa had boarded the barge standing tall.

He drew one slow breath. Then another. Johann watched him from the corner of his eye. He saw the moment Karl's shoulders lowered. Saw the slow, deep breaths. Saw his younger brother choose steadiness. Johann said nothing.

He simply matched Karl's pace when he started walking again. Both were relieved Mama, caught up in her own fears, had not noticed a lag.

It was then that Karl redirected the walking route. His first attempt at taking care of Mama came in the form of choosing a path home that would guide them near the waterway where trumpeter swans gather, their white feathers gleaming against the gray tide.

The presence of swans brought an unmistakable joy to Mama, and the delight was rooted in old Hamburg lore. Generations had spoken of swans as symbols of peace and freedom, creatures that graced the waters only when the city enjoyed calm and prosperity. To see them gather was to believe that, even in uncertain times, life could still hold beauty and promise.

Karl knew this folklore well, and he recognized joy in Mama's face every time they paused at the wharf to take in the scene. For a moment at least, on the most trying day in family history, Mama and Johann and Karl basked in peace beside the river, drawn in by creatures that promised brighter days yet to come. Karl hoped Papa would be proud of him for thinking of the swan-filled path home.

Fittingly, Mama's most prized possession was a small wooden swan Papa had carved for her before the boys were born. The swan sat in elegance beside the family Bible. Whether or not real swans brought peace, Karl sensed this little carving brought a certain serenity to Mama.

The swan was carved from a dense, dark wood, the grain so tight it felt heavier than it looked. Papa had shaped the neck in a graceful arc, so that the head bowed as though in quiet thought. The wings bore delicate scoring that suggested feathers caught in a breeze. To Karl, it looked like a living thing caught in stillness, a token of Papa's devotion and Mama's hope, guarding a corner of their humble hearth like a quiet protector.

Finally at home, Mama went straight to the Bible without removing her shawl. She flipped past the genealogies with a practiced thumb, eyes searching for a verse that might steady her. Whatever she found did not seem to soothe her spirit. Her brow raised and the page trembled faintly beneath her fingers.

Closing the book, she pressed her lips together and slipped the wooden swan into her dress pocket, as though it were a guardian angel. Karl watched from the doorway, unsure whether the swan was meant for comfort or courage. He sensed Mama was wrestling with words that demanded trust when trust felt elusive.

The days after Papa's departure passed unevenly. Some moved quickly, filled with tasks and forced optimism. Others dragged, heavy with waiting. Mama kept the house orderly, as though neatness might summon Papa home. "We will not believe any news we hear until it reaches our doorstep," Mama said daily, her words echoing in the small home.

Karl lay awake each night listening for boots on cobblestone, repeating Papa's words like a vow he wasn't sure he understood. *Adapt. Stay positive.* He whispered them into the dark until they sounded less like comfort and more like a challenge. He did not know who he was meant to become or how he might adapt. He did know that he would now have to stand taller in the house.

The river had carried his father away. One day, he suspected, it would call him too.

Chapter 3

Winter came early to Hamburg that year. Frost clung to thatched roofs and turned the fields stiff under a sky the color of pewter.

In the Steinheimer house the hearth burned steady and the shutters stayed bolted against the wind. Johann and Karl hauled wood twice a day, breath fogging, fingers burning. At night Mama mended by the fire, eyes twitching toward the door whenever a gust rattled it—half expecting a knock, fully afraid of one.

Papa's promise note lived on the kitchen shelf, a single sheet of paper sealed with careful signatures. Every day Karl took it down and read it. Before putting it back, he whispered the line aloud. After weeks, the words came thin and frayed: *I promise I will return.*

Karl hadn't known ink could wound. The letter began to sting behind his eyes. He thought he noticed the ink on Papa's name beginning to fade.

Johann would shake his head. "We shouldn't have made him sign it. A soldier can't promise something like that." Karl had no answer. His anger had turned inward at himself for believing a piece of paper could pull a man safely from a battlefield.

It was mid-November when word finally came. A courier arrived at dusk, cloak pulled tight and boots white with frost. Mama opened the door with the boys pressed close behind her.

"From the Kingdom's postal office," he said, handing over a sealed packet. "By direction of the War Ministry."

Mama thanked him in a voice barely there. The house went still. She stared at the black wax seal stamped with the Prussian eagle, holding it as if it might cut her. Karl felt his stomach twist. Johann sniffed beside him. They opened it by candlelight, shadows shaking across the parchment.

To Frau Steinheimer,

We regret to inform you that your husband, Musketier Matthias Steinheimer…

The rest was orderly. Cold. Condolences from men who had never seen Papa's face, or his laugh, or the way he carved toys for the boys when wood was spare. Mama read until her voice cracked. Then she folded over the table like someone struck from behind. Karl touched her back, unsure whether to speak. The letter blurred in his vision until the ink looked wet again. Outside, the wind banged the house as if winter wanted inside.

Papa's note of promise remained on the shelf the next day, the ink neat and certain, like it had not yet heard the news. Johann stared at it a long time. Karl couldn't look at it at all.

"What good is a promise if it dies?" Johann said, voice cracking on the last word. He snatched the letter from the shelf. Karl didn't stop him. Didn't say a word. The anger in the room breathed on its own. Johann folded the page once, twice—hard creases like he meant to hurt the paper —then shoved it into the stove box.

The letter resisted the flame. Karl watched Johann strike the tinder again, hands focused, until the flame licked the corner. Karl's eyes welled with tears as he saw Papa's signature curl in flame. He didn't speak until the signature vanished in ash. "He didn't lie," Karl whispered, throat burning. "He just… couldn't keep it." Johann slammed the stove door. "Same thing."

Afterward, neither boy looked at the shelf where the letter had lived. Mama never asked where or how the promise letter vanished. She only dusted the empty place.

Two more long weeks passed before the second letter came—rough-edged and tied with twine instead of sealed with wax. It was from Sergeant Mohr. Mama unfolded it at the table. Her voice trembled at first, but steadied as she read. Mohr did not write like a clerk. He wrote like a man with dirt under his nails and grit in his throat.

He said Matthias had not fallen running or afraid, but holding the line along a muddy embankment where smoke was so thick Mohr could not see his own hands. He wrote that before the musket ball struck him, Matthias had dragged a wounded soldier up the slope. He wrote that he did not suffer long, and that his last words were for his wife and boys, spoken low so the younger soldiers would not frighten. He comported himself with honor, the letter read, and gave heart to younger men. We buried him at day's light. I prayed for him, and for you.

Mama stopped there. The letter slid onto the table. Johann stared at the floorboards. Karl held his breath, afraid to move in case something delicate in the air shattered. Mohr's letter stayed on the table long after Mama stopped reading. Johann wouldn't meet anyone's eyes. Karl stared at the words *last words were for his wife and boys*, and felt his body tremble.

When Mama finally left the room, Johann leaned close and whispered, "He tried… even at the end. He was a hero. We shouldn't have burned the letter we made him sign. We should have kept it. For Mama.

For him." Karl didn't answer at first. His throat scraped dry. "He didn't lie," he said finally. "He did come back. Not the way we wanted."

Johann placed Mohr's letter in the Bible. They both looked at the stove—closed, heavy, quiet. Karl imagined sifting the ashes for a piece of Papa's handwriting, some scrap of the promise. They had fed the fire well and too many days had passed. Nothing remained. Karl wished fiercely for the promise letter back, not to believe it, but to honor the man who signed it.

The spirit of the house shifted in ways Karl couldn't yet name. Mama no longer cried like she had the day the first letter came. Instead she moved through rooms, uncertain of what belonged where. The quiet was sharper. Even the tasks felt different—hauling wood, carrying water— everything heavier without Papa's shadow in the doorway.

At night, Karl saw Mama kneel beside her bed, shoulders shaking. Not praying. Not exactly. It looked like trying to speak and finding no words at all. Karl hovered in the hallway, afraid to interrupt, afraid to leave, afraid of what she might be saying without sound.

On Sundays they walked to the chilly church together. Pastor Linde spoke of suffering, shaping through trials, and God's will. Mama stared at the pastor with eyes that glistened but did not soften. She no longer sang the final hymn. She slipped out early, gripping the boys' hands too tightly. The house was fatherless now and quieter where faith had once lived.

Spring thawed the fields. Grief stayed frozen.

One morning Mama found Karl behind the barn, fists slamming into a tree trunk until the bark was slick and his knuckles bled. "I am not Father," he hissed when she touched his shoulder. "And I cannot be him." Mama knelt and kissed his torn hands. "No one asked you to," she whispered. "You only have to remain you." The words, though encouraging, didn't steady either of them.

That night, after the boys slept, Mama sat at the hearth with Mohr's letter in one hand and the black-sealed notice in the other. She tried to pray. The prayer never came. The language of faith had left her. She lit a candle instead. At last she folded both letters and whispered into the empty room, voice raw as scraped wood: "Lord, I cannot raise them alone."

Help arrived two weeks later in the form of Franz, one of Mama's brothers, who burst through the door in a gust of salt and spring air. He stayed two nights. He saw the thin stores, the French patrols, the way Mama's face had gone hollow, and he said: "You're coming with me. All of you. Gardelegen has work and bread. We leave tomorrow."

Mama agreed at once. Johann nodded too. Karl didn't. He just stared at the floorboards. It felt wrong, adults deciding the future of a family in two sentences. Hamburg was where Papa worked, where the harbor smelled like tar and fish and adventure. Gardelegen sounded like a cough.

Franz lacked Papa's size and tried to make up for it in volume. He entered rooms like a man announcing ownership. He had burst into Papa's house carrying himself the way Papa once warned against: "A real man doesn't need everyone to know he's in charge," Papa had said during some quiet evening by the stove. "The moment he tries to prove it, he's already lost."

Karl remembered that now, watching Franz. He felt a tightness in his chest that had nothing to do with hunger. Papa had been rough around the edges, salt-rough, but his affection was easy to spot. You never wondered if Papa loved you. He built that certainty with his hands and voice every single day.

Watching Franz now, Karl realized he felt no such certainty. Instead he sensed rules, corrections, and something brittle that looked like control based on fear. He was missing Papa in a new and even more aching way, if that was possible.

After supper, Franz brought in wood from the yard and stacked it beside the hearth. He talked about fields and cows you could milk every morning. Johann's eyes followed him around like a dog's. Karl folded his arms and glared at the fire until the colors blurred. Franz noticed. "There's honest work there, Karl," he said. "Work that builds a roof and keeps a family fed."

Karl kicked at the wood basket. "Papa worked near the sea. That's real work." Franz straightened, eyes narrowing. "Real because you've seen it?" Karl lifted his chin and said, "Real because real men work at sea." The words came too fast, sharpened by resentment, and the moment they hit the air Karl felt proud and sick in the same breath.

Mama's needle froze mid-thread. Johann's mouth pinched. Franz's eyes flared, hot with boiling anger. He stepped toward Karl, not crouching, not soothing, his voice rising. "Selfish talk from a boy who's never had to earn his supper," he snapped. "Your father worked in the harbor because he had a gift and he needed coin. Don't make him into a hero so you can sneer at the rest of us."

Karl's face went red. "I'm not sneering!"

"You are," Franz shot back. "And you're wrong if you think a family is fed by dreams and saltwater. You think I enjoy mending fences? You think I want Johann mucking stalls at dawn? But someone must. Someone has to keep a house standing while you dream of foolishness." Karl stared at him, throat tight. Franz's hands trembled as he shoved the last piece of wood into the stack. "You want to call men at sea 'real'? Fine. Then call the others a fraud. Call the farmers, the carpenters, the mothers, the brothers—useless." His voice cracked like dry wood. "That's childish, Karl. Childish and selfish."

Karl wanted to shout back, to defend Papa, to defend the sea, but the words tangled in his stomach.

Franz dragged a hand over his face, trying to throttle down his temper, but anger still smoldered in him. "I loved your father," he said. "Matthias was brave, but bravery isn't measured only in dying. Some men stay. Some men dig in their heels and keep families alive. Remember that before you decide who counts as a 'real' man."

Karl said nothing. He heard Franz's words as accusation. Going with Franz meant letting the world decide who you are. Going meant becoming small.

Mama threaded her needle again, but her voice was bare: "Karl, enough." Karl pressed his lips tight. He didn't look at Franz. He didn't look at Mama. He stared at the floorboards so they wouldn't see the pain in his eyes.

Later, when Franz stepped outside to cool down by inspecting the horse's hooves, Mama rested her hand on Karl's back. "Not every good man is drawn to the sea," she whispered. "Not every good man has saltwater in his veins." Karl wanted to say Papa would never have lived in Gardelegen, never traded ships for milk cows. The words seemed too sharp for Mama, so he kept them inside, unspoken.

Gardelegen lay far inland, and to Karl it might as well have been on the dark side of the moon. There were fields instead of masts, cows instead of sailors, mud instead of tidewater. Papa would never have exchanged the sea for soil. Karl wasn't sure he could either.

That night he lay awake listening to the howl of the wind creak the beams. He thought of Papa—strong and sure, laughing over salt and wind—and he thought of Klaus Störtebeker, the local legend who lived by daring instead of orders. Thinking about both at once made it feel as if knots were being tied inside him. He pulled the blanket over his head so Johann wouldn't hear him breathe hard. "I will come back stronger," he said to himself. "I will come back as a man with coin."

Karl made his choice. It was the choice of a confused and heartbroken eleven year old.

At first light he rose without lighting a candle. The house felt fragile, as though even floorboards might protest his leaving. He dressed in the dark, fingers clumsy with cold and doubt.

He took with him what a young boy could. A crust of bread. A spare shirt. He hesitated over the small table before taking Mama's wooden swan. Taking it felt like theft. Leaving it felt like abandonment. He closed his fingers around it. The wood felt heavier today.

On the table he left a note in his stubborn, careful hand: *I'm not running away. I'm following my heart. Don't be angry, Mama. I'll write someday. —Karl*

The ink splotched where he pressed too hard. He slipped out without awakening anyone.

The harbor was already stirring when Karl reached it. Nets slung over shoulders. Crates thudding on the docks. Gulls screaming their complaints into the gray. He slowed.

Suddenly, the enormity of his decision was pressing against him. Behind him lay Mama's quiet breathing, Johann's tangled blankets, the empty place on the shelf where the promise once sat. Ahead of him lay uncertainty. Maybe if he worked hard enough men would not ask his age.

A brig sat low in the water, battered hull streaked dark with years of tide. Sailors shouted from her deck, preparing to cast off. Karl stepped toward it. Then stopped.

The wind shifted. For a moment he imagined turning back. He pictured Mama finding his bed still warm. He pictured Franz scolding but relieved. He imagined slipping the swan back on the table and pretending he had only gone for air.

The image lingered. He could still return. No one had seen him yet.

He felt inadequate. He felt like an eleven year old.

Then, another sharp thought emerged. If you turn back now, you will always be the boy who turned back. The words hovered inside him.

He looked down at the swan in his hand. Its wooden curve fit into his palm with quiet encouragement. Strength isn't loud, he thought. Action overtakes despair, he remembered Papa saying.

A shout rang from the brig. "Cast off!" The ropes splashed free. Decision collapsed into a single breath.

Karl ran. He jumped onto the brig as the gap between the dock widened. A startled dockworker glanced down, then returned to his rope, unaware he'd seen a boy leave his home, maybe forever. Karl slipped below deck and found a place to hide.

Mama found Karl's note before the morning fire caught. Her strength folded inward, not in anger, but in a low, terrible whisper: "He has lost his faith… and I do not know how to get mine back."

Franz ran to the harbor, Mama and Johann trailing behind, all three calling Karl's name, but the tide had outrun them. A battered Hamburg brig glided into the fog, sails shrinking. No boy waved. No voice called from the deck.

Johann cried. Mama stood rigid on the pier, shawl clenched tight. Franz steadied her. "Your boy isn't dead," he said. "He's stubborn as Matthias—chasing the world he means to see. Grief won't haul him home." Mama's tears left salt on her cheeks. "He is eleven," she whispered. "What world will take him?"

"Most worlds take boys sooner than they should," Franz said gently. "But the sea grows them into men." Mama pressed Johann into her side and tried hard to pray. The words wouldn't form. Only longing did. Mama never mentioned the missing swan.

Karl's escape was only part rebellion. Truth be told, he was running *toward* something, something he didn't understand. Faith had failed Mama. He sensed faith was failing him too. Maybe the sea held answers to prayers.

He was about to learn the lessons of the sea, and the costly manner in which they are taught.

Chapter 4

Karl's first day aboard the *Wodan* was a blur of wind, salt, and escalating fear. Bound for the Caribbean by way of English ports, the brig groaned under straining timbers while rigging snapped like whips overhead. From the darkness of his hiding place in a coil of wet canvas, Karl heard the crew long before they heard him.

At dusk they dragged him up from the hold, a stowaway hauled into the fading sun like vermin from a trap. Someone's fist stayed locked in the collar of his shirt as if afraid he might slip back into the dark. Kapitän Reimer stood waiting at the rail. The brass speaking trumpet hung from his belt like a weapon. Broad as a doorframe, jaw squared like a cut stone, he looked Karl over the way sailors look at spoiled meat.

"A rat," someone muttered.

Reimer's lip curled. "Rats go overboard," he said.

Reimer's hand closed around the back of Karl's collar, hauling him toward the rail with the casual intent of a man discarding refuse. The crew barely looked up. Boys vanished at sea all the time. Karl saw nothing but the gray chop of the cold water below. Before Reimer could finish the motion, a man stepped in. He didn't bark or shove. He simply stepped between Karl and the rail with the quiet authority of a man who understood leverage. One hand settled on Reimer's arm—light, but immovable. "Keep your poise," the man said to Reimer.

Reimer's head snapped in anger. "He's a stowaway."

The man gazed down at Karl, recognition surprising both of them. "Aye," Nathaniel Harwood murmured, "I've seen him before. Down at the wharf last month. Helped me with the rope slings. Didn't run off with the pay either." Karl shifted under Reimer's grasp, stunned that Nathaniel had remembered him and thankful that he embellished the encounter in a way that painted Karl as valuable.

Reimer looked unconvinced. "That make him worth feeding?"

Nathaniel shrugged. "Better to have a boy who can coil line than feed the sharks for amusement. Put him to work. If he's useless, the Gulf will decide soon enough."

Reimer hesitated and then spat over the side of the brig. He released Karl with a shove that sent him sprawling across the deck planks. The crew went back to their business. Mercy, usually absent aboard a ship, had just been spent for the month.

Nathaniel crouched beside Karl long enough to speak without being overheard. "You shouldn't have boarded a ship run by fools or desperate men," he said quietly. "This one's both." Karl dipped his chin. "I didn't know."

"No one ever does at your age." Nathaniel straightened, voice still low. "Listen well. Keep your head down, your hands busy, and your mouth shut. So long as they see you working, they won't see you dying." Nathaniel didn't wait for an answer. He simply turned and walked toward the forward hatch, calling over his shoulder, "Up, boy. The sea won't wait for you to find your courage."

Karl pushed himself upright, knees stinging. For an instant, in the wake of humiliation and the heat of Reimer's fury, a strange thought whistled through him. Reimer was worse than Franz.

He had been onboard for just a few hours and already learned that the Kapitän barked orders like cannon fire. Franz needed to appear in control. Reimer ruled by fear and had no need of disguise. He appeared to want to control every breath aboard his ship.

Karl's head sunk to his chest. Maybe he made a huge mistake by leaving Mama and stepping onto a floating world ruled by men who cared only that the work was done and done fast.

He steadied himself against the deck rail, trying to swallow the sudden ache behind his heart. The sea—vast, blue, endless—stretched out in every direction. Freedom, he had thought. Adventure, he had dreamed. Now the spray tasted bitter, and he wondered if he had traded one kind of prison for another.

The tide had long since carried him beyond the point of return. A tear streaked down his face. Maybe he could still make Mama proud. Maybe he could honor Papa by securing what Papa had died to provide for him, a better life.

At that moment, it seemed unlikely. He lifted his chin. "Adapt," he whispered.

Day by day, with survival as his motivator, Karl earned his place by the sweat of his back and the skin off his knuckles. The hours were a cruel schooling fueled by rope-burned palms, tarred trousers, cold saltwater down the spine. Deckhands mocked his size but watched, wary, when he climbed. Karl moved with the reckless grace of the newly wounded, unafraid of heights because men below had already disappointed him.

He scraped decks, hauled lines, polished brass until he could see a stranger's face snarling back. At night he slept among damp coils that smelled of mold and brine, and in the dark the faces of Mama and Papa and Johann drifted over the waves until they tore apart in the wind.

Lessons came daily, usually reinforced by anger. One morning, a squall came on faster than the lookout called it. The wind snapped the mainsail so hard that it groaned like it was wounded. Men scrambled for lines. Someone moved too slow. Thankfully, it was not Karl.

It was Anders, a broad-shouldered deckhand who had sailed voyages longer than Karl had been alive. His fingers fumbled the reefing knot. The canvas bellied wrong. For a breath too long, he hesitated.

Reimer saw it. He crossed the deck in three strides. No shout. No warning. His hand struck Anders across the face with a crack that carried even over the wind. The man staggered, nearly losing his footing. "You hesitate," Reimer said, voice level as iron, "and men drown."

Anders opened his mouth—perhaps to explain, perhaps to protest—but Reimer seized him by the coat and hauled him to the rail. Not over. Not yet. Just enough that the sea showed its fury below.

"Look," Reimer barked. The ship pitched. Spray drenched them both. "That is what waits for softness." He shoved Anders back onto the deck. "Finish it."

No one moved to interfere. Not Harwood. Not the quartermaster. The storm did not pause for mercy, and neither did the captain.

Karl worked the line beside Anders in silence. He kept his eyes on the sail, but he felt Reimer's presence sweep the deck like a blade. When the knot was finally secured, Reimer did not praise them. He simply gazed menacingly at the knot.

As the squall passed and the crew resumed their stations, Karl understood something that tightened his spine more effectively than fear. Nathaniel Harwood might save a boy from the rail, might steer a course truer than any compass, but this ship belonged to Reimer. Every plank, every breath, every life aboard answered to him. And Reimer never overlooked a weakness.

Karl took it as a small kindness of fate that two boys near his own age were already aboard. Lukas Engel and Otto Steger were older by a couple of years, louder in every gesture, but at least they were not men yet. In their presence, he allowed himself the hope of companionship.

Lukas and Otto watched Karl with narrowed eyes from the very first day, whispering between themselves when they thought no one noticed. As time passed, neither liked the way Kapitän Reimer barked orders at Karl instead of them, nor how Nathaniel Harwood sometimes paused to correct Karl's knots with patient hands while saying nothing to either of them. Jealousy was a quiet thing at first, but quiet things on a ship often grow.

Karl hoped, foolishly, that they might become friends. One week in, he offered them a share of his rationed bread, and Lukas accepted with a grin that never reached his eyes. "Not bad, Hamburg," he said, as if Karl were a dog that had done a trick. Otto only laughed.

By the end of the month Karl understood the truth. Lukas and Otto did not want friends. They wanted someone to blame. When the deck officer found a belaying pin left loose or a coil fouled, Otto shrugged and pointed at Karl. "The Hamburg boy was working that line." Lukas nodded along, solemn as a priest. Karl protested once, but Reimer silenced him with a glance sharp enough to cut bone.

One gray morning they decided to do more than point fingers.

"Karl," Lukas hissed as the bell clanged for mid-morning watch, "the quartermaster wants the tackle moved from the forward hold to the main hold. Said you should do it quiet-like. He's in a temper." Karl hesitated. Moving tackle alone was dangerous. The blocks were heavy, ropes were frayed, iron fittings could crush fingers. "Why not both of you?" he asked.

Otto snorted. "We have our orders. Unless you'd like to explain to Reimer why you disobeyed the quartermaster?" Karl's stomach knotted.

He didn't want another accusation hanging over him. So he descended into the dim forward hold alone, lantern swinging, the smell of bilge thick and sour.

The quartermaster wasn't there.

Almost at once the ship lurched on a swell. A barrel rolled, slammed into his shin, nearly sent him sprawling. An iron block skidded across the boards, clanging, and the tackle swung free from a hook above. One wrong move could've broken an arm or worse. Karl reacted without thinking— Papa's voice in his head from long-ago days at the Hamburg docks: *Mind your balance, boy. The sea hates the bold, but it saves the careful.* He wedged the barrel with his boot, lashed it fast, and then secured the block with a quick hitch that would've made Harwood proud. Only after the danger passed did his hands start to tremble.

When he climbed back on deck, bruised and breathless, he found Lukas and Otto lounging against the rail, smirking. "No quartermaster down there, was there?" Lukas drawled. Karl's pulse thudded in his ears. Part of him wanted to swing a fist. Part of him wanted to cry. Instead he took a slow breath the way Mama taught him when tempers ran hot at home.

"Next time you try to get someone hurt," he said, voice steady, "be sure they're not faster than you are." Before either boy could reply, Harwood emerged from the companionway, wiping his hands. His eyes moved from Karl's bruised shin to the guilty smirks of Lukas and Otto. Harwood was a man who missed little.

"Engel. Steger," he said mildly, "since you've time to laugh, you've time to scrape barnacles off the quarter rudder. Both of you. Now."

Their faces soured at once. They obeyed, because men aboard obeyed Harwood, even when he whispered. Karl watched them go, then met Nathaniel's gaze. The navigator didn't praise him, didn't ask what happened. He only said, "Good hands don't shout about themselves," and walked on.

Karl carried those words with him the rest of the day. Near dusk, the deck settled into the dull rhythm that comes after labor but before night watch. The quartermaster sent Karl below to fetch a folded chart from the navigator's berth.

Harwood's quarters were narrow as a coffin and twice as orderly. Instruments were lashed in place with care: the navigator's arc wrapped in oilcloth, compass secured in a fitted box, charts weighted flat against the swell. Nothing shifted without permission in that space.

Karl found the chart where he'd been told and turned to leave.

A drawing caught his attention. Pinned above the small writing desk, tucked between a tide table and a scrap of canvas, was a square of paper browned at the edges. The drawing was simple and awkward, a ship with sails too large for its hull and smoke curling from a crooked chimney. The sea beneath it was a row of uneven blue lines. In one corner, pressed hard enough to tear the page, were careful block letters: FOR PAPA.

Karl stared only a second before sensing someone behind him. Harwood stood in the doorway. He did not raise his voice. He did not step quickly. He simply moved into the small space and, with quiet deliberation, removed the paper from the wall. He folded it once and slipped it inside the front of his coat. "That'll be all," he said evenly.

Karl looked down, unsure why he felt he had trespassed. He climbed back to the deck and handed over the chart to the quartermaster. The ship pressed on as if nothing had altered. Yet something had.

Men like Harwood, Karl realized, did not belong only to the sea. Somewhere beyond the gray line of the horizon, there was someone small enough to draw him awkwardly and call him Papa. That meant the navigator carried more than charts across the water.

Before long the older crew members noticed Karl's resolve. The quartermaster tossed Karl extra salt pork at supper. Nathaniel gave him a nod one morning that meant more than praise.

One evening, as the crew settled into the slow rhythm before night watch, the sailmaker handed Karl a scrap of cured leather. "For your palms," the man muttered. "Or you'll bleed through the week." Karl hesitated before taking it. He was learning that everything came with a cost. A favor meant obligation. A kindness meant weakness seen and stored for later use. He searched the sailmaker's face for mockery and found none. "Thank you," Karl said carefully.

That night, instead of wrapping the leather around his hands, he tucked it beneath his coil of canvas and slept on it like a thing borrowed rather than given. It was not until the next morning, when the rope bit deep and reopened a half-healed burn, that he realized he did not yet know how to accept protection.

Lukas and Otto saw it all, and hated Karl for it. Karl knew his choice was an easy one – better to earn respect than scrape for affection that soured as soon as it was granted. Maybe Mama's prayers were being answered. Maybe he was becoming a young man that would make her proud.

Sometimes, when the cold crept bone-deep, Karl whispered the Lord's Prayer. Mama used to whisper it in the kitchen, as if God required secrecy. In those last months her faith had wavered. One day, Bible clenched, her voice would be hot with certainty. The next day she would be hollowed by doubt. Watching her belief split down the middle had frightened Karl more than his current living arrangement.

One night, with the sea black as oil and the wind shaking the shrouds like a rack of bones, he curled tight against the salt-stiff canvas and forced himself to remember Mama's table, those evenings when she made the boys speak blessings before they ate. The ritual felt small now, maybe even foolish, but he tried.

"I am alive," he whispered into the cold. "I can work. Reimer didn't throw me in."

The words steadied him less than he hoped. He couldn't tell if he had fled the unknown of Gardelegen or the slow terror of watching his mother lose the certainty that once held their world upright. Perhaps he was running after the shadow of Papa, slowly learning it would always outrun him.

By the end of the month, the crew grudgingly stopped calling him *Ratte* and started calling him *Kleine Sperling*—the sparrow—for the way he slipped through rigging and shot up the ratlines faster than men twice his age. Papa would have laughed at the nickname. A sparrow survives by being small enough to bend. And sometimes small enough to avoid detection.

Like all deck hands, Karl was still prone to making errors. One morning, he left a coil imperfectly flaked near the mainmast. Not yet dangerous but sloppy. He knew he had been the last to handle it. He had meant to fix it after securing the forward line, but the wind shifted and someone shouted, and the moment passed.

An hour later the deck officer noticed. "Who left this fouled?" Silence hung thick as pitch. Karl felt a lump gather in his throat.

Before he could speak, Otto shrugged. "Engel was working that line."

Lukas stiffened. "I was at the braces."

"Were you?" Otto replied lightly.

Reimer's gaze cut across them. "Which of you?"

Karl could have ended the confusion with one word. Instead, he held still.

Lukas's jaw tightened. "I suppose I touched it last." Reimer stepped close enough that Lukas had to tip his head back. "Then you'll spend your off-watch correcting every line on this deck until your hands remember how."

"Yes, Kapitän."

It was not a beating. Not blood. But it was punishment.

Karl kept his eyes on the planks.

Later, near the stern, Harwood approached him without pretense. "You were the last at that coil," he said quietly. It was not accusation. It was fact.

Karl met his gaze. The lie rose easier than he expected. "No, sir." Harwood studied him for a long moment, long enough for the sounds of the deck to fade. "Very well," Harwood said at last. Then he walked away. A few days would pass before Karl could once again look into Harwood's eyes.

That night, Karl lay awake longer than usual. He told himself it was survival. Lukas had tried to see him hurt. Otto had pointed fingers before. This was balance. He had stayed silent to protect himself. He shouldn't be asked to interfere with the version of himself the crew had begun to respect. After all, respect aboard a merchantman was clawed out of the spray and survived in silence.

The Caribbean waited somewhere beyond the gray horizon. Karl hoped it was a promise. Maybe it was a reckoning.

The sea had not yet decided.

Chapter 5

By late summer the *Wodan* sailed warmer waters. The Atlantic deepened to a luminous blue, and flying fish skittered across the surface like skipped stones. Beauty did not soften the trade routes. It only disguised them.

Two days later, the disguise disappeared. A schooner rose out of the dawn haze. Low in the water. Lean. Moving with a predator's patience. Too fast for a trader. No colors flew from her mast. No signal gun. No courtesy of distance. She angled toward them without haste, canvas trimmed close, hull slicing the sea in a narrow wake that spoke of discipline.

"Strange sail larboard quarter!" the lookout called. Reimer did not lift his spyglass immediately. He studied her with his naked eye, measuring the set of her sails, the confidence of her line. "Hold course," he said.

The schooner altered course immediately to match them. The crew moved without chatter. Powder was brought up. Swivels primed. Axes set near the rail. Karl felt a tightening in his chest.

The first shot came without ceremony. Roundshot skipped across the water and struck the *Wodan's* rail, splintering oak in a spray of sharp white shards. The deck jumped under Karl's feet. Outrunning the schooner would be fruitless.

Hooks flew. The pirates boarded not as wild men but as sailors accustomed to violence. Their weapons were clean. Their clothes were patched but not ragged. One wore a faded naval coat stripped of insignia. Another carried himself like a former officer.

Karl froze. Only for a breath, but long enough to feel the shame.

Then the deck erupted. Smoke rolled thick as wool. Pistols cracked at arm's length. A man screamed near the foremast — not theatrically, but with the wet, confused sound of real injury. The smell of burned powder mixed with salt and blood.

Karl loaded muskets with shaking hands. Twice he spilled powder. The third time he steadied himself. A boarder lunged toward him — a young man, not much older than Johann. Sunburned. Hollow-cheeked. Desperate.

Their eyes met. The pirate hesitated. Karl did too.

Karl was expecting to see hatred. He did not. He saw hunger.

The moment broke when Harwood fired past Karl's shoulder. The shot took the young man cleanly through the chest. He collapsed without a sound.

Karl stared at him longer than he should have. "Move!" Harwood snapped. Karl moved.

The fight did not last long. The schooner had misjudged the *Wodan*. Reimer's crew fought like men who had too much invested to lose. Or maybe like men who dare not disappoint the Kapitän. Within minutes, the remaining attackers were disarmed, three dead, two wounded, and four bound at the rail.

One of the prisoners spat blood and laughed. "You call us pirates," he said in accented English. "Who do you think sells your sugar?"

Reimer regarded him without expression. "Throw the dead back," he ordered. "The rest we keep."

Karl helped drag the body of the young man shot by Harwood to the rail. It was lighter than he expected. When it struck the water, it did not sink immediately. It rolled once in the swell, face up, eyes open, as if surprised by the sky above him. Karl turned away before it vanished.

He saw Harwood approach. Smoke still drifted between them. "You hesitated," Harwood said quietly. "Yes, sir," Karl said. "So did he." The words did not carry triumph. Only fact.

For a moment, neither spoke. The sea resumed its rhythm, slapping against the hull as if nothing of consequence had occurred. Harwood's gaze remained on the water where the body had disappeared.

"He was young," Karl said before he could stop himself. Harwood's throat shifted. A muscle twitched in his face. "Yes," the navigator said. He exhaled slowly. "You learned something today," Harwood continued. "Bravery doesn't keep a man alive. Decision does." His eyes moved to Karl. "You wait for clarity out here, you die waiting."

Karl's stomach felt hollow. Harwood rested a hand on the rail. "I did not fire because I hated him," he said, voice lower now. "I fired because he would not have spared you." That was the closest Harwood came to confession. He walked away before Karl could answer.

Karl's attention turned to the far side of the deck, where other deckhands were celebrating the trappings found in the schooner's hold: a chest of milled Spanish dollars, a keg of cocoa, and several bales of fine indigo cloth evidently bound for Jamaica. It was small treasure by buccaneer standards, but to the *Wodan's* crew it sparkled as if meant for a king. They ferried it aboard while Karl watched wide-eyed. He would remember every detail — the stink of powder, the shrieks of the wounded, the silver coins that chimed like bells in their wooden chest. Mainly, he would remember the electricity that danced along his veins. And the way the exhilaration had unsettled him.

Harwood took the schooner's ledger and flipped through the pages. "Privateering commission," he said quietly. Reimer's jaw shifted slightly.

"So… not pirates," Karl said too quickly. Reimer glared at him. "Call them what you like," he replied. "They boarded my ship."

That night, Karl lay awake listening to the prisoners coughing near the stern, wrists bound. He tried to summon righteous anger. Instead, he saw the young man's face as Harwood's shot struck him. He retched next to his mat, trying to decide if he was cut out for this life.

The pirate attack kept the crew on edge. Tension lingered. Lukas and Otto had not spoken to Karl in days. Their silence felt deliberate.

The following day, the afternoon sky was rustling with just enough wind to make carelessness dangerous. Karl was securing a tackle near the mainmast when he felt something wrong in the give of the line. Too smooth. Recently handled. A block above him jerked loose.

He barely twisted aside in time. The iron-edged wood clipped his shoulder instead of his skull. Pain exploded down his arm. He hit the deck hard. Laughter cut through the wind behind him.

"Don't be so clumsy, Hamburg," Otto said smiling. Karl rolled to his knees. His arm burned. He could not lift it properly. The line had been cut halfway through. Not frayed. Cut.

He looked up slowly. Lukas met his gaze and did not look away. This was new. This was not mockery. This was a challenge.

Before Karl could speak, a gust snapped the unsecured line violently. The loose tackle whipped toward the rail where two older sailors were bracing. If it struck, it would take one, maybe both, overboard.

Karl did not think. He threw himself across the deck, seized the trailing rope with his uninjured arm, and hauled with every ounce of weight he possessed. The fibers tore at his palm. The wind howled. "Hold it!" someone shouted. Three men joined him. The line went taut just before the tackle cleared the rail. Silence fell heavier than a storm.

Reimer descended from the quarterdeck. He examined the cut line. Ran his thumb along the clean edge. "Who touched this last?" No one spoke.

Karl opened his mouth. He could name them. He was certain now. But something in Lukas's stare stopped him. Not fear. Calculation. This would not end with one accusation.

Karl stepped forward. "I secured it, Kapitän," he said evenly.

Reimer studied him for a long moment. Then he struck Karl across the face, not viciously, but decisively. "You secure nothing halfway," Reimer said. "You want to live? Finish what you touch."

"Yes, Kapitän," Karl said.

Reimer turned to the others. "If I discover deliberate damage to my rigging, I will not ask twice." His gaze passed over Lukas and Otto. They looked down. But they did not look afraid.

That night, Karl lay in his hammock unable to sleep. His shoulder throbbed. His cheek burned. He replayed the moment again and again. He could have spoken. He had chosen not to.

Not from mercy. From strategy. The line had been cut cleanly. That meant intent. And intent meant this would happen again.

Across the dim hold, Lukas lay awake too. Their eyes met in the lantern's dying glow. No words passed between them. None were needed.

Karl drew his small backpack closer and felt beneath his spare shirt until his fingers brushed smooth, familiar wood. He took out the small swan and turned it in the lantern glow. He noticed things he had never seen before. The wings were slightly lopsided. The beak was dull. He traced the grooves Papa's knife had left and saw Mama standing at their window, smiling, as Johann sketched by the fire.

Karl closed his hand around the carving and breathed in the sour blend of sweat and wet rope. He tried to pray but found he was unable. Now he knew how Mama must have felt.

He had chosen this path—salt over soil, wind over quiet—but in the dark he wondered how long a heart could stretch before it tore.

Chapter 6

Months after leaving Europe, the *Wodan* crested the horizon and revealed Hispaniola, a gleaming crescent of emerald against the Atlantic. The port city of Cap-Français emerged like a jewel laid upon the water, a harbor of impossible contrasts.

Bright blue waves lapped at docks lined with whitewashed mansions. Balconies overflowed with bougainvillea and ironwork imported from Paris. Fortifications jutted from hillsides, their walls catching the sun like burnished metal. The air was thick with the perfume of sugar, citrus, and something harsher—gunpowder.

Karl's eyes widened. He pressed closer to the rail, mouth slightly open, palms moist. The island shimmered, yet beneath its beauty was a current he had not seen. Harwood came to stand beside him. "You have the sea in you now," Nathaniel said. "Your father would be proud."

Karl did not know if it were true. He only knew that he had survived. Sometimes, when he lay awake listening to the sea breathe, he wondered if Mama's God had followed him, or if he had traded heaven for salt and thunder.

Cap-Français was captivating. Ships of every size creaked as they rose and fell with the tide, masts straining under weight. Crates and barrels crowded the docks, stacked high, wobbling with every shove of a passing sailor.

Karl darted between barrels, careful to keep his balance on the slick planks. A cart toppled nearby, sending sugar barrels crashing into the water with a roar that made his ears ring. Sailors swore in German, English, and Spanish, stamping and slipping as they tried to right the toppled cart. One barrel rolled straight toward a small boy chasing after it. Without thinking, Karl lunged, catching it just in time before it could tumble into the canal.

A loose plank slid beneath his boots, nearly pitching him over the edge. Nets swung wildly from the rigging, brushing shoulders and heads. Sparks flew as a dockworker hammered a crate too close to a lantern, and a wisp of straw caught fire before a sailor stamped it out. Barrels of indigo spilled their powder over wet planks, turning them blue. Karl dodged, slid, and leapt, weaving through the chaos like a thread in a storm.

In the middle of it all, he felt something growing inside him. Courage. When a sailor called for help with a rope snagged under a rolling cart, Karl didn't hesitate. He grabbed the rope, pulled it free, and righted the cart enough for the crew to secure it. The sailor clapped him on the shoulder, laughing, and Karl's chest swelled with pride. He was beginning to understand that bravery didn't always mean swords or guns. Sometimes it meant moving before thinking, trusting your hands and your wits.

When the chaos finally slowed, Karl leaned against a piling, soaked, scraped, and trembling. He had just arrived and the harbor already had tested him and thrilled him. He glanced toward the skyline, white mansions glinting against the gray winter sky, and a thought struck him with sudden tenderness. *What would Mama think if she could see this?* The smell of salt and smoke, the cries of sailors, the dazzling chaos. It was a world apart from the calm of St. Catherine's pews and her careful counting of blessings.

He had promised, quite earnestly, that he would write. He would send a letter to Mama full of assurances and stories and proof that he was not lost to the world. But days became weeks, and weeks became months, and pen and paper somehow burned hotter than flame. What could he say? That the sea made him feel alive? That danger exhilarated him? That he was changing in ways she might not recognize? So he wrote nothing, alleviating his conscience with the idea that correspondence would not reach Mama regardless.

Regret stirred. He imagined Mama waiting at Franz's window after evening prayers, hoping she might see her youngest son walking toward Gardelegen. He hoped she would understand, someday, that he was seeing life as it truly was: fast-paced and messy. He wasn't forgetting her. Or her guidance. Instead, he was becoming someone he did not yet know how to describe. Maybe he was becoming who he was meant to be.

Karl quickly noticed the sharp and wary glances exchanged between men in uniform, and the quiet tension in the way merchants counted their coins. The island's heartbeat was uneven, detectable even by a boy fresh from the open sea. Karl learned that Hispaniola was at war with itself, and he was on the edge of its fire. The revolution that had begun with slaves and sugar now devoured governors and generals alike.

"The French lost the island once," he heard a sailor mutter. "They won't lose it twice."

"It isn't France's to lose anymore," someone answered.

Indeed, the French had been pushed out in many regions and new factions vied for power in an uncertain birth of nationhood. Confidence was a currency as real as silver. Karl carried himself with just enough of it to be noticed.

It was near the dock that he first saw the man with the ink-black hair and the linen coat too fine for the humidity. The man stood apart from the dockside shouting, observing rather than bargaining. He had the posture of someone accustomed to being obeyed. When their eyes met, the man gave a small measuring nod.

"You are not French," the man said in careful German as Karl passed. Karl stopped. The familiarity of the language felt like a hand placed lightly on his shoulder. "No," Karl said.

"Nor English," the man said with a faint smile. "But you serve both, I think." Karl stiffened, then relaxed. A perceptive merchant, he assumed. Perhaps even useful. "I serve the *Wodan*," Karl replied.

"Of course you do," the man said as his gaze lingered on Karl's rope-burned hands. "Ships like yours require… discretion." Karl mistook the pause for admiration.

The man introduced himself only as Herr Bauer. He spoke of shifting allegiances and how quickly information traveled from Saint-Domingue to Havana to New Orleans. He knew names, too many names. He knew which captains could be bribed and which governors pretended not to see certain cargoes.

Karl felt a flicker of pride that he could follow the conversation. He offered his own thoughts, enough to appear informed. Bauer listened carefully. Encouragingly.

When they parted, Bauer clasped Karl's shoulder with easy camaraderie. "Ambition is not a vice, young man," he said. "It is only dangerous when it lacks allies."

Karl walked away feeling older. He did not notice that Bauer had not offered a ship, nor a warehouse, nor a partnership. The only information exchanged came from Karl's own tongue.

Two days later, Reimer summoned him to the quarterdeck. "You've been speaking freely in town," he said. It was not a question. Karl's pulse quickened.

"A man approached Harwood this morning," Reimer continued. "Knew precisely how many muskets we unloaded. Knew we would be ready to sail by nightfall." The Kapitän's eyes were colder than anger. "You are learning quickly," Reimer said. "But not yet quickly enough." Herr Bauer had never been a merchant. He had been weighing Karl. Lesson learned.

Soon enough, Karl regained the grace of Reimer, if such a thing existed, and began running messages and cargo manifests for the Kapitän. Because boys are invisible to most men, Karl heard everything. He learned that in this strange corner of the world, former slaves now rode on horseback as generals and governors, escorted by guards who had once been their masters. He heard that French officers drank themselves sick in shuttered cellars, poring over charcoal maps and pledging oaths to restore *l'ordre ancien* with blood and steel, if need be. He watched merchants wager fortunes on sugar or coffee before breakfast, only to claw at their own hair by sundown as markets collapsed or warehouses mysteriously burned.

In the counting-houses the whispers were sharp enough to cut:

"Toussaint's shadow still rules here."

"Murat will send ships—just wait."

"Spain wants the west, Britain wants the ports, and the devil can have the rest."

Through it all, ships came and went like omens—brigantines from Jamaica heavy with rum, French corvettes limping from skirmishes off Guadeloupe, American schooners with their flags rolled tight because neutrality depended on silence more than cloth. Karl carried papers through taverns thick with tobacco smoke and rum breath, past men with sabers on their belts and pistols tucked into sashes, and realized that this island was not merely alive. This island was armed, divided, and trembling under a dozen different ambitions.

With each message delivered, he carried back knowledge. Some knowledge he shared, some he kept to himself. Karl had survived storms at sea, but Cap-Français was a place where he felt danger walking the streets in broad daylight.

One evening just after dusk, a French merchant came aboard the *Wodan*, moving like a shadow along the slick deck. He whispered of a "midnight transaction," and the words carried the weight of secrets, lawlessness, and peril.

Lanterns swung in the wind, their flames flickering over the sailors' tense faces, casting leaping shadows across crates and rigging. Every creak of the deck sounded louder than it should. Every slap of water against the hull clanged like a warning drum.

Karl crouched behind a coil of rope, heart heavy in his chest. He had never seen a night so alive with danger. Muskets and powder were transferred from the skiff to the *Wodan* with quiet grunts, each movement deliberate. A slip, a dropped crate, even a careless footstep could send cargo, or a man, into the dark water below. The merchant hissed instructions, and the sailors obeyed, eyes darting toward the shore, wary of potential patrols.

Karl's hands itched to help. When a crate of muskets teetered on the edge, threatening to tip into the canal, he lunged, steadying it with a shove of his shoulder. The merchant glanced at him sharply, but did not scold. He tapped Karl on the shoulder with approval.

The crates contained powder, shot, and muskets, all illegal under the new regime and dangerous in a colony already trembling with tension. Karl wondered if the muskets would arm rebels who would kill civilians.

He decided not to ask.

Finally, the last crate was secured, ropes tied fast. Karl learned that men tie knots faster when afraid. He slumped against a piling, soaked with sweat, lungs burning, eyes wide. The *Wodan* rocked gently under the lantern glow, but the danger of the night lingered in his pulse. He had kept the cargo from falling, but, more importantly, he had moved with purpose. He had survived the tension of the night. Courage was acting when fear clawed.

He looked across the harbor and a single thought surfaced: *What would Papa think?* The chaos, the risk, the thrill. Would he embrace me or scold me? Would he be proud? Would he compare me to Störtebeker?

The illicit cargo was buried snugly beneath tarps, but secrecy in Saint-Domingue burned about as long as a half-inch fuse. The next morning, gunshots cracked from the pier. Armed men, Black soldiers in ragged uniforms mixed with French deserters, rushed the docks shouting that the muskets belonged to the state, that Reimer was a thief, that the crates were evidence.

Kapitän Reimer swore every curse word known to sailors and roared for the crew to set full sail. Karl scrambled up the shrouds as the crew cast off. Cannon from the battery boomed. The air tore open with iron. Splinters whipped across the rail. The *Wodan* took to open water under a storm of iron, her hull bleeding wood but afloat.

They didn't return for days. The guns had driven them too far to risk doubling back and Reimer feared privateers lurking in the shallows. So they rode the tides east with canvas low and profile lower, letting the sea swallow their wake.

Freshwater grew precious. The last barrels had to stretch, so Reimer sealed the casks and tallied every ladle. Men drank in turns, half-cups at dawn and dusk, just enough to keep throats wet and tempers dull. Hardtack softened with a few drops was their only meal. Karl soothed his salt-crusted lips by licking rain from the rigging without shame.

Three days later they offloaded their cargo. Reimer paid his crew and granted two nights' liberty. Karl celebrated his free time by following Harwood to a waterfront tavern—*La Taverne des Pavillons Brisés*, the Tavern of Broken Flags. Torn banners hung from the beams, trophies taken from ships that had changed hands more than once. Sailors drank beneath their ruins as if nations were merely cloth.

It was there Karl first saw Jean Lafitte.

Lafitte wore no gaudy scarves or jangling blades, only a dark coat, polished boots, and a white shirt open at the throat. More merchant prince than pirate. The room seemed to bend around his movement, as though men unconsciously adjusted their course around him.

Karl guessed Jean to be ten years older, about the same age as Harwood. He wondered what ten years could make of a boy who refused to drown. Would Karl carry himself like Jean in ten years?

Lafitte's eyes swept the crowd—sailors, merchants, soldiers, freebooters—and then paused, without hurry, on Karl. It wasn't a long look, but it was measured, as though Lafitte was entering Karl's name in a ledger. Harwood noticed. "Don't stare," he muttered. "That's Lafitte. Smuggler, corsair, trader. Whatever yields profit." Karl whispered, "He looks like a nobleman." Harwood snorted. "Maybe once. Now he's the king of men who answer to wind and powder."

When Lafitte moved on, talk resumed—dice rattled, a fiddle scratched a tune, someone cursed over spilled rum—yet Karl felt changed by the simple fact of having been seen. He also felt slightly exposed. Admiration and mistrust tangled in him. Lafitte was French, formed from the same soil that had engulfed Papa at Jena. Should he admire such a man or despise him?

Later, Harwood swapped news with other sailors while Karl lingered near the bar. A fight erupted, two French planters against a British privateer. Chairs smashed, mugs burst, and someone drew steel. Karl ducked as the British privateer lunged past, striking him across the cheek with the back of a knife-hand. Light burst behind Karl's eyes. The man squared to deliver another blow to Karl. A hand – lean and strong, rings flashing in lamplight – caught the privateer's wrist.

Lafitte.

"This boy is no threat to you," he said in smooth, unhurried French. "He tripped me!" the privateer spat. "Then find surer footing," Lafitte replied, voice calm as a loaded pistol.

The privateer was gone a moment later. Pushed or escorted, Karl couldn't tell. The tavern gave Lafitte space without instruction. Lafitte turned to Karl, studying him with unnerving patience.

"You climb rigging like a spider," he said. "And you keep your head in a brawl. How old?"

"Fourteen," Karl managed—fudging by two years so as not to appear child-like. He recoiled in his heart, wishing he had started this encounter with honesty. Mama always said, "when in doubt, start with the truth." It was too late. He was becoming aware of how often he was on the wrong side of Mama's wisdom,

"German?" Lafitte asked. Karl moved his chin up and down. "Germans make good soldiers," Lafitte said. "Sometimes good sailors too." He studied Karl longer than necessary, as if measuring future usefulness.

From the corner of his eye, Karl noticed Lukas and Otto edging closer, trying to catch Lafitte's attention. Lukas fumbled with a dagger, flipping it between his fingers, while Otto cleared his throat loudly and jabbed at a loose knot on the deck. Both boys grinned, hoping to look capable, but Lafitte's eyes barely lifted toward them.

"Tell your captain Jean Lafitte has a proposal at first light. And you…" His eyes narrowed, amused. "Karl, is it?"

Karl was astonished. "How did you—?"

Lafitte smiled—small, precise, dangerous. "A captain knows his crew. Even the smallest ones."

Lukas and Otto exchanged wary glances, pride deflating. Every gesture meant to impress the pirate leader had failed. Karl felt a quiet thrill, not arrogance, but the satisfaction of having earned Lafitte's notice on his own terms. Lafitte vanished into smoke and laughter. Harwood appeared pale. Karl was baffled. He thought Reimer was his captain.

"You just swam with a shark," Nathaniel murmured. "Keep your wits sharp."

"I thought Reimer was our captain," Karl said.

"He is," Nathaniel said, "but here everyone reports to Lafitte, one way or another."

Karl pressed a cloth to his cheek. Pain throbbed, but beneath it stirred something stranger. Possibility. Confused possibility. He had come to sea searching for faith in waves, in stars, in the roar of canvas. So far, he had mainly found indifference and silence.

Now, as Karl watched Lafitte slip out the tavern door, he felt the world tilt, perhaps permanently, as if someone had nudged his keel toward a future no prayerbook would care to name.

A week later, Karl was on deck at dawn, checking ropes and rigging with practiced care. The wind was brisk but steady, the schooner cutting cleanly through the waves.

Behind him, whispers threaded the air. Before Karl could turn, Lukas lunged from behind a barrel, fist arcing toward Karl's jaw. Otto came from the other side, seizing Karl's arm and wrenching it backward. "Time to see who's really in charge, Hamburg," Lukas sneered.

Karl stumbled but did not fall. He dropped his weight, twisting hard. His elbow caught Lukas beneath the ribs. Otto's grip tightened, fingers digging cruelly into muscle, but Karl pivoted and drove his heel backward. Otto slipped on the damp planks and went down hard. The deck erupted in shouts. Men in the rigging leaned out to watch.

Lukas charged again, wild with embarrassment. Karl ducked, drove his shoulder forward, and felt the solid thud of impact. Otto scrambled up and came at him with both hands, teeth bared—more animal than young man.

Karl moved with the rhythm of the ship. He let Lukas overcommit, stepped aside, and sent him stumbling toward the rail. He seized Otto's sleeve and twisted, slamming him against a coil of rope. The breath rushed from Otto's lungs in a harsh grunt.

They had misjudged him. Karl had bested both of them.

"Enough!" Reimer's voice cracked across the deck. His fist slammed against the rail. The vibration seemed to travel through the planks. "All of you," he said, voice low and harsh, "back off."

Karl stepped away first. Lukas spat blood onto the deck and wiped his mouth with the back of his hand. Otto did not move immediately. He stared at Karl. Not panting, not cursing. Just staring. There was a new level of calculation in his eyes.

Reimer's gaze passed over them. "A ship is no place for grudges. The sea holds enough grudge for all of us. Learn that now."

Lukas muttered something crude and staggered away. Otto lingered. As he passed Karl, close enough that their shoulders nearly brushed, he leaned in and spoke softly, too softly for the others to hear. "You won't always have him watching."

Karl felt the words more than heard them. Otto's mouth curved. "This isn't finished, Hamburg."

Within a week, Reimer made his choice of how he would resolve the grudge. Lukas and Otto were transferred to a merchant brig bound north. Lukas departed loudly, swearing about favoritism and a captain who coddled children. Otto said nothing at all.

As the brig pulled away, Karl watched from the rail. Lukas stood at the stern railing, gesturing angrily. Otto stood completely still beside him, hands folded behind his back. He did not look at the crew. He looked only at Karl. When their eyes met, Otto touched two fingers lightly to his temple, not a salute. A promise.

The distance between the ships widened. Otto's look did not.

Chapter 7

After the night in the tavern, Kapitän Reimer and Jean Lafitte met. No one knew what was said. No one dared ask. But the *Wodan's* contracts shifted. They made more nighttime landings, more deliveries inland, and hired extra guards. Karl didn't ask questions. Sailors learn early: cargo that travels by moonlight is never discussed.

On a humid night thick with cane and salt, Lafitte himself came aboard with a posse as mixed as the Caribbean itself: Creoles with silver signet rings, Spaniards with scarred knuckles, free men of color with muskets slung across their backs, and two pale English deserters wearing mismatched French coats.

Reimer jerked a thumb at the rigging. "Ratlines. Look sharp. Eyes open." The ship hugged the coastline without lanterns, silent except for the distant roar of surf. Karl spent the night in the shrouds scanning for patrol boats. At some signal he never heard, Lafitte's men unloaded crates into longboats and vanished upriver into the cane.

Only later did Harwood explain, quiet in low German: "Muskets for rebels. Lafitte sells to whoever pays—French, Spanish, revolutionaries, governments. He is a merchant of wars."

Karl absorbed the words with the solemnity of someone mapping adulthood. Mama would have called it sin. Lafitte called it business. Sometimes, Karl still whispered prayers before sleep, half-remembered verses Mama taught him, but each night the words felt smaller against the vastness of this new world.

Weeks later, Lafitte summoned Karl directly, an honor that made other sailors pretend not to stare. The meeting place was a sugar warehouse near the docks, sweet rot mixing with gun oil. Lafitte stood over a map spread across crates, sleeves rolled up, a quill behind his ear. He did not look up.

"Tell me what's wrong with this map," he said.

Karl hesitated. "I don't understand."

"You've sailed that coast for months," Lafitte replied. His voice was low, controlled. "Something is missing. Tell me what."

Karl studied the map. After a moment he pointed to a blank stretch of shore. "There's an inlet west of here. Small. Hidden. We sheltered there in a storm. It's not marked."

Lafitte's eyes lifted in a manner of appraisal. "How far west?"

Karl measured with his hand. "There. A league, maybe. You won't see it until you're almost on it."

Lafitte's mouth twitched into what might have been approval, or calculation. "You see what others miss," he said. "That is a rare gift. And a dangerous one, if misused."

He said it almost kindly, yet Karl felt a chill. Mama spoke of gifts from God. Lafitte treated gifts like weapons.

Lafitte never called himself a mentor. Too binding, too sentimental. But in the coming months, he had a way of making Karl learn without ever admitting he was teaching. Lafitte valued silence in young men. Silence meant their thoughts had room to sharpen. Karl listened more than he spoke.

So Jean tested Karl, quietly. Sent him to weigh cargo at the warehouse instead of swabbing the deck. Had him copy manifests and study charts. Asked what he *saw* when a vessel entered the harbor—its trim, its crew, its purpose. Never praise, only nods, a raised brow, the faintest curve of approval. In that way, without vows or proclamations, Lafitte began shaping Karl for a world where nations mattered less than nerve and where a sharp mind could be more dangerous than a cannon.

Before long, Lafitte's influence was woven into the air Karl breathed. Jean started with language. Not conjugations or polite introductions. Lafitte barked French curses across the deck when a line tangled, and Karl learned quickly which ones meant "duck" and which meant "pull."

Later, in the tight heat of a Spanish port, Karl heard Lafitte switch tongues as easily as changing a coat, issuing sharp Spanish commands that made dockhands move twice as fast.

Then came navigation. On quiet nights, when the Gulf was dark and glossy, Lafitte would nudge Karl toward the rail and ask him what the tide was "saying." Karl learned that currents pulled stronger near the sandbars and that stars slid across the sky in predictable clocks. "Maps lie," Lafitte would mutter, tapping the water with a finger. "This does not."

Commerce and codes followed. Karl watched smugglers count coins on the barrels stacked in the warehouse behind the town hall, watched gold slip into one pouch and silver into another. Bribes shifted hands as casually as greetings exchanged—five percent for the guard who pretended not to see, ten percent for the official who stamped a paper that meant nothing. Loyalties, Karl learned, were purchased like rum, always measured, never trusted.

Then there was war. Not the king's war of drums and uniforms, but a pirate's war—fast, dirty, and decided before anyone could shout a prayer. Karl learned how to choose a bend in the marsh grass where musket smoke vanished into the reeds. He learned to reload while kneeling in mud that sucked at his boots. Lafitte corrected him once, silently shifting his elbow so the rifle rested steadier on the root of a cypress tree.

In all of it, Lafitte never said he was teaching. He only set the stage, pointed once, and let the world do the rest. It was the sharpest kind of mentorship, the sort that never asked for gratitude.

Karl watched Lafitte negotiate with planters, revolutionary generals, French officers, and Spanish merchants. Lafitte rarely threatened. He offered *choices*—each profitable, each subtly coercive. He survived because he understood men, not merely cannon. Karl found himself studying Lafitte's manner the way a theologian might study scripture.

Mama had given him prayer. Lafitte was giving him pattern.

In quiet moments Karl still felt the ache of missing Mama's hymns at dawn. Divine will seemed distant here. The Caribbean did not reward humility. It rewarded nerve. Lafitte believed in different laws, ones not written in a king's charter. He would say, almost casually, that "kings come and go," usually while sliding a crate of contraband sugar beneath a customs official's nose.

Karl once watched Jean drink wine in a tavern while news spread that a Swedish king had fallen. The sailors whispered like the world had tipped over. Lafitte just raised his glass and counted his earnings from the week's trade. "Kings are temporary," he murmured, tucking a ledger into his coat. "Profit is not."

As for fate, Lafitte made his thoughts unmistakably clear during the storm season. He had little patience for men who surrendered themselves to heaven while the sea demanded hands and nerve. The lesson was reinforced one night when a squall fell upon them without warning. A green crewman froze at the wheel as the ship reared and bucked, mast groaning like a wounded beast. Rain slashed sideways across the deck. Men shouted prayers—to saints, to mothers, to whatever god they hoped might still be listening.

Karl clung to the rail, knuckles white, heart in his throat. For a breathless moment he felt the old instinct rise, the one Mama had taught him, to bow his head and pray for mercy.

The ship lurched. "Turn her!" someone screamed. The next gust struck like a fist. The young man at the wheel lost his footing. His hands slipped. The wheel spun wild beneath him. He stumbled backward, boots skidding across the flooded planks. The rail struck his hips. Not a scream. Not even a word. Just a flash of pale face and open mouth devoured by black water.

He was gone. "Man overboard!" someone yelled too late.

Karl surged toward the rail, but Lafitte was already moving. He shoved past the men at the helm, seized the wheel, and forced it against the screaming wind. "Hold her!" he barked. "Hold her steady!"

Karl expected to hear an order to lower a boat. To turn back. To search.

The order never came.

Lafitte's arms locked against the wheel, eyes narrowed into the rain. "God favors motion," he roared over the storm, forcing the bow one brutal degree at a time. "Not pleading."

The schooner resisted. Shuddered. Fought them. Then, inch by inch, answered.

Behind them, the black water closed without ceremony. When at last the worst of the squall passed, the deck lay wrecked with loose lines and torn canvas. Men stood breathing hard, faces washed clean by rain and fear. No one spoke the boy's name.

Lafitte handed the wheel to another sailor and wiped seawater from his eyes. He didn't speak of miracles. "Fate," he said evenly, "is like wind. It can be used. It can be resisted. Or it can take you." He glanced once at the empty rail. "It does not care what you hope."

Karl looked out into the dark where the crewman had vanished. He could not remember whether the crewman had mentioned a family or a hometown. The sea had erased him faster than prayer.

Karl remembered Jean's words long after the deck dried. Mama counted blessings after danger passed. Lafitte acted inside the danger. From that night on, Karl began to understand that destiny did not arrive like a letter from God. It came like weather. And a man either learned to take the helm, or he was swept aside.

Freedom, to Lafitte, carried a price. Karl saw it the night Spanish soldiers blocked the narrow street leading to the warehouse. Shots cracked. Smugglers scattered like startled birds. Lafitte didn't run, he covered their escape, firing twice before vaulting over a shuttered stall.

Later, bruised and breathless in the swamp grass, he checked to make sure they had all made it out. "Freedom isn't granted," he said, as if noting a change in the weather. "It's paid for—one way or another."

Those were his laws. No parchment, no seal. Just actions that made the meaning unmistakable.

Lafitte simply lived, and men followed. The simplicity of it embarrassed Karl's old prayers. Perhaps Mama's God governed heaven. Lafitte governed outcomes. He felt guilt for thinking it, and guilt for liking the thought.

A few nights later, Karl discovered two sailors stealing powder kegs from Lafitte's armory. They saw him. He could have shouted, or fled. Instead he shadowed them silently, watching where they hid the crates. Only when they left did he seek Lafitte.

"They plan to sell it to French officers tomorrow," Karl said. "I saw where."

Lafitte did not praise him. He merely nodded, sent two men, and by morning the thieves were gone from port—claimed by the sea, the cane fields, or quieter ends.

Later Lafitte paused beside Karl on the pier, watching surf break over pilings. "You did not try to stop them. You did not run. You observed and informed." His voice was almost reflective. "Wars are won that way. Not with muskets, but decisions." Karl tried not to glow under the attention. He knew enough to hide hunger for praise.

Lafitte invested in nothing that lacked return. For reasons Karl couldn't yet see, the pirate was investing in him.

Jean embraced the way Karl rose before dawn without being ordered. While the rest of the crew staggered from hammocks, Karl had already scrubbed the deck and coiled the lines with the stiff precision of a Prussian soldier. Lafitte paused beside him one morning, tapped a boot against a neatly coiled rope, and let a slow smile spread across his face.

"Hamburg," he said, calling him by his nickname to keep him humble, "I admire the way you seize the day. Not because you follow orders. You don't need orders. You take what comes and shape it, just as a man must shape his own destiny. That's rare on any ship, and rarer still in life ashore."

Karl's hands stilled on the ropes, a warm flush creeping up his neck. Lafitte's quiet nod seemed to illuminate a truth he had felt but never fully grasped. Maybe a boy could seize the day, and steer his own course through a world that often tried to dictate it. He remembered Mama's gentle encouragement to him and Johann – embrace each day. Rise with purpose. The memory came to him as if carried on the wind. This small mastery of morning, of action, of choice must have been what she meant.

Jean's lessons intensified. When they scouted a new inlet along the shore, Karl traced the curve of the sandbars with his finger, quietly noting where a schooner could slip in on a rising tide. Later, while smugglers argued over ciphered messages in a tavern back room, Karl deciphered the system faster than the older men. Lafitte watched without comment, but his eyes darted with interest.

When the fighting came, and it came as timely as the sun, Karl didn't fold into fear. He reloaded when told, ramming powder and ball with trembling precision even as shots hissed overhead. When smoke stung his eyes and iron tore at his flesh, he kept quiet, wincing but never stopping.

Through it all, Karl carried struggle like a well-worn pack. Whether it made him brave or numb no longer mattered. In this life he had chosen, there was no time to sort the difference.

Then there was the trait Lafitte valued most. Loyalty.

It showed one night when a delivery collapsed under Spanish patrol fire. Shots cracked through the cane fields. Men scattered without orders, vanishing into alleys and marsh grass, each saving his own skin. Crates were abandoned. Gold was left behind.

Karl ran with the others at first. Then he stopped. He turned back.

Smoke drifted low along the street. Somewhere ahead, Lafitte's voice cut sharp and controlled, directing men toward the boats. Without weighing it further, Karl slipped against the flow of fleeing sailors and pushed toward the sound. He found Lafitte covering the retreat, firing once, twice, calm as a man tallying accounts. Karl seized a fallen musket and took position beside him without being told. They withdrew together.

Later, when the crew reassembled in the mangroves, breathless and soaked, the silence around Karl felt different. It was not gratitude. It was distance.

"You doubled back," one man muttered, not quite looking at him.

Karl said nothing. Another spat into the mud. "Could've drawn them straight to us."

"You trying to prove something, Hamburg?" a third asked. Not loud. Not joking. The question hung heavier than accusation.

Karl learned what no sermon had ever prepared him for: loyalty upward is often seen as betrayal sideways. He had not meant to expose them. He had not meant to show them up. He simply did what he thought was right.

Across the clearing, Lafitte met Karl's eyes only briefly and gave the smallest nod. Approval. Karl learned that every allegiance has a price. Most times, the first payment is trust.

Unfortunately, trust on the island was a tricky commodity. The nighttime arrangement had always been simple. Lafitte would get what he needed by delivering a crate of sugar and two bottles of brandy to the patrol cutter captain. He had successfully handled such mathematics for years. On this night, however, the lantern signal from shore did not appear.

Lafitte's band of men waited offshore longer than caution allowed. "Perhaps the wind shifted it," one of the men muttered. Lafitte did not answer. He studied the shoreline through his glass, expression unreadable. Finally, he gave the order to proceed.

The longboats cut silently toward the dock. Halfway in, the trap sprang. An entire row of lanterns flared along the dock. Muskets cocked in unison. Spanish soldiers stepped from behind stacked barrels that had not been there that afternoon.

"Down!" someone shouted. Shots split the dark. One of Lafitte's men pitched forward into the water without a sound. The crew scrambled back toward the boats. Oars splintered. A crate burst open, spilling powder into black water.

Karl felt a jolt of disbelief. This was not how Lafitte operated. They barely escaped.

Back aboard, men counted wounds in tight silence. One dead. Two bleeding. Three crates lost. Lafitte stood near the rail, soaked and still, eyes fixed on the burning shoreline signal they had mistaken for welcome.

Harwood approached carefully. "They knew."

"Yes," Lafitte said. No anger. No visible fury. Just a narrowing of thought.

"The customs clerk?" Harwood asked. Lafitte shook his head once. "No. I misjudged the lieutenant." Karl watched Jean closely. "New man at post," Lafitte continued quietly. "Young. Ambitious." A pause. "I assumed hunger meant greed." Another pause. "It meant promotion."

Lafitte believed every man had a price. Tonight, he had discovered one who preferred advancement over coin. He turned to the crew. "We adjust," he said simply. "We do not repeat mistakes."

Karl felt the Lafitte myth shift. For the first time, Jean had not been orchestrating the board. He had been moved upon it.

Later, as the deck was scrubbed clean of blood, Karl stood alone at the stern. Mama had said no man sees the whole pattern. Tonight, Jean Lafitte had missed a thread. The thought frightened Karl more than the muskets.

The next night at the Tavern of Broken Flags, Harwood warned Karl: "You've become his eyes and his ears. Be careful. Lafitte rewards well, but he does not protect the weak."

Karl understood. He did not want protection. He wanted meaning, the thing Mama's God once promised before they lost Papa and war tore childhood open.

After Harwood departed, Karl rubbed his hands together and whispered, not sure why he was speaking to himself.

"Papa did what he was told," he said to no one. "Kings and captains and priests, always someone above him. Papa never broke a command in his life and it got him killed just the same."

The words fogged in front of his face and vanished.

"Mama says a man's duty is to work. To keep his head down and his hands busy." He paused. "That's not enough. Not for me."

He twisted a mug in his hands, watching it catch the moonlight. "I don't want to be anyone's tool," he said. "Not a king's. Not a priest's. Not anyone who won't speak plain." The admission startled him. He tried again, slower. "If a man's going to follow anything," he said, "he ought to choose. And it shouldn't be… empty. It ought to mean something."

The tavern was loud but Karl was lost in his own thoughts. He wasn't sure why his mind had pivoted to form a life code. When he rose to leave, his feet were numb and his boots stiff, but something in him moved easier. Like a compass needle had stopped spinning. That night as he closed his eyes to sleep, he whispered in the dark: "A man ought to choose."

Chapter 8

Karl was carrying charts from Lafitte's warehouse to the docks when shouting erupted near the Spanish quarter. A knot of men were yelling in rapid Castilian surrounding a young woman clutching a cloth-wrapped parcel to her chest.

She was maybe eighteen—olive-skinned, dark-haired, slender in a green dress that belonged to a better neighborhood. Two Spanish sailors circled her. One grabbed her arm. She fought like a cornered animal until his hand sent her to the stones.

Karl froze, caught between fear and instinct. He never had the chance to do what he'd vowed he would—choose. A pistol cocked nearby, smooth and unmistakable. "Let her up," Jean Lafitte said from behind the crowd. He did not shout. He didn't need to. Men parted around him without knowing why.

The sailor who had knocked down the girl spat, "This is not your affair, corsair." Lafitte smiled, all cool civility and hidden steel. "Everything in this town is my affair," he said. The man drew a knife. Lafitte didn't flinch. He lifted his pistol and fired once into the air. Far down the street, a line of soldiers turned their heads.

"You have two choices," Lafitte said calmly. "Run, or explain to the guard why you are abducting a young lady." Cowardice and calculation circulated for a heartbeat. Then the sailors fled down the alley, swearing in Spanish as they went.

Lafitte holstered the pistol and knelt beside the fallen girl. "Élise," he said softly, his voice as soft as velvet. "You walk dangerous ground." She glared up at him, still clutching the parcel. "I have yet to find ground that repels danger," she said.

He offered his hand. She hesitated, then took it. Karl saw a tenderness between them, the easy familiarity of two people whose story had begun long before this afternoon. Watching them, Karl sensed that love had its own navigation.

The story of Élise Moreau reached Karl in fragments over the following weeks. She was the daughter of a French merchant murdered during a plantation uprising, and she possessed something half the city coveted—the last merchant notes her father left behind, enough currency to change her fate or destroy it.

Lafitte arranged protection without announcements or ownership. Soon men who answered only to him watched the roofs above her street. Jean never claimed Élise, never confined her, never announced his guardianship. Yet he courted her in ways unmistakable to anyone with eyes. In the market he offered his arm. She took it without hesitation.

When a dockhand mocked her accent, Lafitte stepped forward with a sudden, dangerous stillness. Élise touched his wrist before he could speak, and his anger evaporated as quickly as it had risen. She leaned in and whispered something that made him laugh—a warm, unguarded sound Karl had never before heard. Then she tugged his collar straight, and Lafitte kissed her temple in front of half the harbor without embarrassment.

In every gesture Karl saw how a man might treat a woman—with strength that protected and touch that reassured. Their affection wasn't secret and wasn't reckless. It was deliberate, witnessed, and instructive.

One evening he found them on the warehouse roof, overlooking the harbor at sunset. Élise sat between Lafitte's legs, her back against his chest, stitching an embroidered kerchief. She worked intently as his fingers brushed little circles along her shoulders. She sighed at his distraction, but she didn't move away.

Karl tried to retreat. Lafitte heard him. "Come," Lafitte said. "Sit." Karl did, careful as a shadow.

Lafitte glanced toward the harbor. "What do you see?"

Karl squinted. "Ships. Sailors. Plantation smoke."

Élise tilted her head back slightly to look at Lafitte, and he kissed her forehead with a smile that held both pride and amusement. "And what does Élise see?" Lafitte asked.

Élise didn't stop her stitching, but her voice softened. "I see the sails of French ships. I watch for a ship that will take me away from this island." Lafitte's fingers went still against her shoulder. For a moment something unguarded crossed his face. Not anger. Not pride. Disappointment.

"A ship to take you away," he repeated, purposely looking away from Élise as he tested the weight of her words. Élise continued stitching. He withdrew his hand slowly, folding both arms across his chest, reclaiming his composure. He had carved out a future here. He naturally assumed she would remain in it.

"You see the present," he said at last, turning to Karl. "She sees the past." His mouth curved faintly, but the smile did not reach his eyes. "The past is done. The time to be happy is now." He let the words hang in the humid air. "Only this moment is real," he continued, his voice low and steady, "If happiness waits for permission, it never comes. You take it."

Jean's eyes stayed focused on Karl. "You rise before dawn, scrub the deck, coil the lines. You seize the day without waiting. That is freedom. Happiness is earned by taking hold of life, not granted by some mystical force."

Karl wasn't certain if those words were meant for him. Or Élise. Or maybe Jean himself. Karl shifted in his seat. Embrace the day. Choose happiness. Jean was beginning to sound strangely like Mama.

Jean leaned closer to Élise, voice low but still at a level meant for Karl, too. "Occasionally it can be wise to glimpse the future. I hope the future is sitting with me." Élise's needle paused mid-air. She turned and kissed him. When she drew back, her voice was low and steady. "We shall see."

Karl watched, a lump rising in his throat. After a long moment he blurted, "And…what is love then?" Élise paused. Lafitte didn't laugh or mock, he gently brushed a thumb under Élise's chin before answering.

"Love," he said, "is wind you cannot chart. You let it carry you, or you break against it. And a man," he added, glancing at Élise with a crooked smile, "must never pretend he commands it."

Élise rewarded him with another kiss. "For once, Jean has spoken wisely," she teased, wiping a smudge from his cheek with her thumb.

After a hesitant silence, Karl dug into his coat and produced the small wooden swan—Papa's carving, Mama's cherished keepsake. He held it out awkwardly, sensing the gesture was foolish. "It was my mother's," he managed. "My father carved it for her. She said swans meant peace…and keeping faith."

Élise set aside her needlework and took the carving lightly, as though it might disturb the memory it carried. Her thumb traced the wing-feathers.

"Que c'est beau," she whispered, French for how beautiful it is. "So small, and yet…so fierce in its grace." Lafitte leaned in, studying it without mockery. "A craftsman made this," he said quietly. "A man who cared for the woman who carried it."

Élise looked up at Karl, her dark eyes warm. "This is not a toy. It is… how do you say…an inheritance of the heart." Karl beamed. He had expected curiosity, maybe amusement, not reverence.

Élise returned the carving with both hands, as though restoring something sacred. "Then keep it well," she said. "Peace returns to those who guard it."

Karl slipped the swan back into his pocket. He stored away moments like this, knowing Mama would approve of tonight's lesson. He was basking in the conversation, longing for it to continue.

"Jean," Karl said suddenly, "have you heard of Klaus Störtebeker?" Lafitte tipped his head, more curious than annoyed. "Ah," Lafitte said, "the Hamburg corsair. Hero or villain depending on who pours the ale."

Lafitte stretched his legs as though settling into a tale he hadn't planned to tell. "Störtebeker frightened merchants and irritated princes," Jean said. "That alone earns him a place in my heart."

Karl hesitated, his thumb rubbing the seam of his shirt. "My father admired him," he said quietly. Lafitte glanced over. "Your father had taste."

Karl tried not to smile, but Jean's response had encouraged him. "Hamburg keeps Störtebeker's drinking mug in the town hall," Karl said. "Papa took me and my brother there when I was small. Said a man who could empty a full tankard in one draught deserved to be remembered."

Lafitte leaned back against a crate, considering the thought. "Stories are the only coin a man keeps after the state takes the rest," Jean said at last. "No ruler has yet found a way to tax a tale."

Karl felt the conversation stitching itself into him, thread by thread, until he no longer wished to leave the rooftop. With Jean and Élise beside him, the night air seemed warmer than any memory of home.

"Why did Störtebeker have to die the way he did?" Karl asked, hoping to re-ignite the exchange. Lafitte's dark brow arched. "Freedom, my boy, is a currency. Störtebeker bought legend but he paid with his head."

"So you respect him?" Karl asked. Lafitte chuckled low in his throat. "I respect any man whose enemies remember him after several centuries. But I do not envy him. He emptied mugs. I prefer to fill coffers."

Élise nudged him with her shoulder. "In other words, Karl, Jean admires courage so long as it does not interfere with commerce."

Karl laughed, but his spine tightened. He wondered what Papa would think of Lafitte, this corsair who spoke of freedom as currency and affection as strategy. Would Papa approve? Would he call it wisdom? Folly? And Störtebeker—would he have followed a man like Lafitte, or slit his throat in the night?

Karl said nothing. His fingers closed around the wooden swan in his pocket. Lafitte had ships and power. Störtebeker had legend. Karl had a wooden swan with worn wings.

Karl was about to speak again when a lantern flashed in a window across the square. One blink. Two. Three. Darkness.

Jean had stopped breathing before the third flash.

He did not move. He did not speak.

He simply watched the dark where the light had been.

Chapter 9

The morning market in Cap-Français was a riot of color and sound. Stalls bristled with sugar, coffee, and indigo, their fragrant powders mingling with the salt air. Merchants shouted over one another and the clang of bells from the distant cathedral punctuated the chaos.

Élise moved through the market like a shadow, eyes sharp beneath the wide brim of her bonnet. Every glance seemed meant for her. She understood why. The word of her inheritance had spread like wildfire.

A Spanish agent, donning an immaculate coat, asked after her in persuasive tones, his questions wrapped in flattery. French officers greeted politely, but the glint in their eyes betrayed their intent. Everywhere, whispers chased her footsteps.

As evening fell, a merchant approached with a cordial bow, offering an invitation to a private dinner, his eyes bright with covetousness. She smiled, weighing the greed behind his courtesy. She could not trust appearances. She declined the invite politely but completely.

Her inheritance promised wealth, yes, but it delivered a merciless world.

One night Karl found Jean on the gallery, sharpening a knife against a whetstone. Sparks leapt with each slow stroke. "They will come for her again," Lafitte said, eyes on the blade. "Men who believe gold grants them license."

"What will you do?" Karl asked. Lafitte tested the edge of the blade with his thumb. "What I have always done, guard what others would devour. Even if I cannot hold it." At the time, Karl thought Jean meant the money.

The unease surrounding Élise deepened her bond with Jean. Their affection grew quietly—glances spoke volumes, dangers were shared without complaint.

One afternoon Karl asked Harwood what he made of it. Harwood scratched his beard. "Love makes men fools—and sometimes heroes. Watch Lafitte awhile. You'll see both."

So Karl watched and something stirred inside him. Not jealousy, or desire, but a vision of some future shore where a voice might call him back from danger. Love, he decided, was like the sea itself. Beautiful, perilous, and worth learning.

One night, with little warning, the world shifted beneath them.

Bootsteps thundered on Élise's gallery. She had just snuffed her lamp when the lock gave way with a crack. Three men burst in. One seized her wrists, another clapped a scarf over her mouth, a third caught her ankles as she kicked. Her sewing basket overturned, needles skittering across the floor.

Across the hall, Lafitte's door splintered as shapes stormed in with clubs and short sabers. Lafitte fired once from the pillow and missed, then he was struck from behind before he could reload. He fell face first to the floor. He twisted and flailed on the ground until they bound his wrists with sailcloth.

Élise was carried barefoot down the exterior stairs. Lafitte stumbled in the grasp of two men, blood on his lip and murder in his eyes. They were dragged to the wharf beneath tarred canvas. Lafitte tried one last time, throwing his full weight sideways and toppling two men. A club answered, driving the air from his lungs. Élise screamed behind the gag, her whole body straining toward Jean.

A waiting schooner rocked at the pilings, lanterns waving. The prisoners were shoved aboard. The ship slid into darkness before the harbor patrol realized a mooring had been cut.

Karl heard of the struggle too late. By the time he reached the docks with a pistol trembling in his hand, the schooner was already fading into the night. He fired once—aimless, furious—and the shot dissolved in the wind.

For two days he searched without sleep, bargaining with cutthroats and pleading with officials. The American vice-consul shrugged. Privateers were inconvenient rumors.

Karl did not leave the matter alone. He requested an audience with Don Esteban Valera, a Spanish customs magistrate whose patience was said to be shorter than his temper. The clerk tried to dismiss him twice before Karl forced the matter with a quiet insistence that did not fit his youth.

The magistrate received him in a shaded office that smelled of ink and citrus oil. Valera did not offer a seat. "You are a German clerk," the Spaniard said, studying him as if he were flawed merchandise. "Why do you trouble Spanish authority with French problems?" Karl lowered his gaze. He let silence hang just long enough to imply reluctance.

"Because," he said softly, "the men who took prisoners were not acting for Spain." That made Valera look up. Karl stepped closer, lowering his voice. "They claimed Havana backing. They wanted it known. Loudly. In taverns. On purpose." He let the implication breathe. "If that is false, it suggests someone profits from making Spain appear… disorderly."

Valera clenched his jaw. Karl continued, measured and respectful. "If it is true, then it means the bounties are no longer contained to certain waters. That is a matter for governors." He did not blink.

The lie was elegant. He had no proof of tavern boasting. No certainty the kidnappers wanted Spain implicated. But he was beginning to understand pride. And pride, once provoked, was more powerful than law.

Valera studied him. "You presume much," the magistrate said.

"I report what I hear," Karl replied. It was not entirely untrue.

"Be careful, German," Valera said. "Men who understand pride often provoke it in the wrong direction."

When Karl left, he knew two things. First, Valera would make inquiries, not for Jean's sake, but for Spain's reputation. Second, he would remember the young foreigner who dared suggest that Spanish authority might be losing control of its own shadow networks.

Karl felt no triumph in the manipulation. Only the quiet, hard understanding that truth alone did not move men in power. Reputation did.

The captors of Jean and Élise were no common thieves. They belonged to Spanish-aligned syndicates paying blood prices for certain names. For months the taverns whispered that Lafitte had been raiding ships bound for Havana rather than neutral ports. His raids were choking a Spanish artery that moved sugar, weapons, and worse. Unable to strike openly, the governors paid in gold instead. Gold for silence. Bounty for bodies.

Élise had unknowingly worsened matters by showing Jean a packet of letters left by her murdered father. The letters named Spanish officers who financed privateering suppression through Creole intermediaries in the islands. "These are not smugglers," she had said. "They are agents." Lafitte had laughed, dismissing the letters without regard.

Far beyond sight of Cap-Français, the captors put Jean and Élise ashore on a barren spit. They left a keg of water, two knives, and the promise someone would "come fetch the bones."

Élise wept, not from terror, but from shame that Jean was made to suffer for her father's letters. Jean brushed sand from her hair. "They erred," he murmured. "They left me alive."

On that nameless rock Jean Lafitte proved why men followed him. He moved with the calm certainty of someone who had stared down worse fates and refused to blink. He scraped holes into the sand until the earth bled brackish water. He lined the shallow wells with stone and coconut husk, letting the sea's bitterness drain until the water ran sweet enough.

He hunted the tidal pools at dawn, wading through knee-deep surf with a sharpened spar of driftwood. Jean drove the spear clean and quick, tossing his catch onto the rocks with a predator's efficiency. He dried the fish on racks so that provisions lasted longer than appetite.

At night, Lafitte carved signs in the sand—crosses, stars, letters— wide as sails, bright under the moon. Even on a forsaken scrap of rock, Lafitte behaved as though rescue were inevitable, not because he hoped for it, but because he intended to compel it.

Élise refused to sit idle while Jean labored. She gathered driftwood and insisted on carrying what she could. When he tried to take the load from her, she held fast. "I will not be freight," she said. "If we live, we live because we both worked for it." Jean acknowledged her words and set her to sorting shell from stone, a purpose less strenuous.

Despite Jean's watchful eye, Élise weakened with each passing day, not from hunger alone but from the sun's relentless authority. By the fourth day, the sun was working on her patiently, hour by hour, draining her faster than Jean could restore her. By the seventh day the sun had begun to hollow her. By the tenth day she no longer rose without swaying.

When the heat peaked, she drifted in and out of wakefulness, lips dry, breath shallow. Her body was no longer cooling itself.

On the eleventh day, the island's silence broke under the harsh cries of seabirds. Lafitte climbed the island's highest crag, hands scraping against coral stone as he gained the vantage. He spotted a sail, square-rigged on an easterly course, scarcely a mile from shore.

He descended at once. Within minutes, a signal fire was laid. He tore his shirt into bands and fixed them to a spar of driftwood, fashioning a proper sign of distress. He returned to the height and waved until his arms burned. He bellowed in French, in Spanish, in English, his voice growing hoarse in the salt air.

For a time the ship held its course, either not seeing or else judging the signal to not be worth the trouble. Élise watched from below, white as linen and barely upright.

Finally, miraculously, the vessel backed its topsails, bow canting toward the island. Canvas took a new line. A boat was lowered. Oars flashed.

Only then did Lafitte's posture slacken. He sank to one knee on the sun-blasted rock, breathing hard as though he had won a duel. He permitted himself the smallest laugh. He had wrested his survival, and the survival of the woman he loved, from stubbornness and a clear understanding that the Caribbean seldom grants second chances.

Élise left the shore changed, lighter, slower, her strength thinned. Even with help, she struggled to board the rescue vessel.

Survival was not recovery.

Chapter 10

When the schooner returned Jean and Élise to Cap-Français, the wharf filled with sailors and idlers drawn by rumor. Karl pushed through the crowd until he saw Jean—shirtless, salt-stung, lean as an island cat, his eyes bright with a private victory.

Élise followed, supported by two crewmen. Her feet barely touched the planks, and when she lifted a hand toward Karl, it trembled and fell. Karl helped carry her to a physician on Rue du Cap, shutters half-open for sea breeze and gossip.

The thin French doctor said little, feeling the flutter of her pulse as he fed her broth. Jean paced outside the exam room, refusing comfort. At last the doctor emerged, spectacles fogged with sweat. "She needs rest," he said. "Rest. Nourishment. Time. She has been given too little of each."

They lodged her above a tailor's shop with blue shutters and a courtyard where children played. Karl visited daily, bringing fruit, broth, and anything that might tempt her appetite. Élise drifted in and out of fever, speaking once of France, once of dance halls, and once, smiling faintly, of the beaches of Cap-Français.

On the fourth night, the fever broke, but her breathing grew thinner, not stronger. At dawn, before the bells, Jean felt Élise's hand go limp and slip from his. He did not call for the doctor or move her arm from her chest. When Karl arrived with bread and tea that morning, Jean's eyes were red and swollen. He was still seated near Élise, but his gaze was distant. For a long time neither spoke.

When Jean finally rose, he drew the sheet over Élise's face with a tenderness Karl had not known he possessed. "In every life," he said, voice low, "there are women who stay and women who go. Élise was both."

They buried her near the old fort that overlooked the harbor where cannons rusted and goats wandered between graves. A few Spaniards, some freedmen, and several smugglers attended at Jean's request.

As the last clumps of earth settled, Jean placed a silver locket atop the mound. The gesture hardened him. The man who taught Karl how to read the measure of other men now seemed tempered in a hotter forge. Less swagger, more steel.

After the shovels were returned and the crowd dispersed, Karl and Jean stood beneath a salt-stunted tree. Karl stared at the sea until it blurred. He said softly, almost to himself: "I am alive… I have work… I am not alone." Jean glanced sideways, a brow lifting. "What is that?"

"Counting blessings," Karl said, cheeks warm. "Mama said it keeps a man steady in storms." Jean considered the thought. "Sounds dangerous," he said. "Reminds a man how much remains to be lost."

Karl did not trust himself to speak. He had been wanting to ask Jean about the deserted island. What does a man do in that situation? The timing was wrong. He would wait for another day to ask. Jean brushed dirt from his palms with the care of a man closing a chapter.

"I cannot stay," he said quietly. "Every street chases me with her laugh. Cap-Français was ours. Now it's a city of shadows." Karl stared. Storms had not shaken Jean. Muskets had not shaken him. Grief plainly had. "Where will you go?" Karl asked. Jean hesitated only a breath. "New Orleans, where my brother keeps a house on the river and trades—of a sort. He'll take me in." A humorless smile touched his mouth. "Or at least he owes me a drink."

The news struck Karl harder than he expected. Lafitte belonged to motion, asking him to remain would be like asking the tide to stay in its basin. Yet the thought of losing him swirled in Karl's chest. "How soon?"

"Soon," Jean said. "The sea does not wait." Karl didn't voice the plea that lingered on his tongue. Jean was not a boy, and begging never turned a tide. "When you go," he said instead, "don't leave without telling me." Jean looked at him fully then, measuring the request, weighing its dignity. He inclined his head in agreement.

Two weeks later, Karl stood on the shore at dawn, watching Jean Lafitte oversee the loading of the ship. The loaders moved quietly, sure-footed, mindful of Jean's loss. Jean spoke seldom, yet every command cut like wire. Whatever he had been before, he now looked like a man preparing not for flight but for reckoning.

Karl admired him for it—the poise, the certainty, the way grief had hammered him into something harder. But admiration did not quiet the unrest in Karl's chest. His mother's voice cut through him like a bugle at dawn: *Vengeance is the Lord's, not ours.*

Harwood walked up and stood beside Karl, arms folded. "You'll go with him," he said. Not a question, merely fact observed. Karl hesitated. "Jean means to destroy a kingdom. That is not my fight." Harwood's beard twitched with something like a smile. "A man doesn't choose his fight. The fight chooses him. Sometimes it waits."

Karl looked at the ship. The black hull cut against the brightening sky. Jean moved among the crew with a purpose that belonged to the wounded and the unafraid. Karl muttered, "Mama would call this the devil's work."

"And you?" Harwood asked. Karl had no answer. He admired Jean's devotion to Élise, and his refusal to bow to the crown. There was a clarity in Jean that felt almost holy.

Jean spotted him and came over, gait uneven from his weariness, eyes clear. "You're thinking too loudly," Jean said with a faint smirk. "That is dangerous on an island like this." Karl tried to hide his thoughts, but Jean's eyes were too sharp.

"I'm evaluating regret," Karl said. "I think I will regret going with you. And I think I will regret not going with you." Jean smiled.

"You do not owe me anything," Jean said. "If you stay, I will not think less of you. If you go with me, you will be part of something the world will remember." His gaze drifted toward the horizon, darkened by his grief. "The Spanish believe they own the Gulf. I intend to show them otherwise."

Karl studied him. The sharp light behind Jean's eyes was love. Love that was lost and now weaponized. Softly, Karl asked, "Why does God let kings grind the poor to dust?" Jean did not pause. "Because He leaves men to their own courage."

The simplicity struck Karl like divine scripture. Jean's God breathed fire into broken men and gave them reason to rise.

Karl closed his eyes. He saw Mama praying by candle flame. He saw Élise torn from Jean. When he opened them again, the world looked crueler. And clearer.

He pulled the wooden swan from his coat and kissed it once. "Forgive me, Mama," he whispered. Then, louder, to Jean: "Save me a berth." Jean smiled. "Good," he said. "New Orleans will sharpen us both."

Karl ambled up the gangway, everything he owned in one small satchel. He could feel Mama's teachings shrinking inside him, though not without a fight. He whispered a prayer to himself, not for an answer, but that he hadn't crossed an irreversible line.

In the distance, he heard the familiar ring of church bells.

Chapter 11

Jean secured passage on a swift Bermudan schooner named *Étoile Marie*, whose captain owed Pierre Lafitte favors stretching back to Cádiz. The ship was fast, nimble, and well-manned, but Jean warned Karl of the dangers that lay ahead.

"The Spanish patrol these waters like hungry wolves," Jean said. "They will fire without warning. Follow my lead. Otherwise, you will wish you never heard of New Orleans."

Karl wondered why Jean hadn't shared the potential perils before departure. Maybe that was the lesson. Freedom does not announce its price in advance. Few men would pursue freedom if they knew its price upfront.

Jean stood at the stern, face to the wind. He had not looked back at the island. Not once.

Karl was beside him as the coastline thinned. Behind them, a smaller vessel appeared. No flag flew from her mast. Her sails were trimmed tight. She kept her distance, then slowly began to close. Jean watched without expression and said, "We have a shadow."

On the quarterdeck of the pursuing ship stood a narrow man in a

Spanish officer's coat. Spectacles caught the shimmer from the water. In his gloved hand he held a folded paper. Jean's voice lowered. "Valera," he said. Karl knew the name.

The Spanish ship fired a single warning shot across their bow. Not to sink. To halt. Jean did not ask for return fire. Instead, he turned to the crew and said, "Bring us alongside." Karl looked at him. "Jean—"

"Bring us alongside," Jean repeated. The vessels drew near, hulls groaning as they touched. Grapples flew. Wood struck wood. The sea pressed them together like unwilling partners.

Valera stood waiting. "You were reported dead," the magistrate called across the narrowing gap to Jean. "An inconvenience needs to be corrected."

Jean stepped onto the rail before the gangplank settled. He crossed first. No pistol drawn. No haste. The Spanish sailors shifted uneasily. Valera raised a hand and they held.

"This need not end poorly," Valera said. "You mistake Spain's discipline for cruelty."

Jean stopped three paces away. "You sent them," Jean said.

Valera did not bother to deny it. "You had become disorder. Disorder spreads."

"And the girl?" Jean asked. Valera's expression remained emotionless. "She was a complication," he said. "Complications are costly."

The word fell between them. Complication. Not a name. Not a life. An accounting error.

Jean remained surprisingly calm. "You left us to starve," he said.

"You survived," Valera replied coolly. "Clearly my assessment was incomplete, which is why we meet today."

Jean drew his pistol then. Slowly. Almost thoughtfully. Valera did the same. The men locked eyes.

Jean fired first. The sound was sharp, not thunderous. Valera's spectacles fell and shattered when they hit the deck. He staggered but did not drop immediately. He looked down at the spreading dark on his coat.

"This," he breathed, "changes nothing." Jean stepped closer. Close enough that no one else could hear him. "It changes Élise." He fired again. Valera's body struck the deck once before rolling against the drain. Blood slid between the planks and dripped into the sea.

The Spanish crew did not advance. They followed authority. Authority was gone.

Jean bent to retrieve the folded paper from Valera's slack hand. A list of names. His was first. Karl's was beneath it.

Jean folded the paper twice, and tucked it into his coat. Then he turned his back on Valera's body and walked calmly to the rail. He stepped back onto his own ship without looking down.

"Cut loose," he said. The Spanish vessel drifted, leaderless.

Karl stared at the widening space of water between the vessels. He realized Jean didn't kill Valera in anger. He killed him like a man balancing an account.

He shifted his gaze from the water to Jean, who was back at the stern. Jean had avenged Élise, but his appearance was not one of triumph. Yes, he had closed a ledger, but the pain in his face remained. Maybe Mama was right. Vengeance was not meant for men.

Karl spent his days among the rigging, learning every rope and spar under the first mate's sarcastic instruction. In the evenings, Jean taught him the invisible arts of their new reality: how to gauge a man's price and how to tell a privateer from a pirate by the tilt of his hat and the condition of his boots.

It was during the third week, somewhere between Havana and the

Mississippi Delta, that Karl faced another test of nerve, again from the Spanish. A cutter, dark and swift, appeared on the horizon, guns glinting, moving as if it had scented prey. The *Étoile Marie's* crew froze, realizing too late that the patrol had spotted them.

The captain barked orders, but a stray shot from the Spaniard's bow cannon tore through a coil of rope, flinging the first mate across the quarterdeck. Karl's stomach dropped as the mate crashed into the hatch. The cutter's guns thundered again, splintering the railing near the bow.

Jean's voice cut through the terror. "Karl! At the wheel—now!" Karl bolted across the slick deck, boots sliding. He seized the wheel with hands trembling, as the *Étoile Marie* lurched under the first broadside. Cannonballs smashed the water alongside, sending sprays that drenched him to the bone.

"Hard to leeward!" Jean roared, climbing the rigging to keep the sails from tearing. "Keep her bow to the guns!" Karl fought the wheel with every ounce of strength. The schooner twisted, but he held her steady, bow into the Spanish fire. The crew followed his lead, trimming sails and manning the small swivels.

For an hour he steered through the hail of cannonfire, each shot a drumbeat of dread, until at last the Spanish, either frustrated or unwilling to risk the shallow shoals, fell back and melted into the horizon. Karl sagged over the wheel as Jean approached and clapped him on the shoulder with a grin.

"You kept us alive," Jean said. "That was command."

Karl's chest heaved. "I just did what had to be done."

Jean tilted his head. "That's what command is."

When the *Étoile Marie* finally slipped into the mouth of the Mississippi, the sailors treated Karl differently. They didn't say much, sailors rarely did, but they made room for him at the galley table and listened when he spoke. This life wasn't what Mama had envisioned for her youngest son, but Karl was reveling in belonging.

The schooner wound through the muddy arteries of the river with New Orleans blossoming ahead—church spires rising above French balconies and a hundred secret fortunes exchanging hands in the shade.

Jean leaned on the rail beside Karl and pointed toward the bustling port. "There," he said. "That's where a new chapter begins. With luck, with cunning, and with a few sins along the way… we might yet make something of ourselves." Karl would have felt more comfortable had Jean not mentioned sin.

As they stepped onto dry land, Karl took in the sights of New Orleans and sought for comparisons to Hispaniola. The docks of Cap-Français had smelled of rum and blood and sea. Here, the air tasted of mud, spice, and smoke. Colors collided in every direction. Shutters painted blue, green, and gold, banners fluttering above narrow streets, the glare of sunlight bouncing off tin roofs. Smoke from grills and forge fires curled into the air, mingling with the scent of sugar, citrus, and the river.

The city clashed together like a song played too fast and too loud, yet somehow beautiful, alive in a way that made Karl's palms sweat. "Close your mouth," Jean teased. "You'll catch flies in New Orleans. Nothing here stops long enough for gawking."

Karl grinned, but his eyes never ceased moving. Street vendors shouted in French and Spanish. English sailors brawled near a tavern. Women in bright skirts dodged past them with baskets of eggs and oranges. A cart loaded with sugar barrels lurched dangerously across a street. Karl dodged instinctively. Jean kept his stride, confident and steady.

Karl's gaze snapped to the alley, and his stomach tightened. A trio of men stepped forward, shadows stretching long. One swung a velvet pouch idly, but the weight in his hand seemed threatening. Jean pressed a hand to

Karl's shoulder. "Stay steady, Karl. Don't give them a reason."

The men hissed words too low for Karl to understand. Then one of them lunged. Karl reacted on instinct, dropping the satchel of his belongings and ducking beneath the man's grasp. Jean caught the attacker's wrist mid-reach and twisted sharply, stepping inside the man's balance with fluid precision. The man rattled the cobblestones with a thud.

The second trader drew a short knife, its blade flashing in the sun. Karl reached for a crate lid and thrust it between them just as the knife came down. Steel shrieked across the wood. Jean did not retreat. He pivoted, seized the man's collar, and drove him back into a stack of sugar barrels. The blade clattered away.

A third man circled behind them, aiming again for the satchel. Karl spun, elbow catching ribs. Jean's voice cut through the uproar, sharp and commanding in rapid French. The words snapped like musket fire. Whatever he said froze two of the men in place. Karl caught only fragments, but he saw fear flicker across their faces.

Jean stepped forward, advancing just enough to make his dominance clear. "Messieurs," he said evenly, the single word weighted with warning. No one moved. Then Jean turned slightly toward Karl, not breaking eye contact with the men. "Pick up the satchel," he said quietly. "And walk."

Not run. Walk. Karl obeyed. He bent, retrieved the satchel, and had an uncomfortable feeling. He thought this to be a thief's petty hold-up. Maybe it was something else entirely. A test of newcomers, perhaps. They exited the alley and turned onto the broader street where vendors shouted as though nothing at all had occurred.

Karl waited until they had put a full block between themselves and the alley before speaking. "They risked broken bones," he said, glancing down at the satchel in his hand. "For this?" Jean did not slow. Karl continued, "There's not enough in here to tempt a hungry dockhand."

Jean's mouth curved with acknowledgment. "They did not want your satchel," he said. "They wanted to see how we would respond. New faces do not move through certain quarters without being measured."

"Being measured for what?" Karl asked.

"Composure. Allegiance. Nerve." Jean glanced sideways at him. "Whether you run. Whether you fight. Whether you shout for authorities who are not welcome."

Karl exhaled slowly. "So what did they learn?"

Jean's expression remained unreadable. "That you walk when told." There was something in the way he said it—approval edged with instruction. "They know you stand beside me."

Karl had fought pirates. He had survived storms and cannon fire. But this invisible lattice of tests and unspoken rules was different.

Jean marched him through the rattling crowds until they reached Rue des Tanneurs, where the smell of worked leather and horseflesh drifted from stables. At the end of the street stood a blacksmith's shop, honest enough in appearance, with a wooden sign etched with a simple horseshoe and the name:

P. Lafitte — Maréchal-Ferrant

Jean grinned. "My brother plays at respectability."

Inside, the forge roared. A broad-shouldered man stood bare-armed before the anvil, hammering a glowing horseshoe. He had the same sharp Lafitte features as Jean—dark hair, hawk's nose, and black eyes that seemed to weigh a man before deciding what he was worth.

When he heard them enter, Pierre quenched the iron with a hiss and turned. "Jean," he said, flatly at first, then the corners of his mouth curved. "You cursed devil. I thought you rotted in Cap-Français."

Jean threw his arms around his brother in a rough embrace. "I nearly did." Pierre's smile faded as he studied his brother's face more closely.

"Something happened."

"Later," Jean replied, voice low. "This is Karl. He sailed with me."

Pierre gave Karl a single assessing glance. A look that seemed to strip away ego, pretense, and fear. "You're young."

"I am," Karl managed. He had turned fifteen, without fanfare, on the voyage across the gulf. "Good. Young men learn faster." Pierre pulled a shirt over his head and wiped his hands on a rag. "Come to the back. There's wine, and I have news."

Pierre poured dark wine into three cups. "To surviving," he said. They drank, and Jean finally spoke of Élise, of the kidnapping, of the island and the rescue. Pierre listened without interruption, though his knuckles whitened around his cup. When Jean finished, there was silence.

Pierre set his cup down. "You were right to leave. This city is tonic for grief. It will either drown you or sharpen you. Better than rotting on that cursed island."

Karl glanced around the room at the crates stenciled with foreign markings. For a blacksmith shop, there was a great deal of merchandise that had nothing to do with horseshoes. "Your business seems… successful," Karl ventured.

Pierre smirked. "The shop keeps Sheriff Morales content and the Americans blind. But the real coin is in the Bayous. Guns. Powder. Sugar. Coffee. Whatever moves at a profit."

Karl wasn't sure what to say. "You smuggle?"

Jean chuckled. "He organizes smuggling. There's a difference."

Pierre shrugged. "Call it commerce. Call it survival. This city hungers, and I feed it."

Pierre stood and clapped Jean on the shoulder. "You're home now. There's room for you here. Work, ships, men loyal enough not to slit your throat while you sleep." Jean raised his brows slightly. "And for Karl?"

Pierre studied the young German again, slower this time. "If he's useful." Karl straightened, heart pounding. "I can sail. I can fight if needed." Pierre waved the words away. "Anyone can fight. Can you listen?" Karl paused, then responded with a nod. "Yes."

Pierre leaned forward. "Then you might survive New Orleans. Which is more than I can say for half the captains in this harbor."

Karl considered recounting the survival of alley chaos, then decided some stories were best left unspoken. He was thankful that Jean hadn't mentioned it either.

Pierre finished his wine. "Rest tonight. Tomorrow, we introduce you to the Bayou."

He turned back to the forge, where the fire still glowed, waiting to shape iron, or maybe men, as it pleased.

Karl followed Jean outside. The streets of New Orleans pulsed with unruly, irresistible life. Karl was on the threshold of a world more dangerous than any sea, where honest blacksmith shops hid profitable sin, and where his future would be forged on anvils of fire and ambition.

Mama would hate this place.

Chapter 12

Karl soon learned that New Orleans was two cities. One built of brick, balconies, and bustling markets, and another made of water, shadow, and whispered deals. It was into the second one that Pierre Lafitte introduced him.

They set out before dawn, taking a narrow skiff from a hidden dock behind the blacksmith shop. Jean lounged in the prow with a long gun across his knees, while Pierre poled them into the Mississippi's murky embrace. The river air smelled of rot and magnolia. Before long the city faded behind them, replaced by cypress knees jutting from black water, draped in Spanish moss. The bayou seemed to swallow sound.

Pierre finally spoke. "This place is older than any king or empire. It remembers the French, the Spaniards, the Choctaw, and whoever comes next. We move quietly. It hears everything." Karl gripped the side of the skiff.

They reached a cluster of stilted shacks half-hidden in the brush. Men emerged with crates that smelled of molasses and gunpowder. No one greeted them with words. Pierre traded hand signs and nods before pushing off again with half a dozen crates aboard.

When the skiff was deep in the bayou once more, Karl finally asked, "Where does this go?" Pierre kept his eyes on the water. "To a certain Spanish colonel's estate upriver. His soldiers are short on powder. Morale dips when a man feels the city has forgotten him."

Karl frowned. "But Spain is the enemy." Pierre's eyes glanced back, amused. "Which enemy? The Spanish who govern? The Americans who want the port? The French who want their colony back? Or the Creoles who want them all to go to hell?"

Karl was surprised Jean would supply the Spanish. He was about to say something, but Jean grunted before he could. "Nations change," Jean said. "Money stays."

Pierre continued poling them through a curtain of reeds. "Politics here is simple, Karl. Americans, Spanish, and French all fight for power. And pirates—well…" He glanced toward Jean. "We control whatever they forget to guard."

By late morning, they arrived at a tobacco plantation where Spanish soldiers lounged under shade awnings. Pierre oversaw the exchange as calmly as a merchant bartering cloth, though the Spanish officer kept glancing at the knife on Pierre's belt. Not a single helmeted officer questioned why a "blacksmith" had such goods to sell.

Back in the skiff, Pierre handed Karl a small cloth purse that jingled with coin. Karl looked down in surprise. "What is—"

"Your share," Pierre said. "You were our witness." Karl weighed it in his palm. "But I didn't do anything." Jean laughed. "Not doing anything is often the difference between life and death in the bayou."

Pierre added, "You didn't argue. You didn't ask foolish questions in front of the wrong ears. You didn't look nervous. That matters." Pierre pushed the skiff off a mudbank with the pole, watching Karl the way a card player watches a new hand. "Trust must be earned. So must discretion."

As they drifted back toward New Orleans, thunder rolled across the swamp. Pierre's face tightened. "The Americans are coming for this city," he said. "Mark my words. Every governor Washington sends wants this port stripped of French pride."

Karl asked, quietly, "And you? What do you want?" Pierre poled the boat another yard before answering. "Freedom to trade without being lectured by men who never felt a storm at sea." Jean added with a half-smirk, "Freedom to do as we please, and enough reputation that men think twice before crossing us."

Karl sat back as the city's spires reappeared through the trees. This wasn't smuggling, he thought. This was survival in a world where governments shifted like tides.

That night, Pierre called him into the shop after they'd stowed the skiff. "You listened," Pierre said. "You learned. And you did not lose your nerve. That is enough for a beginning."

From a locked cabinet, he set before Karl a small, well-worn pistol. Karl closed his hand around the grip. It felt heavier than expected, not just with steel but responsibility. Pierre lifted his chin, satisfied. "Jean trusts you," he said. "And I trust Jean. You've earned a place here. Don't waste it."

Karl Steinheimer—once a runaway orphan—stood on the doorstep of a life carved by cunning and loyalty. He had earned Pierre's trust. But what exactly did that entail?

A few nights later, Jean summoned Karl to the rear of the smithy, where Pierre waited with three maps spread across an unplaned workbench. Pierre tapped at the first map—of the Gulf—and said, "The Spanish think they can cut us off at sea." He tapped the second—of the

Mississippi delta—"We simply move the war to the swamps."

Jean pointed at Barataria Bayou, a chaotic maze of reeds and tidal channels. "We take our ships there. The Americans do not patrol it. The Spanish cannot find it. We strike from the marsh."

Pierre slid Karl a small packet of letters sealed in wax. "These go to smugglers and planters. Men who owe us favors. Deliver them quietly." Karl signaled agreement with a nod. Letters meant trust. Letters also meant danger.

When the meeting ended, Jean stopped Karl at the door. "You know why we chose Barataria?" Karl shook his head. "Because it gives us what the Spanish never will—room to breathe. And because I intend to make them choke on their own arrogance."

Karl had seen that fire before, at Élise's grave. It frightened him, and thrilled him, and made him wonder what Mama would say to Jean if he were her son.

A few days later, as promised, Jean and Pierre took Karl south—past the mouth of the Mississippi, through winding bayous where cypress knees rose like water-logged cathedrals. Barataria was not a town but a principality of outcasts: smugglers, sailors, escaped slaves, Isleños fishermen, Creoles, and free men of color. It was a world beyond American jurisdiction, governed by two rules: pay fairly and keep your word.

Karl's first sight of Barataria Bay was unforgettable. Dozens of varied ships anchored among the barrier islands like a secret fleet. Blacksmiths hammered iron on makeshift anvils. Gunsmiths cleaned flintlocks by the dozen. Tents and shacks dotted the beach, flying no flags but serving every nation when silver was good.

Jean spread his arms wide like a showman. "Barataria, dear Karl! A city without taxes, a court without judges, and a fleet without a king!"

Karl stared, stunned. "How does something like this exist?"

Pierre answered dryly, "By being just useful enough to everyone."

Not surprisingly, the Lafittes made it a point to be acquainted with everyone. They sold confiscated Spanish goods to Creole merchants. They traded gunpowder to planters terrified of slave uprisings. They provided foreign luxuries to American officers who swore they hated smugglers but loved brandy.

Pierre led Karl through the camp, naming the men who mattered. "That's Captain Dominique—you cross him, you swim home. That's Baptiste—our best pilot through the marsh. Over there, the blacksmith from Salvador who repairs a cannon faster than most men can blink. Learn their names. They may save your life someday."

Karl listened. Pierre began sending him north to meet merchants, to judge character, to negotiate prices. Karl discovered he could read men well. Meanwhile, Jean taught him how to fight with a boarding pistol, and how to spot a false flag before it killed you.

Pierre secured warehouses along the levee, hidden behind legitimate fronts: a tannery, a chandlery, even a modest café that served fishermen and smugglers alike. Jean handled the crews at sea—swift schooners that outran customs cutters and Spanish patrol boats.

From Barataria, the Lafitte operation grew like a storm cloud over the Gulf. Karl improved his stock by being fearless. When the city's customs men began weighing rum and gunpowder shipments with suspicious zeal, Karl and two others spent a muggy night hollowing out molasses barrels, scooping the thick syrup into slop buckets. At dawn they filled the empty cores with gunpowder kegs, sealed the tops with warm molasses, and sent them upriver on a barge smelling sweet as Sunday morning. The customs inspector tapped one barrel, tasted the molasses, and waved the shipment through.

By such daring acts, Karl earned a name spoken with respect, or at least with the kind of envy that counted for respect in Barataria.

Opportunity and betrayal arrived together on a humid night in Barataria. A shipment of powder and muskets was due from Cartagena, destined for American planters desperate to arm militia. Karl was given command of the escort, his first major responsibility. But one of his own men, a wiry sailor named Bruges, had been bought by Governor William Claiborne's agents.

Bruges slipped away to warn the Americans, hoping for reward and pardon. When the schooner approached the cove, two American cutters burst from behind marsh grass, guns loaded. "Stand down!" an officer shouted. "By order of the United States Navy, heave to!" Panic rippled through Karl's crew. Powder kegs lay open on deck. One spark would send them all to the sky. Karl hesitated only long enough to remember Mama's voice.

Then he shouted, "Run up the Spanish flag. They'll hesitate!" The Spanish flag snapped in the wind. The cutters faltered. Firing on a Spanish vessel was murky business without witnesses. Karl seized the moment, barking, "Hard to port! Into the reeds!"

The schooner scraped into marsh, men poling desperately. The Americans could not follow without running aground, and soon Karl's vessel vanished into a maze only Baratarians knew. Hours later, safe in the bayou, Bruges was missing. Karl suspected his misdeed. When the schooner returned to Grand Terre, Jean greeted them with a predator's smile. He already knew.

Bruges was dragged in by two watchmen, his wrists bound so tightly his fingers had gone white. He stumbled to his knees before Jean and Pierre. Jean's face was unreadable as the traitor confessed everything—the Spanish agent, the promised silver, the tavern where the bargain was struck. His voice broke twice. He tried to make it sound like necessity.

Karl expected shouting. A pistol across the teeth. Pierre gave him both. Before Bruges could finish naming the price, Pierre struck him across the mouth. Teeth hit the floor. When the man tried to crawl back, Pierre seized him by the collar and hauled him upright, pressing a blade beneath Bruges' jaw. "You endangered every man here," Pierre said loudly with a violence that vibrated in the air. "You endangered my brother." Bruges began to babble about hunger, about fear, about Spain's reach. Pierre's grip tightened. A thin line of blood appeared at the man's throat.

"Enough," Jean said. Pierre did not move at once. For a heartbeat Karl thought Pierre might disobey his brother. Then Pierre released him with a shove that sent Bruges sprawling.

Jean stepped forward and began asking questions in a calm, surgical voice—names, dates, sums, witnesses. He did not raise his tone. He did not repeat himself. Bruges answered because there was nowhere left to run. When judgment came, Jean did not gloat. He did not threaten. "You sell your fear to the highest bidder," he said. "We sell our loyalty. Only one of us will survive this war."

Pierre dragged Bruges away. The man vanished beneath the mangroves. Karl did not ask where he was taken.

What lingered with Karl was what happened afterward. Jean summoned the crew, opened the day's ledger, and distributed the profits from their latest prize. Every man received his lawful share—no favorites, no cheats, no hidden purses. Even cabin boys received their portion, counted into their hands with the same fairness as seasoned crewmen. Karl watched the men nod and murmur their thanks, and he understood why grown sailors followed Jean Lafitte into storms and gunfire. Jean was ruthless, but never crooked with his own.

Karl sensed Mama would have liked that. She would not approve of the smuggling or the guns, but the fairness—the idea that men were bound by honesty—would have stirred something in her heart. For a moment Karl stood between his two worlds, though he knew which one now claimed him.

After that night, men who had watched Karl command now looked at him differently. He had kept his head, made a flag his weapon, and brought them home alive.

Karl spent the rest of the evening on the levee watching bonfires bloom across the city. He had learned that loyalty, once sold, could never be recaptured. Behind him, in the warehouses and taverns of New Orleans, men were whispering the Lafitte name with respect. Or fear.

Karl turned the small pistol Pierre had given him in his hands. Once he believed purpose came from God, work, and family alone. Now it seemed to come from something else entirely. From risk. From loyalty. From the power of knowing that when danger came, men looked to him.

The thought should have troubled him more than it did. The river kept moving, and so did he.

Chapter 13

In 1811, Barataria thrived like a fever dream—half pirate republic, half merchant empire. Jean Lafitte steered the dream with a gambler's instinct and a diplomat's tongue. Karl was his shadow, keeping cargo manifests, tracking secret ledgers, learning how fortunes moved through mud and water.

The world beyond the bayou was tearing itself apart. Napoleon's armies marched across Europe. Spain bled rebellions from Mexico to Buenos Aires. Britain's navy chased enemies across oceans too vast to police. In Washington City, politicians argued beneath plaster ceilings while whispering about another war with Britain.

Empires fought. Barataria prospered.

Ships arrived under every flag and none. Spanish merchantmen heavy with coin. Veracruz schooners carrying cocoa and silver. Smugglers from Curaçao trading medicine for stolen rum. Each arrival fed the legend, and the legend fed the flow of ships. Where nations saw chaos, Lafitte saw opportunity. Barataria bought low, sold high, and prospered in the panic.

Karl remembered vividly the first time he helped take a prize. The

Spanish brig appeared just after dawn, square sails full and careless. Jean studied her through a brass spyglass. Then he smiled. "Too clean," he said. "She's rich."

The Barataria schooner slipped closer under false colors, her crew silent, every man knowing his place. Karl stood near the foremast, heart pounding in his ears.

This was no dockside story now. "Stand ready," Jean said quietly.

The moment broke loose. The false flag dropped. French colors snapped in the wind. Grappling hooks screamed across the water and bit into Spanish railings. The hulls slammed together hard enough to throw men off balance.

Karl seized a line with burning hands and hauled. "Hold!" someone shouted. Karl held.

Steel flashed. A Spaniard lunged for Jean. Karl moved before he could think. He swung a belaying pin and cracked the man's jaw. The sailor dropped.

Jean stared at Karl with surprise for a split second. Then a nod of approval. "Well done," Jean said. Then he turned back to the fight.

The engagement was over almost as quickly as it began. A warning shot into the rigging. A blade at the captain's throat. Surrender spoken in hoarse Spanish. Silence followed, thick and stunned.

Below deck, the truth of the ship revealed itself. Crates of sugar. Barrels of rum. Bolts of cloth. Chests of silver coins stacked like bricks. Enough wealth to change hands quietly, invisibly, from empire to outlaw. Karl stood among it, hands trembling, not from fear, but from the knowledge that he had helped take it.

By midday, the prize was secured and bound for Barataria. Within weeks, the goods would be everywhere: sugar spooned into respectable parlors, rum poured behind polished bars, cloth stitched into dresses worn to church. The city fathers condemned piracy over roast beef and wine, never asking how the silver reached their tables. The city, always smiling, righteous, and complicit, would take its share without ever dirtying its hands.

Karl learned that day how quickly a life could change. He also sensed that this was not a passing venture. This was his life.

By midsummer, wealth moved through Barataria faster than it could be counted. Gold doubloons, valued at roughly fifteen dollars apiece, clinked beneath tavern floorboards. Silver pesos worth about a dollar each were weighed beside salted mullet, and Bolivian ingots worth hundreds of dollars each were stacked behind barrels of pitch. It seemed nations had finally agreed on one currency—plunder.

The more respectable merchants, those who pretended to despise Jean in public, sent agents in the night to buy captured Spanish cargoes at a fraction of their worth. A single captured Spanish merchant ship could yield twenty thousand to forty thousand dollars in sellable goods, sometimes more, and Barataria seized dozens each year. The city shops filled with pirate goods while respectable men denounced piracy at Sunday dinners.

As is often the case, success has a way of bringing new challenges. The challenge for the boys from Barataria became not gathering treasure, but storing it. One evening Jean and Karl stood over a table with a map of marsh channels and shoreline ridges. "Half the world is fighting," Jean muttered, "and the other half is too busy watching to notice us stealing their pockets." Then, more grimly: "If we keep stacking gold in warehouses, someone will burn us out. Better the marsh keeps our accounts."

Karl helped lead the burial parties. Under moonlight they ferried crates into the backcountry. The crates held ingots wrapped in sailcloth, coins sewn into canvas pouches, and pearls sealed in rum bottles. They dug where the marsh grass grew tall and the water table ran low, marking each cache with signs only they would recognize.

On one such night Karl found himself knee-deep in mud, the brackish scent of the bayou thick in his lungs. Lafitte had sent only nine men. Fewer bodies made less noise, and noise might mean rope or bullet. The men worked by starlight, shovels sliding through wet earth with dull thuds, each sound muffled by the reeds.

"Dig faster," one of the men hissed, glancing toward the tree line. A lantern flickered there. Karl's heartbeat quickened, but his hands stayed steady. As a boy he had been awestruck at the thought of privateers. Now he was burying fortunes while the law stalked the dark.

Karl lowered a crate into the hole. Coins rattled softly. He tamped the sand flat, erasing the shape of fortune beneath the earth. Then he set three oyster shells in a careful row. To anyone else they were nothing. To him they were a map.

When the last crate vanished beneath the earth, the men slipped the shovels into the skiff and pushed off into black water. Karl watched the banks recede, full of glittering secrets no one would believe. He wiped mud from his palms and allowed himself a small, breathless smile.

He did not think of the riches underground. He thought of the night itself. The danger, the silence, the thrill of outwitting men who wore uniforms and claimed the right to judge. In a world carved up by empires, this hidden bayou belonged to no king.

By autumn, there were more graves of treasure in Barataria than graves of men, though both were plentiful. Rumor in New Orleans said Lafitte slept on gold. Rumor in Mexico City claimed he had a vault beneath the bayou. The truth, whispered only among his closest men, was simpler and stranger, the land itself guarded his wealth. Jean called it the bank of the swamp.

By winter's first chill, they had amassed what Jean estimated, half in jest, as a quarter-million dollars in stored plunder, not counting what moved through their hands each week. "Enough to buy a navy," he said, "or a country—but robbing one is more fun." Karl smiled. One day, the secret fortune of Barataria would be unearthed by the hands that buried it. He would know where to search.

Meanwhile, the first cannon blast of the War of 1812 did not shake Louisiana, but news of it did. In June, riders galloped down the Natchez Trace and flatboats slid south with crumpled broadsheets declaring that Congress had voted for war with Great Britain. By the time word reached New Orleans, the city was already braced for trouble.

British frigates prowled the Gulf like sharks. Militia companies drilled in crooked lines. New Orleans was a city of whispers:

"The British will take the city."

"Madison will abandon Louisiana."

"We need friends in the Gulf—not enemies."

One evening, as the docks thinned of laborers, Karl leaned his elbows on a piling beside Jean. For a rare moment, no one was shouting prices, or haggling freight, or dashing off with contraband stitched into their coats. Karl hesitated, then asked, "Are you concerned about what comes next?" He gestured toward the harbor, a reflection of impending war, blockades, and shifting nations. Jean watched the harbor. "Concern is for men who think they control the future," he said. "But I am interested, which may be worse."

Karl frowned and asked, "Why is that worse?" Jean gestured toward the river. "Because the future is like the Gulf. It destroys whoever misreads the tide."

He pointed his chin toward the city. "Britain and America will fight.

Napoleon will fall. And whoever controls this river will control a continent."

Karl had expected a shrug or a joke, not a map of the world spoken like a prophecy. "So what do we do?" he asked. Jean smiled without humor. "We adapt. We prepare. We make allies. When the tide turns, and it always turns, we make certain we are not beneath it."

Karl watched the shadows ripple across Jean Lafitte's face and wondered if he was looking at a pirate, a patriot, or something the world had not yet named.

Jean's ability to adapt was legendary. He was always two steps ahead of any flag that claimed to rule the Lafittes. He never sent a ship without two routes of escape. He never stored powder without a second cache already buried. He paid informants in coin, captains in loyalty, and enemies in silence.

When a rival crew attempted to undercut his price on powder, Jean bought their cargo at a loss, then spread word that British cruisers were hunting that particular brand for seizure. The rumor cost him fifty dollars and bought six months of monopoly.

War was bad for empires but excellent for men who could provide services in the shadows. The Lafittes prospered. Spaniards in Havana and Veracruz needed American goods. Americans needed supplies. Jean and Pierre arranged both—quietly, efficiently, and without tariffs.

The year of 1812 slid by without a shot fired in Louisiana, not officially, but anyone with ears could hear the thunder rolling. British ships hovered in the Gulf. Spanish agents whispered in taverns. American merchants grew uneasy at the thought of Washington lunging at Britain and dragging the Gulf South into the brawl. In that nervous space, Barataria grew fat.

Karl's life blurred into salt, smoke, and coin. Days dissolved into nights along the same muddy docks. He learned the tides better than the calendar. Spring tides for landing silver, neap tides for slipping out of the bay, storm tides for outrunning cutters that feared shallow water. At seventeen he was taller, darker, and brisk of speech. Fewer men asked if he knew his business, and more men obeyed when he said, "Make way."

Jean remained the axis, presiding from his balcony at Grand Terre as though the whole island were a stage. His lieutenants shuffled manifests and spy notes across his cluttered desk, and Pierre managed the warehouses, bribed customs men, and kept books no honest magistrate would touch. Between them, Barataria became a nation in all but name. A nation that paid its taxes in gold and gunpowder instead of signatures.

Ships multiplied. Prizes grew. One Spanish brig taken off Campeche yielded forty thousand dollars in coffee and silver. Another brought eighty enslaved Africans, sold upriver through brokers who pretended not to know their origin.

Karl was on the dock when the enslaved were brought ashore. They came in pairs, wrists shackled, iron rubbing skin raw from salt and sweat. Some were young boys. One man walked upright despite the chain, eyes level and unafraid. A woman stumbled. The guard jerked her upright as if correcting a mule.

The sound of iron striking wood in a rhythmic march stayed with Karl. Not loud. Not dramatic. Just steady.

Jean handled the sale the way he handled everything: efficient, distant, precise. Gold weighed. Papers signed. No speeches.

Karl told himself he was not the one fastening chains. He kept the ledger. He counted. Still, some things are impossible to justify. When one of the captives met his eyes, Karl looked away first.

That night Karl walked the docks alone. Somewhere beneath the marsh lay enough gold to change his life forever. The only sound he heard was iron striking wood. That sound followed him into sleep.

Barataria sat on a world already rotten, and Jean never apologized for surviving the rot. "We did not build this trade," Jean said quietly once, when Karl's silence grew too visible. "We profit from what exists. If we refuse, another man will not."

Karl understood the logic. He didn't know if he believed it.

For a time, no power could spare the strength to stop the Lafittes. Spain bled against Bonaparte. Britain chased Napoleon across Europe and harassed American shipping for sport. Washington barely owned a navy and Louisiana barely wished to be American at all. The Lafittes thrived in the gaps, feeding on distraction.

Grand success eventually makes noise, and noise draws interest. By late 1813, foreign consuls in New Orleans began filing complaints— Spanish, British, even French. Manifests from Cádiz vanished. Coffee shipments bound for Havana simply never arrived. Insurance firms in London shrieked over their losses. Havana's merchants demanded retaliation. A British captain wrote that a "nest of privateers under a Frenchman" was bleeding imperial commerce white.

Letters followed—threats from Washington, warnings from merchants begging Jean to slow down before the Americans made a spectacle of him. Jean read them aloud on his balcony, laughing louder than the gulls.

"If we plundered for free, they'd hang me tomorrow," he said. "Because we sell coffee cheaply, they send letters instead."

Karl believed him, but he saw the shift. British frigates prowled closer. Spanish cutters nosed into the passes at night. American customs men began dragging bayonet tips through barrels as though contraband might leap out and surrender. Pierre paid bribes faster and demanded loyalty oaths from captains he had once treated as cousins.

The Gulf turned into a chessboard. American officers wanted intelligence on British Pensacola. British agents wanted smugglers for their fleets. Spanish officials wanted everyone to stop raiding Spaniards long enough to pick a side. Jean played all three with the calm of a man holding better cards. Karl watched him negotiate with diplomats at noon and raid their allies by midnight, learning that war ran on paper, rumor, and coin more than cannon.

By 1814, the game changed, and not for the better. Too many complaints reached Washington. Too many ships vanished into Barataria's warehouses. Madrid demanded action. Governor Claiborne petitioned for force. This time Washington listened. Bounties were posted.

Jean laughed at Claiborne's five hundred dollar bounty on his head and promptly offered thirty thousand dollars for Claiborne's, payable in Spanish coin. Karl heard it from a drunk militiaman that the whole city laughed for days upon hearing of Lafitte's rebuttal.

Privately, the Lafittes packed for siege. Real maps appeared. The kind of maps governments draw. Pierre shifted treasure inland. Karl helped sink powder kegs in the marsh and bury silver in pits known only to Jean.

Barataria had thrived in the cracks between empires. Empires tolerated pirates until the pirates became a nuisance.

Somewhere beyond the Gulf, powerful men were sharpening their knives.

Chapter 14

Karl first saw her in the March 1814 market on Rue Chartres in New Orleans. Women in cotton gowns were arguing over spices. Trappers had spread pelts across wooden tables. Sugar merchants shouted prices into the warm morning air.

In the middle of the noise stood a girl calmly dismantling a vendor. She spoke French with a faint St. Louis accent. "You expect me to pay that price for sugar?" she asked.

The man grinned crudely. The girl didn't raise her voice. Her next words left the man flushed while nearby women hid their smiles.

Karl noticed something bolder than her beauty. She was enjoying the challenge of argument. Jean nudged Karl. "You're staring." Karl looked down at the pepper bins. "No, I'm not."

Jean laughed under his breath. "You've no idea how to talk to a woman, do you?" Karl ignored him, but he knew Jean was right. He was nearing his nineteenth birthday, yet still a novice in matters of the heart.

Only Élise had stirred more than courtesy in him. Mama had taught him kindness, but neither she nor Élise had shown him how to court. The art of love remained a distant horizon, and Karl stood on its shore, eager but untested.

Against his better judgment, Karl followed the girl out of the market, not too close, just enough to watch the way she slipped through the crowd without ever seeming to touch it. Her movement had a quiet confidence, like she belonged to a finer world.

She reached the gate beside the Old Ursuline Convent and paused. Something, instinct, perhaps, made her turn. Their eyes met. Karl felt the impact like a sudden blow. Hazel eyes. Calm. Curious. Not frightened. Just measuring.

Then the moment ended. A well-dressed young man stepped through the gatehouse. Polished boots. Easy confidence. He greeted her as though the place belonged to him. She smiled and slipped her arm through his. The iron gate closed with a soft click.

Karl stared at it for a long moment. Jean came up beside him. "A convent girl," he said, smiling. "That's trouble."

Karl kicked a loose cobblestone. "She has a boyfriend."

Jean snorted. "Half the women in this city have boyfriends." He flicked his wrist to dismiss the boyfriend. "Karl, if you want the girl, you don't slink away because some peacock owns polished boots. You put yourself out there. You make your place known."

Karl stared at the convent gate as if it held wisdom to help him. "Mama says you shouldn't take what belongs to another man."

Jean chuckled. "That's church talk. I'm not telling you to steal anyone's bride. I'm telling you to decide if you're a man who asks or a man who hides. There's a difference." Karl wasn't sure if Jean was giving wise counsel or encouraging foolishness, but he sensed this much: running away from her would feel worse than looking like a fool.

Behind them, the church bells tolled the hour. Jean clapped him on the back. "Come on. If you're meant to cross paths again, you will. New Orleans is a small city when the heart's involved."

Karl took one last look at the convent, and a thought flickered unbidden: *Mama would approve. This girl follows God.*

Annabelle Dixon belonged to order, education, and faith—the very things Mama wanted for her sons. Karl belonged to Jean, to the docks, to a life Mama never envisioned for him. The idea that Annabelle might ever consider entering his life tightened in his heart. He knew how to treat a woman once she chose him. Papa had made sure of that. Jean too. What he didn't know was how to get a woman to choose him.

Two days later, fate—or more likely Annabelle's curiosity—brought them face to face in the blacksmith shop. She entered carrying a broken stirrup strap.

Pierre greeted her with formal courtesy. "Mademoiselle Annabelle Dixon. Back from St. Louis so soon?" Annabelle smiled and said, "My aunt grows weary of the frontier. She insists New Orleans will be civilized any year now." Pierre's expression barely shifted. "We can only pray, mademoiselle."

Her eyes drifted toward Karl. "Who is he?" Pierre introduced him only as "Karl Steinheimer," with no titles or embellishments. She offered a polite nod. For the briefest moment, Karl wondered if Mama would think her too good for him.

"Your stirrup can be mended by tomorrow," Pierre said. "I would advise keeping it inside. Leather doesn't survive this city any better than reputations do." Annabelle's brow arched. "Speaking of reputations—" her gaze shifted to Karl again, pointedly this time, "—I've heard the Lafittes employ privateers." Pierre wore the faintest smirk. "We employ blacksmiths, sailors, and sometimes men who travel. New Orleans has always enjoyed storytelling."

Annabelle paused at the doorway. "In St. Louis," she said lightly, "privateer is just a polite word for pirate." Then she stepped into the sunlight and was gone.

Karl exhaled slowly. "She hates me and we haven't even spoken." Jean clapped his shoulder. "She doesn't hate you. She fears the sea and anyone who follows it willingly. Besides, I thought you said she had a boyfriend." Karl didn't know which stung more, that she feared him or that she had a boyfriend.

A week later Annabelle convinced her aunt that the best bargains on silk could be found close to the docks. She deliberately walked her aunt to the rough quarter. Deliberately.

As her aunt examined silk, Annabelle's gaze scanned tarred rope, stacked crates, river men moving with careless strength. Karl saw her before she saw him. His shirt was sweat-darkened. A coil of rope hung over his shoulder. When a cart wheel snapped loose near her path, Karl moved before thinking. He caught the axle, steadied the load, and dragged it clear before it crushed a basket of oranges at her feet.

Karl set the wheel upright and wiped his hands on his trousers. The vendor shouted thanks. Only then did he realize she had been watching.

"You're forgiven," she said softly.

Karl frowned. "For what?"

"For nearly destroying the market," she said. For the first time, she smiled. Not politely. Curiously.

Her aunt seized her elbow. "Annabelle." But this time Annabelle did not look away quickly. She held his gaze longer than politeness required.

As the ladies departed, Pierre leaned in, smirking. "That one is above your station, son." Karl watched her vanish into the brightness of the street. "Maybe," he murmured. "But she looked at me." Pierre laughed. "Miss Dixon looks at rainstorms too. That does not mean she intends to marry the weather." Karl said nothing. He was left to wonder why Miss Dixon had made her way to the rough quarter.

The next evening, Annabelle and Aunt Colette sat in the courtyard following evening prayer service. The courtyard glowed with lantern light. Annabelle held her repaired stirrup strap in her hands, running her finger along the seam. The work was smooth, cleaner than she'd expected from a Lafitte shop.

"You are quiet," her aunt observed. "I am thinking of New Orleans," Annabelle replied. "I like it here." Her aunt snorted softly. "Then God bless whatever man first convinces you to remain here." Just as her aunt finished speaking, a soft whistle carried across the courtyard. They both stood to get a better view. Her aunt's gaze followed a young man walking, and her expression warmed with immediate approval.

"Ah," she said, "and speaking of sensible young men—bless Theodore Dubois." She waved as the young man stepped forward, hat in hand. "A finer match for a girl could hardly be imagined. His family has land upriver, a respectable name, and he is dutiful—dutiful, Annabelle."

Theodore approached, smiling politely. "Bonsoir, Madame. Bonsoir, Annabelle." He was the same young man who had escorted Annabelle inside the gates just a few days prior. Her aunt leaned closer, lowering her voice. "There is character in a boy who keeps his promises. And he attends mass without complaint. It is a rare combination."

Annabelle mumbled a lukewarm greeting, masking her thoughts as they drifted elsewhere. She was thinking about the riverfront. She was thinking about the market. If she were honest with herself, she was thinking about a pair of startling blue eyes that did not belong to Theodore Dubois.

Theodore asked about prayer service, about her embroidery lessons, about her aunt's rheumatism. All the things polite boys are trained to ask.

Her aunt beamed at each inquiry as if each were a small bouquet laid at Annabelle's feet. When Theodore took his leave, Aunt Colette declared, "God grant you keep courting with such grace. It is a relief to know there are still proper young men in this city and not only… sailors."

Annabelle smiled faintly, though both women understood sailors were exactly the sort of men New Orleans bred in abundance. The sort of men her aunt prayed would pass by her niece.

Annabelle enjoyed Theodore's company. Part of her enjoyed his sophistication. But she wasn't sure she had chosen Theodore as much as he had been thrust upon her by a meddlesome aunt. More so, she wasn't sure God had chosen Theodore for her. Something was missing. Maybe he was too polished.

Her aunt asked if she would like to invite Theodore to supper on Saturday. Annabelle didn't answer. Her mind was locked in on a blond boy with an unfashionably earnest stare. *Karl Steinheimer.* He had hardly spoken to her, yet he'd studied her as though words mattered less than understanding. Men in New Orleans were never quiet. Soldiers bragged. Traders lied. Priests lectured. But this Karl Steinheimer had said nothing. And somehow revealed more.

Still, she reminded herself, he was tied to the Lafittes — and the Lafittes were trouble. *Privateers,* the city called them. *Pirates,* St. Louis called them. Her mother — God rest her — would have called them *temptation.*

Annabelle folded the stirrup strap and stood, whispering into the darkness, "He looked decent, though. Dangerous men are not supposed to look decent."

"What are you talking about?" her aunt asked. "If I didn't know better, I'd think you were on another planet tonight." Annabelle grinned. The darkness offered no counsel, and she did not ask her aunt for any.

After her aunt retired, Annabelle lingered at the courtyard wall. The river breeze carried distant music. Beneath the music was the low thud of artillery practice from the American batteries downriver. War was no longer rumor. It had a sound.

Annabelle thought of Theodore's tidy promises. Of land, and order, and safety. Then she thought of Karl—sun-browned, quiet, watching her as if she were something worth studying instead of acquiring.

Another cannon boomed. Somewhere along the docks, men like Karl would be preparing for whatever came next. Annabelle pressed her hand against the cool stone and whispered into the dark, "God help me."

For the first time in her careful life, Annabelle Dixon knew the direction of her heart. She sensed it was leading her straight toward trouble.

Chapter 15

Across town, Jean was polishing a pistol beneath lamplight, checking the lock, the flint, the pan. Karl sat at the workbench sorting nails with far more focus than the task required. Jean watched him for a moment before speaking. "Most men," he said casually, "smile when a girl looks at them." Karl nearly dropped a handful of nails. "She wasn't smiling at me."

"Pierre says otherwise," Jean said. "She was wondering if you bite or if you just glare like a church statue." Karl bit his bottom lip. "I wasn't glaring." Jean chuckled thoughtfully. "No, you were brooding. That's different. Brooding is for men who think they're mysterious. Glaring is for men who know they're dangerous." Karl sighed. "I'm neither." Jean holstered the pistol with a flourish. "Exactly. Which makes you confusing. Women adore puzzles." Karl stared at him. "She's from the convent, Jean. She's not… she's not—"

"Not for the likes of us?" Jean supplied. Karl didn't answer. He didn't need to. Jean leaned back in his chair, eyes sharpening. "Listen to me, mon ami. The sea saves no room for doubting men. If you want her, speak. Don't stand idle. Matters of the heart require action." Karl flushed. "I don't *want*— I simply noticed—" Jean's grin widened. "Of course. You simply noticed her hair, and her eyes, and the way she speaks French like a lady but argues like a fishwife.”

Karl couldn’t help it, a small laugh escaped him. Jean pointed at him. “There. Good. You’re alive after all. Élise would approve.” The name dropped into the room like an anchor. The humor faded. The air tightened. Karl lowered his eyes. “Would she?”

Jean busied himself by rewrapping the pistol before answering. Then, he looked intently at Karl before replying quietly, “Yes. Élise believed in love, even though she knew love makes no promises.” Silence stretched between them. Karl shifted on the bench, rubbing his palms against his trousers. “But she already has a… a boyfriend,” he muttered, as if saying it aloud might make the humiliation smaller. “They looked certain.”

Jean’s brows lifted. “And what of it? When I met Élise, she had a boyfriend too. A very proper young officer. Uniform starched, boots polished, the kind of man who salutes mirrors just to keep his form.” A wry smile touched his mouth.

Karl smiled, too, trying to picture Jean losing to anyone, let alone an officer. “What happened?” he asked. Jean tapped the tabletop with two fingers. “You saw what happened. Love happened. Élise chose what her heart wanted. Men don’t decide love, Karl, though they often try. Something stronger than us decides love.”

Karl absorbed that in silence. Something stronger. Not force. Not competition.

Jean noticed the faraway look in Karl’s eyes and nudged him with his boot. “So stop burying yourself alive because she has a beau. Your paths will cross again. And if not, the world is full of other storms worth chasing.” Karl gave a small nod. His embarrassment was fading. He was grateful, and pleasantly surprised, he could speak plainly with Jean.

Karl sensed an opening and asked the question that had lingered since Cap-Français. An image of a vanishing schooner sifted through Karl’s mind, followed by a flash of the miraculous return of Jean and Élise.

"I don't wish to stir old pain," Karl said, "but…how did you do it? How did you and Élise survive on that island?" For a moment Jean did not answer. His gaze stayed on the work bench. When he spoke, his tone held no drama, only the steadiness of hard-won truth.

"I would like to tell you there is a secret," he said. "Some sacred knowledge whispered only to the desperate. There is not." He turned to Karl. "Survival is a simple craft. You strip life down to what matters and discard the rest. You adapt to what the day gives you. You keep your mind from turning on itself. And you choose, each morning, to continue the fight." A faint smile touched his mouth. "It is the same lesson you see me practice every day. Adapt. Stay positive."

Karl sensed there was a lot more to the events of survival than Jean had shared, but he didn't press the topic. Adapt. Stay positive. Something in the words rang eerily familiar. Jean's lessons were beginning to sound like Papa's.

Jean clapped once, breaking the silence. "Now — we find a reason for you to walk past the convent gates. And maybe, if God wills it, you'll remember how to smile instead of brood."

Karl stared at the pile of nails in front of him and pondered a future that felt both thrilling and unholy. He was relieved that for the first time in weeks, he was thinking of something other than storms and graves. Or was it the same?

News moved strangely in New Orleans. Sometimes it slept for months. Sometimes it grew legs overnight. By the end of the week, Annabelle Dixon's aunt had heard that her niece had met a young man from the Lafitte shop. That evening, after supper, her aunt folded her hands neatly and said in the calmest tone she could muster: "Annabelle, have you taken an interest in smugglers?"

Annabelle nearly choked on her tea. "I met a young man at the blacksmith's. That was all."

"Yes," her aunt replied, as though that proved her point. "And he happens to be attached to the Lafittes. Who, in turn, are attached to certain… activities."

"They own a shop," Annabelle insisted.

"They own many things," her aunt murmured. "Some above the table. Some beneath it."

Annabelle felt heat rise to her cheeks. "Karl Steinheimer did not seem —"

"Like a criminal?" her aunt provided. "Criminals rarely do. Especially the ones who smile at convent girls."

Annabelle opened her mouth to argue, then shut it. Karl had not smiled at her. He barely managed a nod. Her aunt leaned forward, lowering her voice. "St. Louis raised you to be cautious. New Orleans will demand you be cunning. Choose your company wisely."

Annabelle lay awake that night, her thoughts drifting to Karl and the wild spark he stirred in her. What unsettled her more — the danger he might bring, or the danger he might not? She hated that she worried over someone she barely knew. Yet, he seemed to ignite a warmth within her that no measured courtesy could cool.

Then there was Theodore. The very thought of him brought order. He was kind. He was proper. He carried the weight of her family's expectations with quiet ease. Could she love him? Should she? Her imagination balked, recoiling from the neat path laid before her. The notion of a life with Theodore left her heart unsatisfied.

She buried her face in her pillow, trying to summon propriety back into her heart. As she did, the memory of Karl and his earnest eyes burned quietly in her thoughts. Sleep eluded her, as it always did when the heart wrestled with a storm the mind could not tame.

Jean, for his part, knew little about restless nights or fretful aunts. What he did know was that Karl had been quieter than usual, especially in his company, and that Karl had watched the convent courtyard from the balcony twice that week with the subtlety of a loaded weapon.

Being a shameless patron of young romance, Jean crafted a scheme.

On Sunday morning he declared they needed to go to the Place d'Armes, "for tobacco of a pedigree superior to anything sold by honest merchants," and to breathe "air unbeholden to commerce." He delivered these claims with the solemnity of a bishop. Karl followed because he could not decide whether Jean was lying or exaggerating. Maybe both.

The square swarmed with life — soldiers lingering after drill, criers hawking notices, Creole families in Sunday finery, and free people of color drifting toward Mass. At the iron fence stood Annabelle with her aunt, in conversation with a priest about travel upriver. Jean saw her first. Then he saw Karl see her. Karl's reaction was small — a breath caught in his throat. Jean noticed Karl's response and smiled.

There she is, Karl thought, then cursed himself for the phrasing, as if the woman belonged to him. He looked away before she could notice he'd noticed her. *Don't stare. Don't approach. Don't make a fool of yourself.* There was comfort in rules. Jean placed a brotherly hand lightly on his arm and murmured, "Well? Go on." Karl frowned. "Go on where?"

Jean pointed his head toward Annabelle while inspecting the cut of Karl's coat. "Toward her, before she sails north and you resign yourself to pining at wharves like a tragic opera singer." Karl stiffened. "I won't intrude. Her aunt—"

"Her aunt," Jean interrupted smoothly, "is presently arguing passage rates. That grants you precisely three minutes of invisibility. Use them, or I shall be forced to intervene more directly." Karl opened his mouth to object, but Jean was already gliding away toward a knot of cigar vendors, cloak flaring elegantly. Halfway there he called over his shoulder, low enough for only Karl to hear: "And for God's sake, stand like a man, not a mule awaiting harness."

Karl stood frozen. *I should leave,* he decided. *This is foolish. I have no business.* Then Annabelle looked up. At him. It was brief, a flicker really, but it startled him. Not surprise or annoyance, more like recognition, as if she'd glimpsed a book she might like to read.

Annabelle was wrestling with thoughts of her own: *There he is again — the serious one. Why does he look as though conversation requires swordsmanship?* A spark of amusement tugged at her mouth.

Karl felt his spine straighten without his permission. His boots carried him forward out of pure mutiny against his better judgment.

"Monsieur Steinheimer," Annabelle said, her voice polite but laced with curiosity.

"Miss Dixon," Karl answered, just slightly breathless. *Too fast. Slow down. Don't sound like you've run from cannon fire.* "I… saw you in the market the other day," he added, instantly regretting it. *Congratulations, fool, a true masterpiece of observation.*

Annabelle's lips twitched. "So did the entire market, monsieur. I was not at my gentlest."

"You defended yourself," Karl said.

"That is a generous interpretation."

Karl hesitated, then chose honesty, his safest weapon. "My mother used to say gentleness should not be mistaken for silence. There's a difference." Annabelle was disarmed by the sincerity. "Your mother sounds wise."

"She was," Karl said softly.

Across the square, Jean watched from behind a vendor's cart, entirely too satisfied with himself. He leaned toward the vendor and murmured, "When two people begin speaking without a proper introduction, you are witnessing either divine intervention or sheer incompetence. In this case, I suspect both."

Karl and Annabelle stood momentarily in awkward silence until her aunt glanced over, eyebrows knitting with suspicion. Annabelle lowered her voice. "I was warned that the Lafittes are dangerous men." Karl answered in the most thoughtful way he could muster. "They are… complicated men."

"And you?" she asked. "Are you complicated?"

Karl wanted to say no, that he was simple, that he prayed sometimes, that he listened more than he spoke. But something in her eyes demanded honesty. "I don't know what I am yet," he said.

The confession surprised them both. Annabelle held his gaze longer than comfortable, the admission leaving her in thought. It was unexpected and revealing.

She turned then, brushing a stray curl behind her ear as if the moment had been too direct for polite company. "Most people pretend to know," she said quietly. "You'll be ahead of them when you finally decide."

Karl was unsure what to do with the warmth her words sparked in him. He kicked at the gravel with the toe of his boot, searching for something sensible to say. Instead, what slipped out was not sensible at all, "Do you… like your boyfriend?" he blurted.

Annabelle's head snapped toward him, brows rising. "That is a rather bold question." He flushed to the ears. "I just—I saw you with him at the gate. I wasn't spying, I just—he looked important."

Annabelle's expression softened into something almost amused. "Theodore is important. To my aunt, to my family, to the sort of future they expect for me." Karl feigned agreement, though the words felt like stones pummeling his stomach. "And to you?" he asked. Annabelle hesitated. When she answered, it was with careful precision, the kind she used when stitching torn seams.

"To me, he is… expected," she said, pausing to take a breath. "Expectation is not the same as affection." Karl had no reply. Relationships appeared to be more complicated than any harbor had prepared him for. He was saved from further comment by her approaching aunt, who was forcing a smile sharp as glass.

"Come, Annabelle. Father Girard will walk us to the docks." She turned to Karl and added coolly, "Good day, monsieur Steinheimer." Karl stepped back and watched them depart through the square.

Jean reappeared at his side, chewing tobacco like a proud matchmaker. "Well?" he asked.

Karl shrugged. "I spoke."

"And?"

"I don't know," Karl said truthfully. "She… sees things. I don't know if that's good."

Jean clapped his shoulder. "It's better than being invisible. Trust me." Karl didn't agree, not yet, but for the rest of the walk home he caught himself wondering what he should make of Annabelle Dixon. She was a convent girl with sharp eyes, a guarded tongue, and a mind that seemed to ask more questions than she answered.

He liked the gentleness but wondered about the fire. Or maybe the reverse.

The next Sabbath, Karl attended Mass outside the cathedral—not out of habit, but out of longing. He stood among Creoles and slaves and soldiers, hearing the Latin that once steadied him when Mama whispered prayers at night. He remained after the dismissal, staring at the painted saints and thinking about Annabelle Dixon. He decided he liked her fire.

Mama had once told him, *"A woman should have a spine, Karl. Heaven doesn't reward the weak."* Karl smiled at the memory.

The town square was crowded with ladies under parasols, gossiping in French as musicians tuned violins for the dancing that would follow. Karl lingered near the edge of the crowd, awkward in his best shirt. Jean had insisted he "try not to look like a dock rat for once." He had just convinced himself that mass was not his world when he heard a familiar voice behind him.

"You don't strike me as a churchgoer." Karl turned to see Annabelle, hands clasped neatly, bonnet tilted, her expression equal parts polite curiosity and guarded friendliness. He answered honestly. "I'm not. But Jean said the music afterward was worth hearing." Annabelle's mouth twitched. "That sounds like St. Louis, not like piracy." Karl surprised himself by laughing. "Jean's full of surprises." She studied him for a moment and Karl felt oddly exposed.

Then she asked, "Is it true what people say? That you… raid ships? Plunder cargo?" Karl looked away briefly. "Not exactly. We seize goods that were already seized by someone else."

"So you steal from thieves?"

"Sometimes from kings," Karl added softly, "which might be the same thing."

Annabelle's eyes narrowed, not in anger, but in thought. "My father used to trade furs downriver. He said piracy makes widows and ruins families." Karl shrugged at the weight of the truth. "War does, too," he said. "Governments, storms, disease. The sea doesn't care who you are."

Something shifted in her gaze. Not approval, just understanding.

When the dancing began, she stood at the edge, watching. Karl knew better than to ask a girl from St. Louis society to dance with a privateer. Especially a girl with a boyfriend. So he didn't ask.

Annabelle surprised him again. "You're going to ask me to dance, aren't you, Karl Steinheimer?"

He opened his mouth — and realized he had no idea. "I only dance when someone threatens me," he replied.

Annabelle laughed, properly laughed, and her wariness melted. They danced one measure, then another, turning beneath the cathedral's shadow. Karl realized two things immediately. He was a horrible dancer. And he did not want the music to end.

He kept glancing over his shoulder, half expecting Theodore to appear. Karl realized he had never felt so alive — and never felt so dishonest. When the tune ended, Annabelle stepped back and restored the careful distance between them.

"I don't approve of what you do," she said quietly. "I don't blame you," Karl replied. "But..." she hesitated, looking down at her gloves "... you are not what I expected." Karl bowed, not mockingly, but with awkward sincerity. "Thank you, mademoiselle." She looked up, startled by his courtesy. Before she could reply, her aunt walked up and whisked her away.

As Annabelle walked off, Karl felt something unfurl inside him. Jean was right, action was required. He did not want safety. He wanted Annabelle.

Discomfort clouded his thoughts when Theodore stepped from the cathedral shadow. He was not smiling.

Karl had the uneasy feeling that Theodore had been watching for longer than anyone realized.

Chapter 16

Aunt Colette had sharp eyes and an even sharper sense for impropriety. She did not miss the faint pink in Annabelle's cheeks nor the oddly respectful bow Karl had given. By the time they reached the convent gate, she had drawn her conclusions—wrong in detail, but close enough to spark concern.

Later that week, during her weekly tea with the Dubois family, Aunt Colette spoke in low, troubled tones over china cups. "…and I assure you, he was no dock apprentice," she said quietly. "He bowed like a young officer. But the coat—threadbare. And he had the sea about him. Salt-water manners." Madame Dubois raised a hand to her chest. "A sailor?"

"Worse," Aunt Colette intoned. "A privateer. Jean Lafitte takes an interest in many things—commerce, war, the governor's affairs—but now I fear one of his men has taken interest in Annabelle." The room fell quiet. The Dubois family had lineage, propriety, plans. And those plans did not include privateers.

Two days later, Theodore Dubois found Karl near the waterfront market, arranging coils of line for Lafitte's crew. Theodore approached with the careful dignity of a young man raised among parlor doors and soft carpets, not salt-scoured decks. Theodore had not wanted to confront Karl, but Madame Dubois had insisted it was the proper approach.

"Karl Steinheimer?"

Karl looked up, surprised to hear his full name spoken so correctly. "Yes?"

Theodore brushed imaginary dust from his cuff, steadying himself. "We have not been introduced. I am Theodore Dubois. My father is Monsieur Louis Dubois, merchant shareholder in the St. Charles Company." Karl wiped his hands on his pants. "All right." He recognized Theodore but was unsure why he was here. He must have seen the dance Karl shared with Annabelle.

Theodore's jaw tightened at the lack of ceremony, but he pressed on. "I have been informed that you spoke with Mademoiselle Annabelle Dixon earlier this week." Karl instantly felt heat crawl up his neck. "We talked, yes."

"She is under the care of her aunt," Theodore said. "And under the expectations of her family. You must understand that her future is… structured." Karl's eyes narrowed. "I understand," he said.

Theodore clasped his hands behind his back, the posture of someone trying desperately not to offend. "Good. Then may I ask politely that you refrain from further familiarity? I do not say this to insult you, but to avoid… complications." Karl considered bristling. He considered telling Theodore that Annabelle was not a parcel on a ledger. Instead, remembering Mama's teachings, he pushed the anger down. "I didn't mean any harm," he said. "I'm just a deckhand."

Theodore exhaled, relieved. "You are a privateer's deckhand," he corrected. "That, unfortunately, matters more."

For a moment, Karl thought Theodore might want to scuffle, not out of hatred, but to prove a point. Karl wasn't sure how he would answer a fight. He knew he could whip Theodore, but had misgivings about how Annabelle might respond.

The moment passed. The Dubois family raised gentlemen, not brawlers. So Theodore dipped his head, as stiff as a musket barrel, and said: "Good day to you, Karl Steinheimer."

Theodore turned and walked back toward the row of carriages, boots clicking the stones. Karl watched him go, unsure whether to feel insulted or amused. Behind him, Lafitte's men laughed over a cask of rum, arguing in French and Spanish about prize shares.

Karl was beginning to understand that warships and pirates were not the only forces that drew lines across the world. Society drew them, too. And defended them just as fiercely.

Karl found Jean later that afternoon on the quarterdeck, checking the rigging as a fresh breeze stirred the river. His boots made no sound against the wet planks as he approached. He was full of words he wasn't sure how to say.

"Jean," he began, hesitating. "Something happened… It's about Annabelle." Jean looked up, eyes narrowing under his brim. "Did someone try to stuff you into a cannon?" he asked dryly. "No, worse," Karl muttered, relaying how Aunt Colette was spreading rumors of privateering and how Theodore Dubois had confronted him politely but firmly. Jean's grin spread slowly, mischievous and sharp. "Ah, the boy with polished boots thinks he can scare you off? And what did you do?"

"I didn't fight," Karl admitted. "I… I just said I meant no harm." Jean laughed, low but hearty. "Good. That's better than a punch. A gentleman thinks he holds the rules of court, but a real man knows the heart can't be fenced. You are curious. Alive. And you made your choice." Karl frowned. "Curious… alive… I feel like a fool." Jean slapped him on the shoulder. "Ah, love does that to a man. It keeps you human. And it keeps your heart honest."

Days passed, even weeks sometimes. Karl learned his best chance of catching a glimpse of Annabelle was on Sundays. Mass spilled out into the square with an assortment of lace veils, parasols, and merchants in rumpled coats. The bells were still ringing when Annabelle descended the cathedral steps with her aunt, sunlight catching the white ribbon at her throat.

Karl stood across the square, pressed near the iron fence around Government Hall, cap in hand. He had scrubbed the tar from his nails, smoothed his hair with river water. He did not know why he had come, only that after first seeing Annabelle he had found himself walking toward churches instead of taverns.

Annabelle saw him. She did not smile, but her pace slowed. A small act, sure, yet enormous. Before she could step toward him, Theodore Dubois appeared, immaculate in a blue coat, hat tucked under his arm. He bowed to her aunt, then turned to Annabelle with restrained delight. "Miss Dixon," he said, "I have secured tickets for the symphony. Signor Valentino performs this Friday. May I offer my escort?"

Annabelle opened her mouth but before she spoke her gaze drifted past Theodore, toward the fence. Theodore followed her gaze. His face tightened when he saw Karl. Not with the vulgar anger of jealous boys, but with something colder — the resentment of a man bred to expect order, encountering chaos.

Theodore strode across the square. Karl braced himself.

"You," Theodore said quietly, stopping an arm's length away. "I told you to stay away. I know of your association. I know what ships you walk on."

Karl was undaunted. "And?"

"You are not to look at Miss Dixon again. This is your second warning. There will not be a third."

Karl's temper flared. "With respect, monsieur," he said, "I do not answer to you." Karl was surprised by his own boldness. His chats with Jean were supplying an infusion of confidence. Theodore paused, stunned that a dock boy would speak to him as an equal. "Then answer to decency," he hissed. "Her family will not suffer scandal."

Karl leaned forward just slightly, enough to show he was not frightened. "And her family decides her heart?"

Theodore recoiled as if slapped. "Her heart belongs to sense."

Karl almost laughed. "Then perhaps it is not her heart."

Before Theodore could retort, Annabelle's aunt called for the carriage. Theodore collected himself with brittle dignity. "This ends now," he said. He walked away quickly, arms moving in pace with his stride.

Karl exhaled and smiled. He thought Theodore had no way of knowing when or how this would end. Annabelle glanced back once before the carriage door shut. Just one glance. Karl felt it long after she was gone.

Later that day, porcelain clinked in the Dubois dining room while men murmured over maps of trade routes showing Caribbean ports drawn in neat ink. Theodore stood beside his father, posture perfect, chin high. Annabelle hovered near the doorway with a tray of glasses, unseen, unacknowledged. Except when needed.

"The embargo has strangled trade," Mr. Dubois said. "But once Madison comes to his senses, commerce will bloom again. We must position ourselves for the aftermath."

"Agreed," replied Monsieur Rousseau, a close friend of Annabelle's father who promised he would look after the affairs of Annabelle and her aunt while they were in New Orleans. "The union of the Dubois and Dixon families would consolidate our capital nicely."

Theodore's gaze slid toward Annabelle, not with affection, but with ownership. His father cleared his throat. "Annabelle, dear. Come forward."

She did. Gracefully. Quietly. The room smelled of ink and brandy.

"Mr. Dubois and I believe it wise to formalize an understanding," Monsieur Rousseau said. "There is security in unity during uncertain times. I have spoken with your father and he agrees."

Annabelle understood exactly what that meant. Her heart dipped in resignation. She had known this threat hovered.

She met Theodore's eyes. He smiled politely, eyes softened only by self-satisfaction.

Annabelle bowed her head as etiquette demanded, but her voice did not tremble. "I will obey my family," she said. "But I reserve the right to speak my mind at a later hour."

The men chuckled, assuming she meant gown colors or dinner invitations. Only Theodore caught the edge beneath her words, and his lips thinned. As Annabelle withdrew, her aunt murmured praise for her composure. When the parlor door shut behind her, Annabelle pressed a hand to her breast, trying to quiet a heart that would not behave.

The garden behind the Rousseau house was dimming into twilight when Annabelle slipped out the side gate, bonnet in hand. She did not know where she meant to go, only that she needed air and time to think. Her feet carried her toward the waterfront, toward a young man who somehow made New Orleans feel less like a cage.

The Lafitte men were easy enough to find. Everyone else was avoiding them. She spotted Karl at the wharf, sitting on a coiled dockline, testing a knot over and over, tightening it until the rope creaked. His hair fell loose, touched with salt. He looked up, startled.

"Annabelle?" The name came awkwardly, touched with surprise. It was the first time he had called her by her first name. He liked the sound. So did she. She drew nearer, breathless. "I… needed to walk." Karl was uncertain if he should stand or stay put. He stood.

"You should not be out alone," he said softly.

"Oh, I am seldom alone," she said with a brittle smile. "My aunt's eyes follow me even in my dreams. But tonight, I escaped."

Karl held in a chuckle, unsure if she joked. "Are you in danger?"

"Of suffocation," she murmured. Silence pulled taut between them. Annabelle tightened her grip on her bonnet.

"My family intends an understanding with Monsieur Dubois," she said, keeping her voice even. "Theodore has… expectations."

Karl's eyes lowered. He stared at the water rather than her. "He seems proper. Educated."

"Yes," she whispered. "Precisely."

Karl took a breath. "You don't want him?"

Annabelle hesitated, then stepped closer, close enough that pitch and tar mingled with her lavender scent. "I do not know what I want. Only that I am not ready to be with a man whose greatest passion is seating charts and levee meetings."

Karl risked a glance at her. "What do you want, then?"

Annabelle looked out toward the dark river. "A life that feels as though it is truly mine. I don't need French salons or dances. I don't need jewels. But I would like to breathe without someone measuring each breath for propriety."

Karl said nothing for a long moment. Then quietly: "If you marry him, would you… find contentment?"

She closed her eyes. "Maybe. But contentment is such a small feeling."

The honesty stunned them both. Annabelle turned to leave, afraid she had revealed too much. Karl reached out and brushed the back of his hand against her sleeve, as if to confirm she existed. She stopped. "You deserve more than contentment," he said.

She looked at Karl. There was no poetry in his face, no practiced charm, only conviction salted by hardship. She realized suddenly that he had never been taught how to lie prettily, and that made him dangerous in a world built on prettiness.

"I don't know what I will do," she whispered. "But I needed someone who would not laugh at me for questioning my future."

"I wouldn't," Karl said. "Not ever."

Annabelle drew a slow breath, as if her lungs had forgotten how. For a moment neither spoke, the only sound was waves lapping tattered pilings. "My aunt would faint dead away if she knew I had come here," she said with a weak laugh. Karl allowed the smallest smile. "Then I'm glad she doesn't."

Annabelle turned to leave. "Thank you, Karl."

"For what?"

"For letting me be uncertain."

She walked back into the lamplight, and Karl watched her go, a new and unexpected feeling of possibility forming where doubt had lived.

The very next Sunday, Annabelle descended the cathedral steps on her aunt's arm, pale blue ribbons fluttering at her bonnet. The Dubois family waited at the base of the steps, Theodore standing straight, ready to claim her for the walk to the carriage.

Karl stood just beyond the iron gate, hat in hand, coat rough from river wind, hair ungoverned. He might as well have been a wolf. Aunt Colette saw him a half-second before Annabelle did and inhaled sharply enough to draw whispers.

"Do not even look at him," Colette hissed. Annabelle's eyes lifted anyway. One glance, one heartbeat, one language polite society cannot regulate.

Theodore stepped forward in splendor. "Mademoiselle Dixon. May I escort you?"

It would have ended there, tidy and dull, if Karl had not spoken. He could have stepped back. He could have let her disappear into the square. Something in him refused. Karl stepped forward, hat in hand. For a moment his eyes moved to Aunt Colette, the proper authority.

That was the rule. Ask the guardian. Seek permission. He hesitated. Then he looked past Aunt Colette.

"Mademoiselle Dixon," he said in a voice that carried across the courtyard, "I would be honored to walk with you to your carriage."

Annabelle froze. Theodore froze harder. Aunt Colette looked as though she'd consumed a lantern. Karl was bypassing societal norms and giving Annabelle the opportunity to decide.

The church crowd gasped, some in half-delighted whispers. Someone in the back yelled, "He didn't ask the aunt!" A fan snapped open like a pistol shot. Theodore regained breath enough for fury. "You presume too much, sir," he spat. "This lady is under *my* protection."

Karl's eyes did not move to Theodore. He kept them on Annabelle. "Is she?"

It was not a challenge to Theodore. It was a question for Annabelle, spoken before half the city. Annabelle's heart thundered so loudly she wondered if the cathedral bells had resumed.

Aunt Colette seized her hand. "Come, Annabelle. Now." Annabelle's feet did not move.

The scandal that followed took shape in that moment. It was not about Karl's brazenness, nor Theodore's outrage. It was about Annabelle's stillness. Society could forgive insults. Forgiving indecision was a heftier task.

Theodore raised his voice. "You do not understand what you're doing," he said. He was looking at Karl, but the words were meant for Annabelle. "Men like you disappear when the tide turns. She has a reputation that demands she not disappear."

Annabelle removed her hand from her aunt's grasp. For a moment the crowd held its breath. "My reputation is not my prison," she said. Another gasp rippled halfway to Barataria.

She did not go to Karl. She simply stood without being steered, which was more than enough to detonate the square. Theodore stared at her as if watching a house burn. "You shame yourself," he breathed, loud enough for nearby matrons to hear. Annabelle lifted her chin. "I never promised you anything."

The words staggered Theodore. Scandal was survivable. Humiliation was not.

Karl still waited beyond the gate. He remained silent. He was dangerous by simply existing.

Aunt Colette whispered urgently, "Annabelle, you will destroy yourself."

Annabelle lifted her chin. "Better that," she said quietly, "than live already destroyed."

For a moment no one spoke. For a moment no one moved.

A priest on the steps heard it. Soldiers heard it. Widows heard it. Society would repeat it for a decade. *Better that, than live already destroyed.*

She turned to Theodore. She wasn't cruel, just truthful. "You are a good man. But I am not a prize to be exchanged between families." Then, the coup de grâce, as the French would call it. Annabelle crossed the small distance to Karl, not touching him, not taking his arm, merely joining him at the gate. Theodore's voice cracked. "Annabelle!"

She did not look back.

Karl did not take her hand. He did not claim victory. He merely tipped his head to her and said softly: "Where to, mademoiselle?"

She moved her eyes to the carriage and Karl walked her there. It was polite. It was bold. It felt like freedom. Behind them, Aunt Colette clutched her rosary as if it might strangle Annabelle back into obedience.

Theodore stood at the cathedral steps, where his upbringing helped him regain his composure. "If you truly care for her," he said with poise, "you will think about tomorrow, not just today."

Annabelle stopped momentarily. Karl stopped at her side. Maybe this was foolish, she thought. But it was too late to look back now.

Annabelle entered the carriage without assistance. The door shut with a decisive thud that sounded louder than it was. Inside, the air felt close. For a moment she did not sit. She stood braced against the velvet seat as the wheels lurched forward, the square's murmurs dissolving into distance. Only when the cathedral vanished from view did she sit.

Her hands trembled. She pressed her fingertips hard against her palms, willing stillness into them. A single tear slipped free before she could stop it. Annabelle lifted her hand quickly, brushing it away with the edge of her glove, as if it were merely a piece of dust from the street. She would not allow herself the indignity of visible weeping. Not for matrons. Not for Theodore. Not for the boy beyond the gate.

She drew a careful breath. Then another. Her reflection wavered faintly in the small carriage window. She studied herself as if she were someone else. She noticed her cheeks were pale.

Was the tear for Theodore? For the quiet collapse of a future long assumed? Or for Karl? For the danger she had just invited into both their lives? Theodore offered safety. Karl offered nothing she could name — no house, no assurances, certainly little protection from growing rumors.

Then the thought flashed into her mind. She did know what Karl offered. He offered her a choice. She pressed her hand briefly against her heart, as though it were a restless creature that required discipline. "Steady," she whispered. When the carriage turned onto a quieter street, she opened the curtain a fraction, not to see who watched, but to breathe.

She knew the city would speak of her by morning. She knew that the moment she refused Theodore. She took another breath. By the time the carriage reached her aunt's residence, her posture was restored, her expression composed. Only the faint dampness at the corner of her glove betrayed that something had shifted and could not be returned.

Meanwhile, something eased inside Karl as he watched the carriage disappear down the street. He was far from certain what path lay ahead, but he had a faint sense that he was choosing well.

By nightfall, the story was outrunning the river. It reached the docks first, where the men enjoyed a hearty laugh. In the taverns, the story was distorted and embellished. The Creole ladies whispered while the priests were quick to disapprove. By the time the story reached Barataria, it had acquired three fainting matrons, a duel that never occurred, and a priest who supposedly dropped his Bible in horror.

The following day, the Lafittes were outlining a cargo transfer when Pierre dryly mentioned, "Apparently, our young Karl challenged a merchant heir yesterday in front of half the cathedral." Jean stilled. "Challenged?" he asked mildly.

Pierre shrugged. "Invited the girl to walk with him. In public. On church steps." After a beat of silence, Jean threw his head back and laughed. Not a polite chuckle, more of a rolling laugh that startled two deckhands.

"In front of the cathedral?" Jean said with a measure of delight. "Ah, the boy is growing up."

"He may have grown enemies," Pierre replied. Jean waved that away. "Enemies are inevitable. Indifference is fatal."

Karl had been lingering near the hatchway pretending not to listen. Jean turned toward him slowly, eyes bright with amusement. "So," he said, folding his arms. "You decided not to hide." Karl shrugged. "I didn't mean to cause trouble." Jean's grin sharpened. "Of course you did."

"I only asked if she was free to choose."

"And was she?"

Karl hesitated. "Apparently so." Jean smiled wide, satisfied. "Then you have done nothing dishonorable."

Pierre arched a brow. "You are encouraging him?"

"I am encouraging him," Jean said smoothly, "to understand that the world belongs to men who step forward." He crossed the deck and stopped before Karl, lowering his voice.

"Listen carefully," Jean said. "Men like Theodore Dubois believe life is arranged like tidy ledger columns. They cannot imagine someone altering the arithmetic."

Karl shifted uneasily. "He looked at me as if I'd broken something."

"You did," Jean said. "You broke expectation." A faint wind rustled between them. Jean's tone softened, still serious but gentle. "You want her?"

Karl thought of Annabelle standing still in the square. He thought of her voice. "Yes," he said.

Jean smiled, slow and confident. "Then go for what you want."

Pierre exhaled through his nose. "And when the Dubois family attempts to use their influence?"

Jean's eyes flicked toward the dark horizon, where the faint glow of

New Orleans shimmered. "Then we remind them," he said lightly, "that influence travels both ways." He clapped Karl on the shoulder.

"Next time," Jean added, almost lazily, "do not wait for Sunday. If a woman crosses a square for you once, she might cross a city twice."

Karl smiled. Somewhere beyond the marsh, a cannon boomed in distant practice. Jean did not look toward it. He was smiling too.

Chapter 17

Summer of 1814 in New Orleans was a season of sweat and secrets. As the river warmed and the city's edges grew wild with humidity, three currents stirred around Karl Steinheimer—sometimes calm, often savage, and never fully understood.

The first current, of course, was Annabelle. A young lady had declined a soft future and seemed interested in him. Now what?

They continued to meet, at the market, outside the cathedral after Mass, once at the riverfront when her aunt hired a boatman to carry letters upstream. Each encounter was proper, threaded with the quiet tension of wondering what the future might hold.

Annabelle remained cautious, even cool. She may have avoided an unwanted union with Theodore but that didn't mean that she was ready to embrace a relationship with Karl, especially not a serious one. She still had reservations about his affiliations. She did, however, grow more curious. She asked about Germany, ships, Karl's faith, about how a man learned to trust the sea. Karl answered as best he could, careful never to lie and never to glorify the Lafittes, whose world did not belong in hers.

Once, as they walked along the levee under the watchful glare of her chaperone, Annabelle said: "I was told privateers serve their country. Pirates serve themselves. Which is Jean Lafitte?" Karl hesitated. "He serves his own rules. I think sometimes he wishes a country existed that deserved him." Annabelle considered that. For the first time, Karl thought he saw approval, small, but real.

Their closeness grew in quiet increments of shared observations and borrowed laughter. One Sunday Karl decided it was time to share more of himself.

He spotted Annabelle in the church garden after Mass, sunlight catching the threadwork in her lap. He tried hard not to stare as he slowly approached, clearing his throat so he wouldn't startle her.

"Monsieur Steinheimer," she greeted, pausing her needle. "Did you find the sermon enlightening?" Karl considered. "Enlightening enough to make me vow to behave better," he said, "though I make no guarantees about succeeding." Annabelle's mouth curved, not quite a smile. "An honest man. My aunt would label that a rarity."

Karl glanced at her embroidery. "You stitch beautifully. My Mama embroidered, usually horses with very long legs and very small heads."

"Anatomical challenges," Annabelle said gravely. "I sympathize." They shared a brief, unguarded moment, nothing dramatic, just warmth and recognition passing between them until Karl's pulse quickened. He shifted his weight, hands suddenly unsure. "There's… something I would like to share with you," he said at last, his voice quieter than he intended.

Annabelle's heartbeat startled her, thudding as though someone had knocked on a locked door. Surely he meant a kiss. What else did boys dramatically announce in gardens after church? Her mind raced. Did she truly like him in that way? Was she prepared for such a step? Was he?

Her body didn't wait for answers. Instinctively, she lowered her gaze, feeling the warmth between them. She lifted her chin a fraction, clearly an invitation, fully expecting Karl to reach for her hand and lean in—

Instead, Karl fumbled in his pocket and triumphantly produced a small wooden swan. "This!" he declared. "It's a swan Papa carved for Mama." Annabelle shuddered at the abrupt change in trajectory, her pulse untangling as she tried to hide her expectations. Then, seeing the worn little figure in his palm—neck slightly crooked, wood smoothed from years of touch—her lips curved despite herself.

"May I?" she asked. Karl placed the swan in her hands. Annabelle held it gently, her thumb tracing the grain as though it were something fragile and alive.

"She called it 'hope on water,'" Karl said. "My mother. She said swans bring peace, and they survive by work you cannot see." Annabelle looked up, and whatever teasing lingered in her expression softened into something earnest. "Your mother was wise," she murmured. "And brave." Karl suddenly stood taller. "I think… she would have liked you. Though I don't think she would like the man I'm becoming."

The words hung there—sincere. Annabelle did not laugh or deflect. She returned the swan, and her fingers brushed his with a quiet tenderness that had nothing to do with carved wood.

"I'm honored," she said. "And you're young. Maybe someone can help you find the right path." Karl tucked the swan away and tried to contain a grin. As they walked back toward the main gate, Karl felt something settle in his heart. He wasn't certain if he should embrace it or try to escape.

The second current surrounding Karl was the Lafitte business, which was growing more dangerous. Pierre met with Spanish merchants by day and Creole captains by night. Jean frightened men with his reputation. Pierre frightened them by remembering everything they said. Jean studied maps with a hunger that unsettled even his brother.

Rumors flickered through taverns and tailors' shops: ... *Spanish patrols increasing near Barataria ... King's agents sniffing for contraband ... Gold moving through Havana under armed convoy.* Jean listened to every whisper. He said little, but his eyes hardened.

The third raging current was the Spanish themselves. Revenge hovered in Jean's plans. The Spanish had not forgotten the Lafittes, nor forgiven the humiliation of Jean surviving in Cap-Français and besting Valera. One evening, Jean said quietly to Karl: "The Spanish are bleeding us. They pay for nothing. They steal what they can. They kidnapped Élise and left both of us to die." He paused. "That account still needs to be balanced." Karl felt a jolt in his chest. He was hopeful vengeance had been gained when Valera died. He was wrong.

Within weeks, strangers appeared in New Orleans taverns—men with spotless boots and accents too refined for dock labor. They asked about smugglers. About the Lafittes. About a fair-skinned German boy working among them.

Karl did not learn this until Jean told him one night while cleaning pistols: "You're being watched." Karl froze. "By who?"

"Spanish agents. Or mercenaries paid by them. It makes no difference."

"But why me?"

Jean sighed. "Because they saw you with me in Cap-Français. They know what happened to Valera. They will try to use you as leverage."

Karl felt his throat tighten. "Annabelle—"

Jean raised a hand. "Don't let them see you worry for her. Worry makes targets."

By midsummer, New Orleans simmered like iron beneath a blacksmith's hammer. The nights were thick with insects and the days with rumors, most of them involving the Lafittes. The Spanish had begun to choke the Gulf with patrols. Three Lafitte schooners vanished near Matanzas. Two of their captains returned with stories of boarding parties and confiscated cargo. Pierre cursed the losses but hid the anger behind his merchant's smile.

Jean did not hide his anger at all. He haunted the wharves at night, questioning sailors, tracing the movements of Spanish brigs as if mapping a disease. Twice he returned bloodied from tavern fights. Once from a Spaniard who called him *perro francés* (French dog). Once from an American who asked too many questions. Karl followed when asked, kept silent when told, and watched Jean's grief harden into a terrible clarity.

Meanwhile, Annabelle's world narrowed. Her aunt's letters to St. Louis were sent with increasing frequency—requests for travel escorts and lodging, for confirmation that the city of her birth was safer than this one dripping with sin.

Annabelle read between every line: *We must flee before the Lafitte boy claims Annabelle.* She did not say so aloud. But she did object— gracefully, cleverly, and always just within the bounds of duty a niece would give to a caring aunt.

"I should stay at least until autumn," Annabelle announced one afternoon. "The convent teaches embroidery only through September, and you know how poor I am with the finer stitches." Her aunt narrowed her eyes. "And what does embroidery have to do with that German boy?" Annabelle lifted her chin. "Nothing, Aunt. Truly."

When her aunt turned away, Annabelle's expression softened—part determination, part confusion. Karl Steinheimer unsettled her, not because he was dangerous, but because he was someone she did not yet understand.

Two nights later, Karl rode across town to deliver letters to a Creole plantation clerk near the river bend. His return took him past the convent, where lanterns bobbed like fireflies beyond the garden wall. Annabelle was there, sitting on a low bench, a sewing basket at her feet. She looked up as he passed and, after a pause, waved him closer with the stitcher's calm that had once humbled a sugar merchant. Karl dismounted, heart drumming.

Annabelle gestured toward the sky. "If you stay silent, you'll see the comet." Karl looked up. A pale streak burned across the heavens, neither fast nor slow, like a brushstroke from a hurried saint. The garden dimmed strangely beneath it. For a moment the lantern light seemed weaker, as though the sky had taken some of its strength.

"They say comets foretell events," Annabelle murmured. "War, death, change." Karl spoke before he thought. "I hope it means change. I've seen enough of the other two." Her eyes softened. "And yet you ride with men who chase death."

Karl opened his mouth, then closed it, ashamed of how little he understood his own choices. Annabelle didn't press him. Instead, she asked quietly, "Do you believe God approves of the company you keep?" Karl flinched, not at the question itself, but at the echo of Mama in it.

He forced a breath. "I don't know what God wants from me. But I know what Jean wants. And I know what I want."

Annabelle studied him. "And what is that?" The garden felt impossibly peaceful, as though the city had fallen asleep. Karl pondered the question, not certain he could form an answer. Not certain he knew the answer. Before he could speak, movement stirred at the far end of the garden. Not the idle shifting of servants.

Two silhouettes detached from shadow near the iron gate. They stood too straight. Too patient. One removed his hat, slowly, as though entering a parlor. Karl felt the disciplined stillness. He had seen it in Cap-Français. Annabelle followed his gaze. "Karl?"

"Don't turn," he said softly.

The nearer man stepped forward into lantern light. Spanish cut. Spanish boots. Clean, deliberate. The second man lingered half in shadow. Beside him, beyond the wall, stood another figure. Not Spanish. American coat. Familiar posture. Watching.

Theodore. He did not move. He did not intervene. He simply observed.

Karl's mind raced. Jean's voice echoed somewhere in his memory: *The present is ours. Act accordingly.*

"You've misread the evening," Karl said. "It's spoken for."

The Spaniard's eyes narrowed. He spoke in courteous French. "You have made yourself difficult to approach, monsieur. We intend to correct that now."

Annabelle's breath faltered. "Karl—," she said. "Stay behind me," he whispered.

Theodore shifted slightly outside the gate. Not stepping forward. Not leaving.

Watching.

The Spaniard continued, almost conversational. "You associate with dangerous men. Your presence complicates matters for certain families."

His eyes drifted briefly toward the street. Karl saw it. Saw the connection. Something cold settled into place.

The man's hand drifted toward his blade. For a moment no one breathed. Karl bent down and came up with a fistful of gravel, throwing hard into the lantern flame first, shattering light into chaos, then into the nearer man's eyes. The garden plunged into a broken shadow.

Annabelle gasped.

Outside the gate, Theodore removed his gloves slowly, folded them once, and placed them inside his coat, as though preparing to remember everything. He took a half step back.

Steel flashed.

Karl lunged low, driving his shoulder into the Spaniard's ribs. The man smelled of oil and salt and foreign tobacco. They crashed to the gravel. The impact rattled Karl.

A blade sliced downward. Karl rolled. Too slow. Fire tore across his forearm. He hissed and slammed his elbow into the man's throat. Cartilage crunched. The Spaniard choked but did not release the knife.

Boots thundered from behind. The first attacker was recovering. Karl groped blindly, fingers closing around his own knife that Jean insisted every man carry just as the Spaniard above him drove steel downward. Karl twisted. The blade meant for his throat sank into the gravel beside his ear.

Karl drove his knife upward. Not clean. But enough. The man stiffened, exhaled hard, and sagged. Karl shoved him back and scrambled up just as the second Spaniard charged, half-blinded, blood streaking from his brow.

The two men collided. Fists were thrown. Gravel flew in the chaos. Karl barely registered that the shape at the gate was shifting. Theodore was stepping back. Retreating.

The other man gazed at the gate, too, and Karl seized the moment delivering a headbutt that staggered the Spaniard. A punch to the gut put the intruder on his knees. Karl struck again with the heel of his boot until the man crumpled.

Silence covered the garden. Annabelle stood frozen, one hand to her mouth, eyes wide. She had kept her composure. Now, she was processing what she had just seen.

Karl's sleeve dripped blood. He looked toward the gate. No shadow remained. Theodore was gone.

Karl turned at once to Annabelle. "Are you hurt?" he asked. She shook her head, but she wasn't looking at him. She was looking at the bodies.

"You didn't hesitate," she said.

"No."

"You knew what to do."

"Yes."

Relief crossed her face. Then recognition. "They spoke of families," she said slowly. "Of inconvenience." Karl followed her thought with a nod. Her voice lowered. "Do you believe Theodore would—"

Karl did not answer. He didn't need to. He knew the truth and he suspected Annabelle did too. Annabelle drew a careful breath. "They would have taken me," she said.

"Yes."

"And you stayed."

"So did you."

She stepped closer, not to cling. To stand level with him. "I have spent my life being escorted," she said quietly. "Tonight, for the first time, I was defended." Her eyes lifted. "Not because I was valuable. Because I mattered to you."

Karl looked down at his sleeve. The blood didn't faze him but he was a little unsettled by how quickly his hands had known what to do.

He whispered, "Be careful. If your aunt sends you away—go. St. Louis may keep you safe." Annabelle grabbed his hand with unexpected fierceness. "And what of you?" Karl looked in her eyes. "I don't think I get to be safe."

He didn't say it aloud, but he wondered if men like him ever got to choose anything. He walked Annabelle to the doorway of the convent.

The comet had been timely. Change was coming.

Chapter 18

Karl did not realize how much blood he had lost until he tried to step onto the dock at Barataria. His knees failed first.

Pierre caught him under one arm, swearing. "What happened?"

"Nothing," Karl muttered. "Two Spaniards."

Pierre's grip tightened immediately. "Alive?"

"One isn't."

Jean stepped out of the warehouse and into the lamplight, wiping ink from his fingers. He stopped mid-step. His gaze dropped to Karl's sleeve.

"Who did this?" Jean asked simply without anger.

Karl tried to shrug. He winced as the movement pulled at the cut along his forearm. "In the convent garden," he said. "They approached me and Annabelle."

Jean closed the distance in three strides and seized Karl's arm, turning it to inspect the wound. His fingers were steady. His eyes were not.

"Deep?" Pierre asked.

"Deep enough," Jean said.

Karl winced again. "I handled it."

"I can see that," Jean said softly.

He released Karl's arm and turned away for a moment, pacing once across the dock boards as if measuring something unseen. "What happened?" Jean asked.

"There were two Spaniards," Karl said carefully. "But there was someone else. At the gate. I think it was Theodore."

Pierre swore under his breath. Jean did not. He stood very still. "Did Theodore do this?" Jean asked.

"No. He was watching."

Jean slowly inhaled once through his nose. Then he began to chuckle. "Of course," he said quietly. "A merchant's son does not stain his own gloves."

Pierre shifted uneasily. "You think he arranged it?"

"I think," Jean replied, "that Spanish agents do not wander into convent gardens by accident."

He stepped back toward Karl and forced eye contact. "You understand what this means."

Karl looked down and said, "They're escalating."

Jean shook his head slightly. "No," he said. "They're negotiating."

"Negotiating?" Pierre echoed.

"Yes." Jean's voice cooled further. "They wish to see what I value."

His gaze moved to Karl's wound. "You bled for me tonight," Jean said. Karl opened his mouth to protest but Jean shook his head to cut him off. "Because they could not reach me."

Then the softness vanished. "Pierre," Jean said, already turning back toward the warehouse, "send word to Havana that the next shipment will not arrive."

Pierre hesitated. "That will cost us."

"Yes."

Jean stepped closer again, lowering his voice so only Karl could hear.

"They believe this was a warning," he said. "They are wrong. It was a mistake."

Karl knew Jean was always calculating. This new level of calculation seemed to be more focused, more intense.

"You will not walk alone again," Jean continued. "Not to markets. Not to gardens. Not even to God."

"I can defend myself," Karl said quietly.

"Yes," Jean agreed. "You can." He placed a hand briefly against Karl's uninjured shoulder. "And that is what they fear. Fear makes people irrational."

Karl watched Jean turn away in the lamplight. Vengeance, he knew, was back on the schedule. It was the type of vengeance that did not shout. It planned.

A week later, Karl and Annabelle were at the riverside wharf below the French Quarter, where ships from Havana and Charleston unloaded rum, tobacco, and gossip. Jean was there too. The Mississippi moved slow and brown beneath the heat.

Annabelle sat on an overturned barrel beneath the shade of an awning where Jean was calculating next moves and Karl gingerly stacked light cargo with his one good arm. Chicory drifted through the wharf air from a nearby vendor's cart.

Annabelle tried to focus on the lacework in her lap, though it wasn't lace at all, just a scrap of sailcloth she pretended required delicate inspection. Anything to avoid looking too long at Karl. Every time she did, she found herself cataloging him. The earnest way he listened when spoken to, as though good manners were honor, not obligation. Most confounding, the way he seemed not to know he was handsome.

She wondered how a mother had raised a boy that sincere without turning him soft. She imagined a woman with work-hardened hands and scripture on her tongue. She saw the silhouette of Mama every time Karl paused before making a decision, as though consulting some unseen authority.

Karl, for his part, kept catching her glances and promptly overthinking them. Was she studying him? Did she find him strange? He busied himself stacking crates, staying active to avoid an unease he would rather not acknowledge.

In truth, Annabelle had fallen for Karl as suddenly as the Spaniards he felled in the courtyard. Naive in matters of the heart, Karl was slow to recognize the depth of Annabelle's devotion. Jean observed both of them like a theater critic who had seen the play many times and still found it amusing.

"Mon Dieu," Jean drawled that afternoon. "Our young Karl works as if the toil will gift him salvation. Annabelle studies him like a scholar of rare insects." Karl froze mid-stacking. "I wasn't—she wasn't—" Annabelle nearly dropped her sailcloth. "Monsieur Lafitte," she protested, cheeks blooming rose, "you mistake simple curiosity for impropriety."

"Ah," Jean grinned, "but curiosity is the polite word for impropriety. Ask any scholar."

Karl flushed, torn between mortification and a tiny thrill that Annabelle found him worth being teased over. Jean clapped him on the shoulder, as though sealing the humiliation into memory. "Relax, mon ami. The girl admires you. It is not a crime." Karl sputtered, "She doesn't — that's not—"

Annabelle stood, dignity recovered just enough to tilt her chin. "I admire anyone who works as earnestly as Karl. The world suffers no shortage of idlers." Jean's eyebrows twitched upward. "There. A confession both flattering and safe. You see? Love, properly phrased, is indistinguishable from virtue."

Annabelle rolled her eyes. "Everything becomes poetry in your mouth, Monsieur Lafitte."

"Of course," Jean replied. "That is the only way to speak of things that matter."

Karl wished he could disappear into the decking.

Later that afternoon, when Jean was distracted with navigational charts, Annabelle stole a quieter glance at Karl. He was sitting alone near the rail, watching the sun sink into the Gulf. His hands rested open, palms up, as though ready to receive instruction. The water moved slowly below him, calm at the surface, hiding its labor beneath.

Jean set down his chart and ambled toward Karl, arriving with a smirk. "You are thinking again," he said. "A dangerous habit."

Karl didn't look up. "Only wondering if I belong anywhere at all."

Jean scoffed, not unkindly. "You belong where you choose to matter. The rest is just weather." Karl pondered the thought briefly. "Is that what you believe?"

"It is what I have learned," Jean corrected. "Beliefs are for priests and mothers. Lessons are for men." Karl absorbed that, letting it settle into the space Mama once occupied. He felt guilty for how neatly it fit.

Jean leaned toward Karl and spoke in a low tone to deliver the next lesson. He did not speak of vengeance. He shared what was about to be orchestrated with his oversight. The first step was to plant false flags.

Within two days, three rumors began moving through New Orleans. No one could later remember who had first said them aloud. None were true. All were useful.

Once the rumors had spread, two schooners slipped out from Barataria without ceremony. A third schooner sailed openly, drawing attention elsewhere. Pierre hosted a dinner for a Spanish broker the very evening Jean slipped out to sea.

As they prepared to depart, Karl said quietly: "I sense this raid has little to do with the capture of silver." Jean adjusted the priming on his pistol. "You are correct," he said. "This is all about adjusting expectations."

The target was real. The *Santa Isidora* appeared in the Spanish registry. Armed. Lightly escorted.

"They wanted to know what I value," Jean said as the brig's lanterns appeared against the dark Gulf horizon. "Tonight they learn what I am willing to remove." Karl stood at his side and asked, "You're certain Theodore had a hand in the attack?" Jean answered indirectly, saying, "Spanish officers do not stroll into convent gardens unless someone assures them of privacy."

Jean's men struck just before moonrise. Two boats slipped from shadow and hooked onto the brig's stern before the watch could register movement. Within minutes, resistance collapsed. The capture was quintessential Lafitte – quick and complete.

Jean gave Karl just one command. "Take the papers!" Not the silver. Not the arms.

Karl understood. The papers had contacts. Names. Leverage.

Jean crouched before the fallen captain. "If Spanish agents are seen again near convent walls," Jean said softly, "paper will not be the only thing I take next time."

New Orleans buzzed the next morning with whispers in the Quarter. A Spanish brig had limped home stripped of intelligence. Certain names had been found in its correspondence. Names of men in New Orleans. Men who met with Spanish officers privately.

The papers were never publicly shown. They did not need to be. Pierre made certain the right ears heard the right fragments.

The name of Theodore Dubois surfaced gently. Never accused. Only mentioned. *Curious coincidence*, someone would say. *He is often seen with Spanish men*, another would add.

In a city balanced between loyalties, even the appearance of divided allegiance was poison. The real blow came at a reception hosted by a French merchant whose favor Theodore desperately needed. The room glittered with candles and silk, rumors drifting beneath violins.

All of the city's leaders were present. Theodore arrived late. Confident.

Jean was not there, but he had already set the trap.

Midway through the evening, the merchant requested a word with Theodore in full view of guests. The conversation was brief. Quiet. Every eye watched as the merchant's expression cooled. Theodore attempted a laugh that did not land.

Moments later, a Spanish officer entered, uninvited, asking directly for Monsieur Dubois. The room went still. The officer removed his hat politely. "Monsieur Dubois," he said, "thank you again for your previous courtesies." Theodore did not reach for the offered handshake.

Someone dropped a glass. Theodore turned pale. It wasn't proof of treason. But it was proof of relationship. In 1814 Louisiana, that was the same thing. Theodore left the reception, no one stopped him.

Details of the evening arrived in Jean's warehouse the next day. "It is done," Pierre said simply. Karl smiled. "You never touched him."

Jean smiled faintly. "I removed his protection."

Theodore had relied on private Spanish backing to strengthen his position in the city. And to threaten Karl. Jean had cut Spain's reach and then illuminated Theodore's connection to it.

It was a psychological duel. No blood. Only isolation. Jean looked at Karl and said, "If he is wise, he will never come near you again."

Days later, Theodore did come near once more — not at a ball, not at a church — but outside the convent. He looked thinner. His eyes were dark with shadows.

Karl and Annabelle were sitting on a bench in the garden. Karl stood when he saw him coming. Theodore stopped before getting too close.

For a moment, it seemed Theodore might challenge. Might attempt to reclaim dignity.

Whatever fight Theodore had in him evaporated quickly. He gave a shallow nod and looked at Karl for a long moment.

"To your future," he said quietly. Then, almost as an afterthought, "Guard it carefully." He walked away slowly, like a man leaving a city that no longer knew his name.

To the surprise of no one, Theodore left New Orleans within the month. Family members said he left to pursue "business opportunities." A kind way of saying Theodore left to escape the silence that met him in every room.

The weeks that followed blurred into a strangely golden chapter. Rumors hovered on the docks, and the Spanish threat seemed to pulse just beyond the horizon. But in the quiet mornings and late-night hours, Karl and Annabelle continued to find each other.

Love lingers quietly before arriving all at once. Devotion revealed itself in the way Annabelle began waiting for Karl when he returned from errands. Affection was evident in the way Karl unconsciously sought her gaze before answering Jean, as if to confirm that his words were suitable for both pirate and lady.

One afternoon, as Jean met with officers in whispers behind closed shutters, Annabelle and Karl walked along the levee. The river rolled toward the Gulf with a slow and inevitable purpose.

"New Orleans is changing fast," Annabelle said, watching a boat unload hurriedly. "Father says the British grow bolder by the month. And the Spanish grow thinner." Karl shook his head. He did not pretend to understand politics, but he understood danger. New Orleans felt like a play awaiting catastrophe. Annabelle hesitated before adding, "My father wants me in St. Louis before winter."

Something in Karl's chest thudded once, hard. He tried to keep his voice level. "You intend to go?"

"I intend to obey," she replied, with a small sad laugh. "We are not all permitted to choose our adventures." The words stung him more than he expected. He imagined life without her and felt an old coldness creep up, the same cold he felt the first weeks he had left Mama behind.

"I'm sorry," he said, because he could think of nothing else. Annabelle stopped walking. She faced him fully, eyes bright in the fading light. "Karl," she said softly, "I did not tell you to hurt you. I told you because I do not wish to vanish from your life without saying it plainly." The blunt kindness of it almost buckled his knees.

"I… I do not wish for you to vanish," Karl managed, the words awkward but true. Annabelle's expression warmed with something unguarded. "Then do not let me." He sighed. "How?"

She stepped closer, close enough for him to smell lilac. "By remembering that I care for you," she whispered. "By letting me return to someone who will still choose me." Karl felt the world tilt with the realization that he could choose something other than survival. He could choose someone. "Annabelle," he said, voice low, "I care for you too. More than I know how to say." She smiled, and for once it wasn't shy or cautious.

The evening ended with a promise that was not spoken like poetry, but agreed upon like a pact. When the war settled, when New Orleans no longer trembled under foreign flags and conspiracies, she would return.

He would be waiting. Or at least he promised he would try.

Chapter 19

New Orleans did not pause for dreams of the future. The British threat intensified, and American officers began to arrive with questions only Jean could answer. Privateers who once plundered Spanish ships now met uniformed generals over maps stained with rum. Jean negotiated with the cool posture of a man who understood leverage. He would fight—not from patriotism, but because he despised crowns and chains, and Spain had taken from him what no treaty could restore.

One night, after a long council in the smithy, Karl found Jean alone behind the shop, loading pistols with slow, methodical precision. "We'll bleed the British before they take this city," Jean said without looking up.

"You hate the British as much as the Spanish?" Karl asked. Jean gave a humorless smile. "I hate anyone who believes the world belongs to them by right. Kings. Empires. Ministries." He paused. "The Spanish took Élise. The British would take the Mississippi. Both commit the same sin— ownership." Karl shivered. Not at the words, but at how calm they sounded.

"Do you believe God will avenge her?" Karl asked quietly, surprising himself. Jean's hands stilled over the pistol. "No, Karl," he said softly. "God does not avenge." The powder horn tipped, dark grains sliding into the barrel. "Men avenge," Jean continued. "And the sooner a man learns that… the safer he becomes."

Karl recoiled. Mama once said vengeance was the devil's imitation of justice. Yet here was Jean, alive and fierce, promising what heaven could not.

Karl walked back toward the forge with a strange feeling. He wondered if his faith had been surrendered or traded away. He knew Jean's hard creed had replaced Mama's prayerful one.

Meanwhile, everyone in New Orleans could smell war riding the currents. The British wanted the mouth of the Mississippi—the keyhole to the continent—and the city knew it. Karl lived on the edges of that tension, splitting his time between Barataria's warehouses and New Orleans alleys. He had learned when to keep his eyes open and his mouth shut.

The first British ship to anchor off Barataria did so under a white flag. It was September of 1814—two summers into the war—and the Gulf crawled with Royal Navy frigates. The British had burned Washington City, seized American ships, and now cast their gaze on New Orleans. Three red-coated officers arrived in a longboat, escorted warily through the bayou by Lafitte's men. They were delivered to Grand Terre, where Jean Lafitte waited in an open pavilion, dressed like a gentleman rather than a pirate. Karl stood at his right shoulder.

The senior British officer, Colonel Nichols, spoke plainly: "Mr. Lafitte, we intend to take Louisiana. We offer you the rank of captain in His Majesty's Royal Navy. You will receive thirty thousand dollars in gold and full amnesty for your men. Guide our forces through these channels and oppose the Americans."

Jean raised an eyebrow. "You flatter me with an empire."

Nichols continued, "The Americans treat you as criminals. We recognize you as privateers. Aid us, and you may govern this place under British protection." Most men would have lunged at the offer. Jean remained silent.

Thirty thousand dollars. The amount was impressive, but Karl knew Jean had ten times that much buried in the marsh. Yet legal protection under the British could be tempting. Jean might be swayed by the promise of legitimacy.

Then Karl's thoughts moved to a dark place. If Jean accepted the British offer, they would no longer be hunted by Americans. Instead, they would be owned by the British Empire. The Lafittes, he sensed, would not report to a superior.

Finally, Jean said: "I am flattered, Colonel. But I am not for sale today. Leave me the proposal, and I shall give you my answer within a fortnight." Nichols, confident, agreed.

When the British departed, Karl leaned closer. "Will you consider it?" Jean's expression didn't change. "No. But I may sell the refusal dearly."

The refusal emboldened Karl. If Jean turned down an empire's gold, perhaps there was a kind of honor that did not wear a uniform.

Jean knew his loyalty had always been to Louisiana, not to Britain or Washington. But he also knew leverage when he saw it.

The next day, at Government Hall, the guards barred the steps before Lafitte reached the door. They knew his face—New Orleans knew its pirates—and they shifted nervously, muskets angled but not raised.

"State your business," the sergeant demanded. Lafitte's smile was razor thin. "A message for the governor, from men with ships."

The sergeant hesitated briefly and then motioned for guards to escort Jean. He knew better than to fire guns in broad daylight. New Orleans was volatile enough without blood on its steps.

Governor Claiborne did not rise when Lafitte entered. "You are under bounty," Claiborne said evenly. "Five hundred dollars."

Jean inclined his head. "And yet I am here." He placed a sealed letter on the desk. "From British officers anchored at Barataria."

Claiborne snatched the letter and broke the seal. With each line his face blanched further. "This—this is treason," he rasped.

"No," Lafitte corrected. "This is war. I bring you this because the British would like Louisiana carried away in pieces, and I prefer it not be. I propose a truce. You will rescind your bounty and cease interference in my operations. In return, I will refuse their gold."

Claiborne stared at the letter as if it might ignite. "Five hundred dollars for your capture," he murmured, as though embarrassed by the paltry sum.

Lafitte allowed himself a dry laugh. "If you wish for a duel of bounties, Governor, I remind you that I have offered thirty thousand dollars for yours. I assure you, there are many in this city who would attempt collection."

Claiborne's face tightened in reluctant respect. New Orleans was a tinderbox of loyalties. He knew Lafitte spoke the truth.

"And what do you expect of me?" the governor asked.

"A truce," Lafitte repeated. "I walk out of this building alive. My men are not harassed. And you will consult General Andrew Jackson about my offer before you drive the finest marksmen in Louisiana into the arms of the British."

Claiborne set the letter down slowly, fingers trembling just enough to betray him. "You give me no choice," he said at last.

"You have every choice," Lafitte replied. "Only some lead to ruin more quickly than others." Silence fell between them. Finally, Claiborne looked up. "I will speak to Andrew Jackson. The bounty will be…

reconsidered. But do not mistake necessity for affection, Monsieur Lafitte. New Orleans is not accustomed to embracing pirates."

Lafitte gave a courteous bow one might give a ballroom partner rather than a governor who had just been strong-armed. "Then New Orleans must learn new habits," Jean said. With that, he left the office boldly, past guards too uncertain to stop him, down steps that had seen revolutions but never a pirate delivering the future like a summons.

Word of the meeting traveled slower than rumor, and the men of Louisiana did not yet know that a truce had been whispered between the pirate and the governor. Within days, militia boats descended on Barataria with cannon smoke and righteous fury, determined to collect the bounty on Lafitte's head.

The attack scattered the Baratarians through the marsh. Jean vanished into the bayous with Karl close behind, both men slipping through channels only smugglers understood. For a week the pirate who had just negotiated with a governor slept beneath cypress shadows and kept no lantern lit, waiting for the city to discover that it had fired its guns at an ally.

Days later, the city welcomed a new commander. Jackson arrived in New Orleans like a thunderstorm wearing a sword. Karl stood in the packed chamber at Jackson's temporary headquarters on Royal Street. Jackson's boots were caked with mud. His eyes were feverish. He had the look of a man in need of a good night's rest. Claiborne handed Jackson the British letter to Lafitte. Jackson read it once, tossed his hat on a table, and barked in a hoarse Tennessee accent, "By God, we will hang the British. The Baratarians we shall hire."

Karl felt the room shift when Jackson finished speaking. Hire. Not hang. For years, the Baratarians had been called thieves, smugglers, rot on the coast. Now the same hands that signed bounty warrants would sign military commissions.

Karl studied Jackson's face. The general had already turned back to the map, one hand pressing flat against Louisiana as if he meant to hold it in place. Karl wondered whether men like that ever let go of anything once they had laid claim to it. He sensed Jackson was not a man who embraced pirates. He was a man who needed them.

Within a fortnight, the city buzzed with word of British ships near the Gulf. Jean vanished into rooms where maps were pinned to walls and futures were gambled in smoke-filled whispers.

In St. Louis, Annabelle's father began a desperate search for immediate passage north for his daughter.

With each arriving cannon, Karl felt Annabelle drifting away.

Chapter 20

In those last hurried days, the tension between Karl and Annabelle became a living thing, visible in the way they lingered after conversations, neither willing to be the first to turn away. Karl found himself eager to see her, then inexplicably clumsy once he did. He wanted every gesture to match the emotion he felt. Too often, his eagerness came across as boyishness.

One evening, after a light supper at a coffeehouse, Karl walked Annabelle back to the convent. The streets were unusually quiet, lamps throwing soft puddles of light across the cobblestones. Their footsteps seemed too loud. Karl kept glancing over his shoulder, half expecting a nun or patrol to materialize from the dark.

At the convent-house gate, Annabelle hesitated as if she had something important to say. From inside came the faint sound of voices. Karl thought she was preparing to say goodnight. "If I leave," she said quietly, not looking at him, "I do not wish to go untouched by my own choosing."

Then she leaned closer and whispered, "Come up"—not an invitation, but a decision already made.

When the corridor fell silent, she slipped the door open just enough for him to pass through, then barred it again. They climbed the narrow stairwell in stockinged feet, holding their shoes, pausing at each landing while Annabelle listened for movement. Once, a door opened somewhere above them, and Karl felt her fingers tighten forcefully around his hand. He had never been so aware of his own size or his own breathing.

Inside her room at last, the door closed with a careful click. The air smelled of candle tallow and lilac soap. A single flame flickered on the small table, throwing their faces into gold and shadow. Annabelle turned to him without speaking and kissed him first—urgent, searching—as if time itself were pressing at her back. Karl kissed her in return, the hunger there startling him, her impending departure for St. Louis now looming like a tide about to turn.

For a moment, the convent ceased to exist. Then a bell rang below for night prayers. The sound threaded through Karl's body like a warning that this moment, like all moments in New Orleans, belonged as much to fate as to desire. Whatever came next would echo.

Clothes fell away in silence broken only by breathing. Buttons fumbled loose, skin revealed in the dim candlelight. They found the bed in a tangle of laughter and trembling. Whatever innocence remained between them slipped quietly away. Karl moved slowly, afraid of hurting her. Afraid of everything beyond that moment.

Annabelle clutched him fiercely, biting her lip to keep from crying out, a single tear slipping down her temple from overwhelm. When the pain faded, she pulled him closer. They moved together with growing confidence. Awkward. Breathless. Exquisitely human. Until both were shaking with the force of it.

Afterward, as they lay tangled in damp linen and cooling sweat, the world returned. Annabelle's face flushed crimson. She turned toward the wall, whispering, "I am tainted," not in despair but disbelief. Karl's stomach dropped as holy dread clamped around him. He imagined God's ledger filling with ink above a bed that smelled of sin and lilac.

"I'm sorry," he said, voice raw. She rolled back to face him, eyes fierce. "Do not apologize for what I wanted." It should have soothed him, but it didn't. He counted the consequences. What if she conceived? What if he had taken something he could never return? He wanted to voice his thoughts, but language failed.

When he finally rose to dress, she caught his hand and placed it against her breast. "Nothing is certain," she whispered, "but everything feels possible." Karl did not fully understand her meaning.

In the days that followed, Karl looked for Annabelle everywhere—market stalls, the convent gates. Yet when she appeared, he struggled to meet her eyes. His eagerness betrayed him. He spoke too quickly, laughed at nothing, fell silent at the wrong moments.

Annabelle noticed. She grew gentler, but also more reserved. Their conversations stalled. Glances lingered too long, then broke away. When they walked together, space opened between them that neither quite knew how to close. The city, which had once seemed to conspire in their favor, now felt crowded with consequences.

Karl replayed that night endlessly, not the warmth of it, but the guilt of taking something he wasn't sure he had properly earned. He feared he had crossed a line he did not yet know how to honor. Worse, he feared she might leave for St. Louis before he learned.

Jean mentioned it before Annabelle could. He mentioned it casually, almost kindly, no malice intended. Annabelle would be departing in a matter of days. St. Louis. Karl knew the day was coming, but the words struck him with a force that erased his fumbling ways. He had a new urgency. He sought her out that very afternoon and, for once, did not circle his meaning.

"I have been a fool," he said, standing before her in the garden. "Not because of what passed between us, but because I've been afraid to stand plainly in it." Annabelle studied him, searching his face as if weighing truth against hope. "I don't know what I can promise," he went on, voice steady now, "except that I will not pretend you are anything less than what you are to me. I will not let you leave believing you were a mistake."

Something in her softened. The distance between them closed. When she finally spoke, her voice was quiet but certain. "I am leaving because I must. But I do not wish to leave unseen." Karl moved his head in agreement. Regret still lived in him, but it had found its proper shape, not paralysis, but resolve. Whatever time remained to them, he would meet it fully. Not clumsily. Not halfway. For the first time since that night, he felt he was standing where he belonged.

As expected, Annabelle's departure came just a few days later, and it was not grand. No crowds, no handkerchiefs waving from docks. Just the two of them in the shadow of a warehouse before dawn as dockhands loaded freight.

Karl reached into his coat and drew out the little wooden swan, the smooth wings warm in his hand. "For peace," he said quietly as he handed it to her. "Someone once told me it's an inheritance of the heart. I want you to have it."

Annabelle's breath hitched from the cruelty of timing. She held the swan briefly, her thumb tracing the curve of the swan's wing once before she closed his fingers back around the figurine and shook her head. "You keep it. I'll come back for it. And for you. We are meant to be together." The words trembled but did not break. "I will come back," she said again, clutching his hands, "when it is safe. When the city stops choosing between chaos and survival."

Karl almost asked her not to go. The words reached his throat and died there. He would not be the man who chained her future to his uncertainty.

Instead, he slid the swan back into the sanctuary of his pocket. His mind drifted to the last promise of return he had known, Papa's voice echoing in the quiet corners of memory. He was grateful that he had not asked Annabelle to offer such a written pledge. Some promises, he now knew, carried too heavy a weight.

The ache he felt was making him bold. "Before you go," he said, voice low, "let's count our blessings." Annabelle, eyes shining, whispered, "I have family waiting. A city that isn't burning. God's mercy for the road ahead… and you, a man who doesn't make me choose between life and love." She squeezed his hands once more, then released them.

Karl watched her step back toward the gangway, then, as though realizing something important, he said, "And I have blessings too. Work that keeps me from idleness. Men who don't vanish when trouble comes… and the hope of your return."

Annabelle stood still for half a heartbeat. Then she kissed him with a passion that overwhelmed them both. She let go before emotion could change her departure plans. Karl watched until the boat became a silhouette moving upriver toward St. Louis. His body ached with longing. His conscience stung with guilt.

Jean appeared beside him, silent as a ghost. "She will return," Jean said. "How do you know?" Karl asked, breath thick with doubt. "Because she said so," Jean replied. "A woman like that does not make promises lightly." Then, with a sly grin, "And because you have given her a reason." Jean said nothing more. He simply stared at the river as if it were a stage where human folly played its acts.

Karl was left with his thoughts, unaware that the consequences of one night were already in motion, unseen and unstoppable, just as surely as the boat upriver.

For a reason she couldn't yet name, Annabelle felt unsettled as the boat moved north. Twice she reached into her satchel for the wooden swan she had almost taken from Karl, only to remember she had left it with him.

For now.

Chapter 21

New Orleans did not pause for Karl's heart. The city strained toward war like a river after rain.

In the days before battle became a certainty, Karl watched Jean move as though balancing powder kegs. He was volatile, hollowed out by Élise's absence. Some nights he found Jean on the levee, staring toward the Gulf as though waiting for a boat that might yet return what had been taken.

Preparations hardened the city. Smugglers' lofts became armories overnight. Warehouse keys changed hands in tavern corners. Men who had cursed Jean a month earlier now sought him with reluctant respect. Jean accepted it all without pride, drilling artillery crews and issuing muskets with Pierre at his side. Cannon that had guarded treasure were trained on the fields east of town.

Jackson, famously stubborn, swallowed his pride and accepted the Lafittes as allies. War made strange business partners of them all.

Karl hauled powder until his shoulders throbbed and hammered shot until sparks kissed his sleeves. When Pierre asked if he meant to fight, Karl answered yes before fear could intervene. He did not know whether it was courage or simply that he had nowhere else to stand.

The morning of January 8, 1815 dawned in fog and smoke. British regulars advanced in red ranks across the wet fields toward the Rodriguez Canal, drums rattling like bones. Jackson's line held behind mud, cotton bales, and earth.

Jean found Karl before the firing started. "You don't have to stand here," Jean said, not as command, but as something close to care. Karl tightened his grip on the musket. "If I don't stand here, then where do I stand?" Jean grinned, an answer in itself.

The first salvo shook the ramparts and sent clods of earth into the canal. British rockets screamed overhead. The Baratarians' guns answered, iron flinging into the advancing columns with terrible rhythm. Karl reloaded until his fingers split, smoke clawing his throat, the earth shivering with each discharge. At some point he realized he had stopped counting the men who fell.

When the first British line broke against the works, he thought of Hamburg. He thought of scriptures whispered over lamplight, and wondered whether God looked upon battle or turned His face away. For an instant, through the smoke, Karl saw not the field but Annabelle's face the morning she left.

Powder kegs ran low along Battery No. 7. Karl dashed down the embankment with two carriers just as a rocket burst, flinging men and kegs into the water. Karl plunged after them, dragging one man up by the hair and heaving a powder barrel clear of the sparks. Jean saw the danger, vaulted from the works, and fired at a sharpshooter sighting on Karl.

"Move!" he roared through the smoke. "Before the Crown blows you to pieces!" Karl obeyed, boots slipping in mud, heart pounding.

When the British attempted a flank toward the cypress line, Jean seized a militia sergeant by the coat and pointed. "There—hold the trees!"

The men bolted, startled into obedience by the certainty in his voice. Jean ran with them, sword drawn, shouting in French and English alike.

Karl joined a line of Choctaw marksmen, firing until the barrel of his musket scalded his palms. The British advance wavered, rallied, then shattered, officers' swords flashing helplessly as the ranks dissolved in mud.

Still the artillery thundered. Jean returned to his guns, sighted a captured long piece, and ordered a double charge. The blast tore into the forming British column, emptying whole ranks in a heartbeat.

By midday the red lines dissolved under rifle fire and artillery that never lost its rhythm. Smoke drifted across the canal and over the fields beyond, settling on heaps of scarlet and white. The Baratarians leaned on their guns, breathing like men who had sprinted across hell.

Andrew Jackson rode the lines like a man inspecting a storm he had survived. His uniform was torn at the sleeve, hat rim darkened by smoke, eyes sharp with the restless energy of a general who trusted chaos more than ceremony.

Jean Lafitte waited beside his artillery crews. His men were smudged with powder, but laughing with the relief of those who had wagered their lives and won. When Jackson reached Jean, he pulled his horse to a snorting stop.

"So," Jackson said, voice low, "the pirate king fights like a patriot."

Jean gave a small bow, mocking but respectful. "Only for today, General."

Jackson stared at him long enough for Lafitte's men to stiffen. Then the general's grim mouth almost formed a smile, as if pain and approval were the same thing to him. "You brought powder when no one else could. Guns when we had none. And you held the line with men who'd never stood in formation." Jackson leaned forward in the saddle. "I won this morning because my army was a patchwork of hellraisers. You, Lafitte, were the most useful hellraiser of the lot."

Jean's dark eyes glanced toward the battlefield where a carpet of red coats and broken muskets were fading under the winter sun. "England thought little of men who live on the margins, General. I hope America thinks better."

Jackson straightened. "America thinks of victory. The rest can be argued later."

With that, he touched his hat brim and rode on, leaving Lafitte standing in the mud, boots stained with the same blood as every man who had held New Orleans. For perhaps the first time in his life, Jean Lafitte felt the reluctant praise of a nation that might remember him for something other than outlawry.

History would remember Jackson, especially after he was elected president. History would largely forget the men who had carried powder to make his presidency possible.

Karl watched Jean, eyes fixed on the field. He sensed Jean had not fought for glory, nor even for the city. He had fought because maybe the fighting could quiet the ache of losing Élise.

After the victory, pardons arrived sealed with the authority of the United States. Congressmen toasted the Baratarians, though none could pronounce "Grand Terre" correctly. On the steps of the Governor's Hall, Karl stood behind Lafitte as Claiborne shook the privateer's hand before a cheering crowd.

But celebration had layers.

New Orleans threw parties for Jackson. Society women embroidered his name on ribbons and praised "American arms" while omitting which hands carried the powder. Merchants bought the Baratarians drinks in taverns but would not seat them at dinner tables. The wealthy praised

Lafitte's "gallantry" but ignored him in drawing rooms where French porcelain and political ambitions lived.

Karl saw the change in Lafitte's eyes, amusement giving way to something harder. "Useful in war," Lafitte said as they crossed the Place d'Armes, "but undesirable at supper. Remember that."

Within months, the city shifted back to law and order. Marshals watched the docks again. Spanish consuls complained about old seizures. Newspaper editors suggested the Baratarians had been pardoned "perhaps too hastily." Lafitte read the papers, folded them once, and set them aside.

Bitter by the lack of recognition, Jean set his jaw against the city that had used him, praised him, pardoned him. Then quietly shut its doors in his face. The war was over, the British beaten back, the papers filled with odes to Jackson and the Kentucky riflemen, with only the barest mention of the "Baratarian auxiliaries" who had given the army its quickest guns and its sharpest scouts.

Lafitte had not expected medals. He was not so naïve. But the cold shoulder of New Orleans society stung like a slap. No invitations. Few handshakes. No acknowledgment that a pirate had done what gentlemen could not. Karl saw the change in him most clearly. After the battle, Lafitte's smile became a mask worn at half-mast, pleasant at a distance and empty up close. At the Maison Rouge, over the din of glasses and music, Jean finally voiced what he already intended.

"Galveston," he said, tapping his hand on the table as if making a decree, "is a place with no Claiborne, no Jackson, no damned committees of gentlemen with weak hearts and softer hands. A free port, built by free men. That is what comes next." Pierre was already calculating what such a place might yield. The other men from Barataria grinned with the weary appetite of wolves who smelled a new forest.

Karl said nothing. He sat at the long table, elbows resting on the rough wood, letting the candlelight paint shadows across Lafitte's profile. He could feel the pivot in the room, not just of plans, but of fate. All wars end differently for the men who fight them. Lafitte had won his war only to lose his true identity.

When the meeting broke, Lafitte beckoned Karl onto the gallery that overlooked the street. Carriages rattled below. "You have a place with us," Jean said, not as an invitation but as a statement of fact. "Men like us do not belong to cities."

Karl felt a knot tighten behind his sternum. "I am grateful," he answered. "Truly. But I will remain here a while longer." Lafitte turned his head, one brow arched. "For what?" Karl did not hide it. "Annabelle."

At that, Lafitte's expression softened into something almost paternal. He clapped Karl once on the shoulder, not as a captain to his man, but as one awkward romantic to another. "Then stay," he said. "Fight your war. A woman is a battlefield no general has mastered." He paused, then smirked. "And no one can accuse me of refusing a man his campaign."

They stood in silence for a moment as the wind carried the scent of the river. Lafitte tucked his gloves beneath his belt and looked down Royal Street as if charting an invisible coastline. "Nations draw borders," Jean said softly. "Men like me live in the margins. In the end, every man must decide whether he sails toward what he desires… or away from what has wounded him."

Karl spoke before courage could flee. "You taught me that," he said. "Those things… and more." He shook his head, almost laughing at himself. "Mama taught me prayers and patience. You taught me wagers and pistols and how the world really works. The lessons don't match, but I think I needed both."

Jean turned slightly, one brow raised in mild amusement. Karl continued, voice rough with sincerity. "I can never repay you." Lafitte snorted softly, as though the idea itself were offensive. "Nonsense. A man repays his teachers by becoming one." He tapped Karl's shoulder with two fingers. "What you learned, you'll pass on. To some fool boy who needs it as badly as you did." Karl smiled, because there was nothing else to say and because it was true. It was as close to a farewell as Jean and Karl ever offered one another.

Within a month, the schooners of Barataria were packed for sea. Lafitte left New Orleans not with drums or crowds but with a quiet exodus of men whose names, other than his own, history would never record. Galveston would be their next gamble, an island republic of contraband and commerce, beyond the reach of Claiborne's proclamations or Jackson's disdain.

For Karl, New Orleans remained, with its heat and perfume, its narrow lanes and convent walls behind which Annabelle still lived in his memory. He was hopeful and stubborn, and fiercely faithful to the girl who had pressed her lips to his and vanished northward.

War scatters many things, but Karl was convinced that love, once thrown to the wind, might yet blow back to its bearer. So he stayed, waiting not for a cause, nor a commander, but for one woman.

The woman he hoped was already traveling south to meet him.

Chapter 22

While New Orleans worked to rebuild, another consequence was already forming along the Missouri River. St. Louis was colder and more gray than Annabelle remembered. The river ran gray and the sky hung low above it. Even the manners of the people she encountered seemed gray. Her father's townhouse sat near the riverfront, respectable enough to avoid gossip but not so fine that it provoked envy. Her aunt fussed with trunks and linens, complaining about the damp. Her father disappeared almost at once into meetings on shipping and insurance, leaving Annabelle alone with silence and propriety.

Days passed. Then weeks. At first, she blamed the nausea on river travel and homesickness, the delicate ailments young women were expected to suffer quietly. But the sickness did not stop. Her clothes grew tighter, though she swore she had not eaten more. Her monthly courses, always precise as clockwork, failed to arrive. Annabelle counted the days, then counted again. The numbers did not change.

One morning, after a breakfast she could not keep down, she slipped from the house and walked to the convent where her aunt once traded embroidery. The sisters recognized Annabelle and sat her by the hearth with warm milk. When Sister Magdalena asked gently what troubled her, Annabelle's composure cracked.

"I have been ill," she whispered, staring at her hands. "For weeks." Sister Magdalena did not rush her. She waited, which was worse. Finally Annabelle asked the question without asking it: "If a woman's courses do not come, and there is no fever… what might it mean?"

The nun's eyes, sharp behind their warmth, moved from the lace of Annabelle's gloves to her trembling lip. "It may mean," she said softly, "that God intends to send a soul into the world." She studied Annabelle a moment longer. "And souls rarely arrive without rearranging many lives." Annabelle bowed her head until it nearly touched her knees.

It was not shame that crushed her. It was certainty.

The certainty that she carried Karl's child across hundreds of miles, from the Mississippi delta to the banks of the Missouri. Sister Magdalena prayed with her. It did not ease the storm.

Returning home, Annabelle found her father in the parlor reviewing bills. He barely glanced up as she entered. When he finally looked up, he noticed only her paleness and said, "You should take broth at supper and rest." Annabelle managed a nod and fled upstairs.

In her room she closed the door, pressed her fists to her mouth, and let the tears come—quiet, fierce tears that soaked her sleeves. She thought of the convent-house room, of Karl's shaking hands and whispered apologies, of the riverboat shrinking New Orleans into a ribbon of smoke behind her. Not regret, never regret, but the weight of consequence wrapped in love and fear.

That night, she could not sleep. She placed a hand beneath her gown over the slight swell that only she could feel. It was not much, perhaps nothing, but her body knew. The child inside her was no longer a possibility but a certainty.

"Karl," she whispered into the dark, ashamed to speak a man's name in her own bed, "I hope you are alive. I hope you would... not despise me."

Her body ached unexpectedly, a protective curl forming as though instinct had already taken root. She was eighteen, motherless, and soon to be ruined in every way the world counted.

She had heard scraps of stories of a battle that had consumed New Orleans, but she did not know if Karl had survived the roar of cannons. She knew only that she carried a piece of that city beneath her heart, and that secrecy would become her shield.

The child would be born in summer 1815. The child would need a name. And if the child were a girl, the name that rose first was Karla. But that she told no one.

When winter finally loosened its grip, news traveled like an ailing bird, arriving slowly, often dying before reaching its destination. Annabelle heard fragments. The British had been defeated. New Orleans survived. Peace, if such a word applied, was spreading through the territories. Had Karl survived? She had no way of knowing.

She packed to return south as soon as the thaw came, but roads were swamps and the river choked with drift ice. Her aunt begged her to wait. Physicians warned of the dangers of travel for a woman in her condition. Her father forbade her.

Annabelle placed a hand on her swelling belly and closed her eyes. "When the river runs," she whispered to the unborn child, "we will go to him."

Annabelle had every intention of returning to New Orleans, every intention of honoring the promise made in a shadowed port before dawn.

But the river has its own calendar, and life has another.

She went into labor on a humid June evening with thunder growling beyond the shutters. Hours dragged like weeks. Her aunt prayed over her in English. The midwife muttered French instructions soaked in old Catholic ritual.

When the wailing finally cut through the storm, Annabelle felt something like joy and grief braided together. "A girl," the midwife said, placing the tiny, squirming infant in her trembling arms. The child gripped her finger with fierce determination. Annabelle touched the newborn's cheek. The infant's brow furrowed in stubborn concentration. She was certain she had seen that look before.

"What will you name her?" her aunt asked. Annabelle took a deep breath. "Karla," she whispered. "For the river. And for someone I hope will see her soon." Her aunt stiffened, propriety bristled against sorrow, but she said nothing.

Annabelle returned to her father's house after Karla's birth. Her father greeted the child with a measured delight reserved for grandchildren and inconvenient miracles. "Another Dixon," he said, squinting at the infant's determined little face. "Heaven help us all." Aunt Colette, less restrained, nearly spoiled the child to death with blankets, ribbons, and wooden toys.

Raising Karla was not easy. Babies do not respect schedules or the longing of a heart to be elsewhere. Annabelle woke to crying at all hours, her own heart aching with names she could not speak aloud. She passed the time by stitching cloaks and tutoring young students in French. At night, she prayed with Karla sleeping against her chest.

Soon, Annabelle was once again asking about returning south. Her aunt shut down the idea with clipped authority. "New Orleans is sin and smoke," Colette said. "St. Louis is stable. You will raise that child here, where the answer to the question is simply, 'Your husband died in the war.' That affords dignity to you. And Karla. And all of us."

Once a season Annabelle tried again, and once a season her aunt gave the same answer. And always, the final blow: "A mother does not drag a child into uncertainty." By then Karla had become an innocent, dependent tether.

Annabelle's promise unraveled, not from lack of love, but from the weight of a newborn in her arms and the iron logic of family members who believed they were helping her. She was told she was being protected. She felt like she was being erased.

Karl, meanwhile, refused to believe silence was an ending. He wrote his first letter in February of 1816. He asked if she was safe, if her family were in good health, if she still meant to return. He sent it upriver by way of a fur agent. No reply came.

So he wrote again. And again. And again—six letters over seventeen months, sent by traders, boatmen, and one illiterate stonemason who swore he had a cousin in St. Louis. Not a single letter reached Annabelle.

The first letter arrived on a chilly afternoon, its edges damp from river air. Her aunt took it at the door before Annabelle could cross the hall. Her aunt opened it in the kitchen next to the stove. She read it once, her expression settling into something distant. That one she folded carefully and locked away in a drawer where the household accounts were kept— debts and balances recorded in a tight, merciless hand.

The second letter came three weeks later. This time Annabelle was nearer. She heard the knock. She stepped into the corridor just as her aunt broke the seal. Their eyes met.

"For me?" Annabelle asked. Her aunt did not answer at once. She skimmed the page, her mouth thinning, then turned toward the stove where the morning fire had not yet died. "It is nothing that concerns you." The paper trembled, whether from her aunt's hand or the draft in the kitchen she could not tell.

"Aunt—"

The letter touched flame. The paper curled but did not burn. Then it caught. The wax seal blackened and split. Annabelle moved forward instinctively, the heat pressing her back. For an instant she thought she saw his hand in the ink, maybe the strong slope of his name, before the fire consumed it.

"You must forget such associations," her aunt said softly. "They lead nowhere." The ashes collapsed in on themselves.

Annabelle stood very still, breathing smoke and anger. She never knew that one letter had arrived previously and more would follow.

By the time the third letter arrived, Aunt Colette knew the pattern: foreign handwriting, southern origins, addressed to "Miss A. Dixon." Each letter carried risk of reputation. It was a risk her aunt was determined to seal away. In her aunt's mind, she was not stealing love, she was preserving respectability.

In time, Karl told himself Annabelle had chosen another life. He told himself Mama would have forgiven such choices. He told himself faith demanded surrender. What he did not know—what no letter or rumor would ever carry southward—was that a little girl named after him was learning to walk along the muddy bank of the Missouri River.

The river kept the secret.

By autumn of 1817 Karl felt the silence like a blade. He took to walking the levee at night, watching flatboats vanish into the dark, and wondering if an incoming boat might one day carry Annabelle, or at least her words, to him. One night at a tavern on Chartres Street he overheard two riverboat captains talking about St. Louis—about its river wealth, its French families, its growing importance on the frontier. One of them mentioned the Dixon name. Karl's heart kicked like a mule.

If the letters had not reached her, then silence was not an answer. Annabelle was not a woman who broke promises. Something, or someone, had broken the promises for her. Interference could be faced. Rivers carried truth eventually. He would follow truth upstream.

Days later, Karl packed a small sack and secured passage upriver. He did not know what he would find in St. Louis, or whether Annabelle would welcome him or turn him away, but the uncertainty no longer frightened him.

He had learned on the battlefield that men could change history. Now he meant to test whether one man could shape his own destiny.

He did not know the river carried more than answers.

It carried a daughter with his eyes.

Chapter 23

Karl left New Orleans at dawn, traveling light—canvas sack, powder horn, and the battered pistol Lafitte had once praised and insulted in equal measure. Fog clung to the river like the breath of a sleeping beast, and the Mississippi ran high and fast from the rains.

The flatboat's pilot braced against his pole, boots slipping on wet planks. "Safer upriver," he grunted, nodding toward the unseen Missouri frontier. "If you've got people in St. Louis, count yourself lucky."

Karl wasn't sure luck was the word. St. Louis meant Annabelle, maybe—but it also meant the end of gunsmoke, ships, and the life he had scratched out for seven years. He let his mind drift to the future. *Annabelle Steinheimer of St. Louis.* The name tasted like home and uncertainty at once.

There were six other passengers: two merchants, a French clerk, an Irish deckhand, and two trappers who smelled of pelts and stale whiskey. They spoke little. Men who knew rivers did not anger them with needless noise.

The clerk squinted toward shore. "Structures on the bank—wing dikes?"

They were not dikes.

Four Choctaw youths crouched in the brush, lean silhouettes against the mud. Before anyone could breathe, a raw war-cry ripped across the water. Dugout canoes shot from the shallows, paddles flashing like blades.

"Down!" the pilot snarled. "No rifles—"

Too late. One trapper panicked and fired. Smoke belched. A Choctaw boy, no older than fifteen, jerked in his canoe, wounded.

The river exploded.

Arrows hissed across the gunwales like angry hornets. A merchant screamed and toppled, clutching his shoulder. Another arrow split the air and thunked into a crate inches from Karl's right leg. The flatboat lurched and slammed into a stretch of riverbank mud as high, piercing whoops split the air.

Choctaws came out of the brush and shallows at a sprint—bare arms painted black and red, knives and short bows, war clubs cut from blackjack oak. These were sons of a people pressed from their lands, testing strength in a world that no longer answered fairly.

Karl did not flinch as the arrows came. He drew his pistol, but froze when he saw one of them, just a boy, collapse with an arrow lodged in his own arm from some panicked volley. Blood striped him from elbow to wrist, yet his chin was raised, pride unbroken. Karl had seen the same defiant fire in Lafitte's men before boarding Spanish brigs.

Karl lifted both hands high. "Arrêtez! Assez!" he barked in rough French. "Stop! No more shooting!"

The Choctaws hesitated. A brief argument—sharp syllables in Chahta Anumpa—cut through the bank. A reed whistle blew twice, and the fighting ceased. Karl and his fellow passengers were yanked from the boat, bound with deerhide thongs, and shoved up the embankment. One merchant wailed prayers in Latin until a war club cracked the dirt beside his head to silence him.

They marched. The woods swallowed them, shadows stretching long through the trees. The Choctaws kept formation, falling into the rhythm of warriors though many shook from fear or excitement. Their leader, Tushkahoma, a tall youth with crow feathers braided into his hair, began to slow, his wound soaking through deerskin.

Karl managed to stand close to him. "Let me look."

"I am fine," the youth snarled in French as he studied Karl. "You shot me?"

"No," Karl muttered. "One of your own did."

For a moment they looked at each other not as enemies, but as men learning the same hard world.

By noon they reached a clearing—charcoal circles from old fires, footprints hardened in the frost. No lodges. A proving ground. A place for boys to show they were ready for war honors… or ransom.

The young Choctaws argued fiercely, gesturing to the captives. Karl caught fragments of the language from fighting beside Choctaw during the battle.

"The scalps of six grown men make us hunters," one of the Choctaw said. "Warriors. Our fathers will sing of us." The others shook their heads —uncertain, afraid of misstepping into dishonor. Captives could be traded, ransomed, or paraded. Killing risked retribution.

The clerk whimpered. The trappers muttered about knives in the dark. The Irishman crossed himself thrice. "Keep still," Karl whispered. "They're testing us, not murdering us."

Tushkahoma called something sharp at his companions—an order? A plea? Their bows lowered a fraction.

Then the forest changed. The afternoon seemed to tense. The

undergrowth snapped, not like animals, but metal. Boot buckles. Rifle hammers. Three frontiersmen emerged, long rifles leveled. The leader, a red-bearded man with a face carved by weather, called out: "Steady now, lads. Bows down."

One Choctaw's hand twitched toward a knife. The merchant shrieked. The Irishman whispered frantic prayers. Karl shouted above them all: "Don't shoot! They're boys!"

The word *boys* cut the clearing in two.

Tushkahoma spat defiantly, straightened, then dropped his bow to the ground. One by one the others followed—furious, ashamed, but unbroken. Red-beard finally lowered his rifle. "Good sense," he said. "Go on home."

The Choctaws vanished into the trees without a backward glance, except for Tushkahoma, who paused just long enough to meet Karl's gaze. Something like respect flashed. Then he disappeared into the pine shadows.

The frontiersmen hacked the captives loose. Karl rubbed his wrists. "Many thanks," he said. "Choctaw youths," red-beard grunted. "Testin' the world. Lucky we were trailin' 'em. Could'a been blood otherwise. I'm certain we will see more of 'em before we get to East Texas."

The pilot eyed Karl and asked, "Why defend 'em?" Karl shrugged. "Boys trying to become men. I've seen worse in ports and battlefields."

The frontiersmen were preparing to depart when Karl asked, "How far to St. Louis?"

"Two days by river," red-beard answered, "if you had a boat. You ain't got a boat."

They introduced themselves as the Mercer brothers—Caleb the red-beard, Ephraim the tall one, and Silas who could not stop grinning.

Karl asked, "What's in East Texas?"

"Good soil," Caleb said. "Bad law. Our brother Isaac's cuttin' a homestead. After that—mustangs."

Silas lit up. "Spanish horses runnin' wild. Thousands. We'll drive 'em east, make ourselves rich."

Karl had heard the tales. Mustang herds rolling like storms across the plains. "Why not head north first?" he asked.

Ephraim spat. "River ain't our road. And we'd reach St. Louis broke." His eyes flicked to Karl's empty pockets. The truth stung. Annabelle felt farther away.

Caleb mounted. Ephraim added, "We'll pay fair for gun work 'n French. Help at the homestead and with the mustangs, we'll see you to Louisiana or Missouri—with coin."

Every instinct Lafitte had hammered into him said *never go into strange wilderness with strangers.* But arriving in St. Louis with empty hands? With nothing to offer but apologies? Annabelle deserved more. Texas seemed his best option. He reminded himself that travel westward would be temporary.

The other passengers were finalizing a plan to return to New Orleans. That wasn't an option for Karl. He lingered beside the river, holstered his pistol, and said: "Fine. I'll go to Texas."

Silas clapped him on the back. "Knew it. Could use a pirate."

Karl stiffened. "I'm not a pirate."

Caleb only smirked. "Sure. Whatever you say."

Karl mounted the extra horse and joined the brothers on the ride west, where the maps thinned and the stories thickened.

Caleb rode in front, straight-backed and watchful, eldest by habit and gravity. He spoke little, but when he did, the others listened.

Ephraim followed at his shoulder, clever-eyed and observant, always measuring angles—of land, of men, of opportunity.

Silas rode in the rear, youngest and least burdened by consequence, whistling tunelessly and grinning as though the world existed largely for his amusement.

Later that day, Ephraim reined in beside Karl while Caleb scouted ahead and Silas ranged wide. "You see that trace?" Ephraim asked casually, pointing to a faint line cutting through the undergrowth. "Shortens the distance by half a day." Karl studied it. The ground dipped strangely. The brush grew too even, too recently disturbed.

"Shortcuts cost something," Karl said. "Lafitte used to say a shortcut invites ambush." Ephraim smiled faintly. "Who?" he asked, before realizing it didn't matter. "What's the cost?"

Ephraim watched Karl the way gamblers watched dice. Karl thought. If it were an ambush, it was lazy. If it were a trap, it was patient. The land smelled damp, which meant rot underneath the green. "Floodplain," Karl said finally. "Looks passable till you're knee-deep and stuck. Anyone following us would have the advantage."

Ephraim spat, then said, "Silas would have taken it."

"And you?" Karl asked.

"I wanted to see if you would," Ephraim replied. He nudged his horse forward. "Courage gets men killed. Sense keeps brothers alive." Karl felt something quiet click into place between them.

That night, as they made camp, Caleb checked Karl's saddle straps with quiet thoroughness. Ephraim handed him a tin cup of coffee and asked a few pointed questions—where he'd learned to ride, who he'd ridden with, what he'd do if pressed. Silas wordlessly tossed him the better blanket.

Karl warmed his hands around the tin cup and considered how much of himself could be spoken aloud. "I left Hamburg when I was eleven," he said at last. The words surprised him with their ease. "Ran, really. My father died trying to stop Napoleon. My mother was never the same." He paused, watching the fire catch and settle. "I thought the sea would raise me better than my uncle."

Ephraim's eyes sharpened, but he didn't interrupt. "I learned balance on decks before I learned it in saddles," Karl went on. "Learned to listen to wind. And to men. Learned that fear passes quicker if you give it work to do."

"And who taught you that?" Ephraim asked. Karl shrugged. "Crews. Captains. Men who didn't ask questions so long as you pulled your weight." He hesitated, then added carefully, "I sailed with Jean Lafitte for a time."

The name moved through the circle like a gust of wind. Silas's grin widened. Ephraim gave a soft, unreadable hum. Caleb didn't look up from the saddle strap, but his hands stilled. "Not a pirate," Karl said too quickly, then steadied himself. "At least, not the sort men like to imagine. He prized order. Discipline. Loyalty." A faint smile touched Karl's mouth. "He believed a man chose his fate by how he stood when things broke loose."

Caleb finally straightened and met Karl's gaze. "And how do you stand?" Karl thought of storms. Of blood on planks. Of choices made too young and carried too long. "I stay upright," he said. "And I don't abandon those beside me."

Silas tossed another stick on the fire. "Good enough for me." Ephraim raised his chin, satisfied—not with Karl's past, but with the shape of his answers. Caleb tightened the final strap and stepped back. "Then you'll do," he said simply.

Karl felt the fire warming his face. For a moment, no one spoke. The night settled back into itself. As always, it was Silas who broke the quiet. "So," he said, stretching his legs toward the fire, "if we're all satisfied you won't sell us out for a sack of coin or a quieter life—why St. Louis?"

Karl looked down at the fire without speaking. Silas grinned. "Don't play dumb now. Men don't fix their sights on a city like that without a reason."

Ephraim glanced up from sharpening a blade. "He's right. You were pushing north with purpose when we found you."

Caleb folded his arms and said, "St. Louis isn't just a direction. It's a decision."

Karl continued staring into the fire. He had faced cannon fire with less hesitation. "There's someone there," he said finally.

Silas sat up. "Ah."

Ephraim's mouth twitched. "Of course."

Caleb waited.

"A woman," Karl added, because there was no point circling it now. Silas laughed outright. "Well I'll be damned. The sea dog's been harpooned."

Karl scowled. "Easy now."

Silas looked down and cheerfully said, "I'm minding how a man who stood firm under Lafitte folds like wet canvas at the mention of a woman."

Ephraim set his blade aside. "What's her name?"

Karl hesitated, then said it. "Annabelle."

Just saying her name aloud made Karl feel like he was lighting a candle in a dark room. Silas tested it aloud. "Annabelle," he repeated. "That's not a tavern name."

"No," Karl said quietly. "She's not that sort."

Silas clutched his chest. "Hear that? He respects her." Caleb cut him a look. Silas grinned but fell silent.

Karl went on, words coming easier now. "We met in New Orleans. She stirs feelings that I didn't know I had."

Ephraim studied him. "Does she know you're coming?"

Karl shook his head. "No."

Silas barked a laugh. "You're chasing a woman upriver without telling her?"

"I'm not chasing," Karl said. "I'm—" He faltered, then tried again. "I'm choosing."

Caleb gave a slow shrug. "That's different."

Silas leaned forward, eyes bright. "Is she worth it?"

Karl didn't answer immediately. He thought of candlelight and lilac soap. Of the night they spent together and her saying *nothing is certain, but everything feels possible.* "Yes," he said. "She is."

Silas whistled low. "Well then. I wish we could go to St. Louis. I'd like to see the look on your face if she turns you away."

Karl laughed. Perhaps he had shared too much. Why was it easier to talk about Jean than Annabelle?

The following day, the men stopped near a creek to water the horses. Silas wandered off into the brush, not an uncommon move for the youngest brother. He returned pale-faced and breathless.

"There's a man back there," Silas whispered. "Hanging from a pine. Fresh." Karl's pulse jumped. He stood slowly, hand drifting toward his knife. Ephraim sucked in a sharp breath and looked away, as though unable to bear the sight. Caleb turned at last, his expression dark. "Show me." They took several careful steps into the trees before the "corpse" dropped from the branch with a thud. Silas had tied his bedroll and coat into a convincing shape, boots dangling absurdly beneath. All three brothers had been in on the prank.

Karl froze—then surged forward with a curse, tackling Silas into the dirt. Ephraim collapsed in laughter, clapping like a delighted audience. Even Caleb's mouth twitched, despite his attempt to mask it.

"You're all dead," Karl said, laughing despite himself. "Every one of you." Silas beamed up at him, laughing the way men laugh who have never buried a brother. "That's the spirit."

The brothers' laughter surprised Karl—how easily it came, how deeply it reached. He wondered if he and Johann would have bonded like this. Probably not, he thought, Johann would have ruined the gag by laughing too early, then apologized while still laughing, incapable of holding mischief without kindness bleeding through. The memory of home ached for a moment, but it no longer hollowed him.

Later that night, footsteps sounded beyond the firelight. Caleb was on his feet instantly, knife drawn. Ephraim slipped to Karl's side and pressed a pistol into his hand without ceremony. Silas went quiet, unnervingly so, eyes sharp in the dark.

"No jokes now," Silas whispered. "You stand with us." The moment passed. The danger thinned back into the trees. When the brothers relaxed, it was together, as though drawn by an invisible cord.

Karl stared into the embers, something steady settled inside him. He would always miss Jean—that bond was irreplaceable. But he was learning that a man might be granted brothers more than once, if he proved worthy of the trust.

By morning, the Mercers no longer tested him. "You ride with us now," Caleb said. "Not beside. With." From that moment on, the Mercers spoke of *we* when Karl was present. He realized he had not heard the word *we* spoken about him since Jean departed.

Karl would learn that the road west demanded payment, no different than the sea.

Chapter 24

Texas did not welcome newcomers gently. The four men crossed into a stretch the locals called the Neutral Ground. No Man's Land. The parcel lay between the Sabine River and the Red River, where Washington claimed one boundary and Madrid claimed another. Neither country bothered to enforce a law. The land had grown used to settling its own arguments.

People drifted here like debris after a storm. Spanish deserters in half-worn uniforms, Kentucky boatmen with warrants at their backs, Choctaw families hunting off the trace, and runaways moving by night with their futures clenched tight.

Traders with mule strings clattered past, offering powder one day and silence the next. A sickly Creole doctor flagged them from a porch, promising quinine for silver and gossip for free. No one lingered long with strangers unless out of necessity.

Caleb warned Karl on the first night beyond the Red River: "This land don't answer to Washington nor Madrid. Settlers hide here, army deserters, smugglers, runaways, anyone who wants to vanish."

Karl had seen the likes of this land before. Barataria smelled of salt and powder. This place smelled of pine and waiting. Barataria lived by coin and rumor of the sea. Here rumor alone ruled and justice traveled on rifle smoke.

The slow rhythm of wind allowed his thoughts to drift. First to Jean. He pictured him on a quarterdeck somewhere, speaking in that measured way that made men feel braver. Karl imagined him ruling Galveston, charming Spanish officers with one hand and outwitting American agents with the other. Karl felt a quiet longing. He wondered if Jean would think him foolish for following his heart instead of the tide. Jean never asked men to follow. He only asked them to choose. Then he watched their choices carefully.

Karl had made his choice. Annabelle. Her face slipped into the same thought, quiet as moonlight over the river. She did not belong to tides. She belonged to measured words and skies that seemed made for silk and parasols. She had listened to him—truly listened—and in her eyes he had seen what he knew was love. He wondered what she would think of him riding dusty trails among strangers when what he had planned was to arrive properly at her family's gate. Would she find it humorous? He could only hope that they would laugh together about it one day. Each passing tree felt like another mile between them. He wondered if she was looking at the same sky.

Texas stretched ahead, harsh and indifferent. By day they rode through forests that smelled of resin and damp moss. By night they camped under stars bright enough to silver the pines. The Mercers moved with quiet coordination—one tending the fire, one hunting, one scouting. Their respect for Karl continued to grow. He met every challenge, whether repairing a jammed flintlock or speaking Spanish with a trading party that had mistaken them for hostile Americans.

Silas was the most curious of the brothers, the sort whose questions came from youthful appetite. He wanted to know how cannons were run out in heavy seas, how a ship turned against the wind, whether powder smelled different after rain. One night, while tending thin strips of venison over the coals, he glanced up and casually asked, "You ever seen the Gulf?"

Karl grinned. "Many times."

Silas's eyes brightened. "They say it's green."

Karl watched the fire flex and settle before answering. "Sometimes. Other times gray as iron. Sometimes blue as glass. Depends on weather, wind," he shrugged, "and who's lookin'."

Silas grinned at that and fed the fire with a pine knot. Sparks leapt skyward, chasing the dark. Silas burned through silence the way sparks burned through pine. "I'm gonna see it," he said. "After we fetch our mustangs."

Karl hoped he would. Everyone should admire the sea once before learning what it demands in return.

Silas flipped a strip of venison toward him, then leaned back on his elbows, his voice more deliberate. "Tell me somethin'… What's a privateer truly like? Folks in Natchitoches say Lafitte's men live on bourbon and gunpowder, marry Creole widows, and bury their gold in cypress swamps."

"People say many things," Karl replied, chewing slowly. "Most of it nonsense." Silas scoffed. "Buried gold ain't nonsense. Old river pilots swear Barataria's just piled with Spanish coin hid under palmettos." Karl snorted. "If there were piles of Spanish coin, Spain would have dug them up first."

Silas laughed—but then his expression shifted, the humor giving way to something intent. "Still. You sailed with Lafitte. You loaded cannon.

You wore pistols." He paused. "That's somethin'."

Karl didn't answer at once. Most days had been barrels of sugar and coffee, endless counting, sweat without song. But there were other moments too—stormlight spiderwebbing the rigging, muskets cracking at dawn, Jean's voice steady when the world pitched sideways. Things no land-born boy would ever believe, even if told plain.

Silas stirred the fire again. "You reckon the Mercer brothers could make it in Barataria?"

Karl looked intently at Silas. At the eagerness in his eyes, the restless hunger, the dangerous belief that bravery alone was enough. "Barataria's not a place for hoping," Karl said carefully. "You don't survive because you're a fine shot or a good rider. You survive because the men beside you don't sell you for an easier future."

Silas went quiet, chewing the inside of his cheek. The fire popped, sending ash into the night. "We don't sell each other," he said at last. "Not for horses. Not for gold. Not for nothin'." Karl believed him.

"Privateers live by tide and rumor," Karl added. "Texas feels the same—dust instead of salt." Silas stared into the fire, nodding slowly. "Sounds like both places got room for men who don't fit anywhere else." Karl didn't argue. He suspected Silas had named truth.

Two weeks later, they reached Isaac Mercer's claim at the edge of the Big Thicket—dense, humid woods alive with insects and birdcalls. Smoke curled from a rough timber cabin still missing half its roof. Isaac emerged shirtless, hammer in hand, beard wild and sunburn fierce.

His face split into a grin. "Caleb! Ephraim! Silas!"

The brothers met him in a tangle of embraces—hard slaps to the back, shouted insults that passed for affection. Isaac's gaze finally slid to Karl, lingering there with open curiosity. "And who's this?" he asked.

Caleb didn't miss a beat. He clapped a hand on Karl's shoulder.

"Must be the brother Mama never told us about." Karl realized he had waited years to hear words like that.

Isaac burst out laughing. "Well, hell," he said, stepping forward and seizing Karl's forearm in a crushing grip. "That explains it. Thought you had the look of Mercer trouble about you."

Silas grinned, saying, "He keeps up." Ephraim added, "And he listens."

"That'll do," Isaac said happily. "Any man who rides with these three and still stands upright is family enough for me." He turned toward the cabin and waved them on. "Come on then. Supper's thin, roof's thinner, but there's room for one more brother."

Karl followed them in, warmth spreading through him that had nothing to do with the Texas sun. He wasn't a hired hand. He felt chosen. It felt good.

Days bled together in hard labor—felling trees, sawing planks, raising walls. Karl proved useful with tools though he had never built a house before.

One afternoon, as they were splitting shingles, Caleb pulled Karl aside. "Two Spanish agents came through last month," Caleb murmured. "Warned Isaac he was settlin' on land claimed by the King."

"Is he?" Karl asked. Caleb shrugged. "Maybe. Maybe not. No one knows where the lines really are." But the message was clear. Isaac needed numbers, rifles, and men who could speak to Spaniards without starting a shooting war. Karl suddenly understood why Isaac had welcomed him so easily. He wondered if hospitality in Texas was ever entirely free.

Caleb continued, "Nothing changes. You stay with us through mustang season—help us make a profit—and we'll see you to St. Louis with more dignity than how we found you. Agreed?"

Karl didn't answer immediately. He looked at the half-built cabin, at

Isaac barking orders, at Silas hauling logs with youthful zeal. He recognized that reaching St. Louis by way of Texas might not have been a workable plan. But his options had been limited. The best way to get to Annabelle would be with the help of the Mercers. A man traveling alone in Texas was a death wish. Plus, he needed time to gather coin. Karl extended his hand. "OK," he said. Caleb shook his hand once, firm and satisfied.

Trouble came just after dawn two days later.

Karl and Silas were cutting saplings beyond the homestead when the thudding of hooves rolled through the trees. Before they could reach their rifles, cavalry swept into the clearing, horsemen in worn blue coats trimmed with red, black leather shakos crowned with brass plates, and muskets leveled. Spanish lancers.

Isaac burst from the half-built cabin shouting, "Hold! Hold your fire!" The lead officer barked orders in rapid Spanish. His men dismounted with disciplined precision, fanning out to surround the homestead. Ephraim cursed under his breath. "Should'a known those agents weren't just talk."

Karl understood enough Spanish to catch the important words:

"Intrusos… tierras del Rey… deportación… ejército…"

Intruders. The King's land. Deportation. Army.

Caleb stepped forward, hands raised. "We're Americans. We're settlers. We mean no—" The officer cut him off, switching to broken English, "Is Spanish land. You build without permiso. You serve for three years. Or you hang as squatters." Silas spat in the dirt. "Serve who?" The officer tapped his own chest. "Serve España."

Before anyone could argue, the soldiers surged in. Hands were bound. The Mercers resisted until rifle butts knocked them to the ground. Karl tried diplomacy. Jean would have tried words before gunpowder. "We are not soldiers," Karl said. "We are settlers." The officer snapped, "Settlers must be loyal. Or they go to Havana in chains. You are lucky."

Karl saw the truth in his eyes. They wouldn't be hanged, but they weren't free. Spain needed bodies. Spanish Texas was thin on troops, and the empire was bleeding men in wars across Europe and Mexico.

As they were forced onto horses and mules, Silas shouted at his brother through bloodied lips: "Caleb! What now?"

Caleb, grim and breathless, was slow to answer. Karl jumped in and said, "Adapt. Stay positive." Silas nodded wearily.

Karl did not know whether Spain had just delayed his future. Or forged it. Either way, the road to St. Louis was growing longer.

Chapter 25

The Spanish column drove them south from East Texas into open prairie, dust choking every breath. Rawhide bindings cut into Karl's wrists with every step, his shirt clinging to sweat, the sun scorching the back of his neck. Each grunt from the Mercers beside him, each flinch at a rod or lance, reminded him patience had no place here. Only obedience.

At night, under scrub oaks, the scent of mesquite smoke thick in his nostrils, Karl's mind wandered despite the exhaustion. He imagined Annabelle reading by lamplight, or Mama insisting obedience and patience were the compass of life, while his body begged for sleep he could not take. He was tethered to the harsh reality of survival, haunted by old choices.

On the fourth night, Karl thought he saw shadows moving beyond the firelight. His heart pounded, imagining the war cries of a raiding party, only for the shapes to vanish in the brush. He clenched his fists, remembering Lafitte's lesson. The world rewards those who pay attention. The world punishes the inattentive.

Water was scarce, one pail for every four men. Bread was hard, dry, and bitter. A corporal hit Ephraim across the back for muttering, and Silas nearly fell into the dust laughing at the absurdity of their treatment. Karl pressed his hand to Silas's shoulder, whispering, "Keep quiet. They won't break us with curses alone."

One night by the fire, the officer finally explained the truth. "Spain fights many enemies," he said, poking the coals. "Mexicanos rebel. In the north, Comanches raid. In Europe, Napoleon still haunts us." He looked at the captives with tired eyes. "You will serve in the presidial companies. Fight rebels. After campaign… maybe freedom."

Ephraim muttered, "Press-ganged by damned Spain." Karl stared into the flames. He had known war under many flags—Prussian, French, American, pirate banners and none at all. Now Spain would claim him too.

After weeks of travel, they reached the Rio Grande near Laredo. The river shimmered like beaten silver, a line between the life Karl had known and whatever waited beyond it. Mexican towns, Spanish missions, and adobe farms dotted the opposite bank. Caleb whispered to Karl as they forded the river. "If we bolt now, we die. If we stay, we might live." Karl nodded. The Mercers did not panic. They calculated. Jean would approve.

On the far shore, the prisoners became conscripts. Their ropes were cut and muskets were thrust into their hands. Spanish corporals drilled them beside mestizo militia, Canary Islanders, royalist creoles, and poor Spaniards far from home.

Karl adapted quickly. He had fought in New Orleans as a soldier, and before that had learned the cruel arithmetic of survival as a privateer. Fear could sharpen the senses. Chaos could be endured. He measured it and absorbed it. So did Caleb and Ephraim.

Silas did not. The youngest Mercer stopped speaking of the Gulf altogether. The allure of the sea vanished from his tongue as if it had never existed. In its place settled something darker and more enduring. His laughter disappeared. The questions ceased. Silas met each day with a clenched jaw and flat eyes. He was tallying every injustice in his mind. He no longer dreamed aloud.

Karl recognized rage. When disciplined, rage could carry a man. When left alone, rage could consume a man whole. He was uncertain which direction rage was taking him. This time, the sea would not be there to take the blame.

The Spanish column continued deeper into the interior, through the dry highlands, then into the foothills of Nuevo León. The air grew thin and sharp. Pine forests gave way to cactus and rock. At Saltillo the truth revealed itself. Spain wasn't fighting bandits alone. Spain was fighting an uprising. Leaflets in the streets called it *la guerra de independencia.* Priests preached rebellion. Farmers whispered of a man named Morelos.

Caleb pulled Karl aside near the stables. "We're not slaves. We ain't criminals. We're stuck in a damn war that ain't ours." Karl answered softly, "It is now." Ahead, soldiers gathered in staging columns, royalists under Spanish generals preparing to meet rebels moving north from the southlands.

One evening, as drums rolled and officers shouted orders, the Spanish lieutenant addressed his foreign conscripts: "Tomorrow we march to meet the insurgents near Patos. All soldiers of the King will fight. Bring honor and earn reward. Flee and you die." He paused. Then, unexpectedly, he saluted them. "El Rey needs every rifle."

That night, Karl lay awake under a sky thick with stars, listening to the camp breathe. He thought of Annabelle in St. Louis. How had he gotten so far off course? Then he imagined Mama at the kitchen table, insisting that obedience and patience were God's compass points. If he had listened, if he had been the dutiful son she wanted, perhaps he would not be lying in a foreign desert with grave danger for company. Instead he had followed the wind, and the wind had led him here.

Karl whispered to the darkness: "If I survive this… I will make my own choices again." His tongue felt too large for his mouth. His thoughts wandered dangerously. He reached into the inner seam of his coat and felt for the familiar curve. The wooden swan. He drew it out and held it against his chest, the pale wood faintly luminous beneath the starlight. For a moment he closed his eyes and imagined Annabelle's hands instead of his own — how she had refused it and how she had promised to return for it. The memory felt impossibly far from this barren stretch of earth.

His throat tightened. "God of mercy," he whispered hoarsely, careful that the others would not hear, "You who see farther than any map… carry me to where she is." He pressed the swan harder against his sternum. "Spare me long enough to reach her. Not for glory. Not for pride. Just… let me reach her."

He had not prayed like this since boyhood. Back then prayer was repetition. Now it was negotiation. He slipped the swan back inside his coat. He turned onto his side, one hand still pressed to his chest, and at last allowed his eyes to close. Dawn would bring battle against an enemy they did not hate, for a king they did not know, on a land that was not theirs.

Dawn always came.

The next day, the sun bled slowly across the scrub plains south of Saltillo, washing the valley in dusty gold. Columns of royalist infantry marched in ragged lines toward the hills, drums rattling. Karl marched beside Caleb, both wearing short Spanish blue coats with mismatched belts and cartridge boxes. Silas and Ephraim followed behind, their faces ashen and alert. None of them spoke. The air tasted of coming violence.

Ahead, a shallow valley opened between two low ridges. A creek ran through it, half dry, lined with mesquite and cactus. Officers raised spyglasses. Shouts rose. *"Insurgentes! En la colina!"* Rebels! Up on the hill!

On the opposite ridge, brown and white uniforms flashed among the rocks, Mexican insurgents in loose companies, flying banners of the Virgin of Guadalupe. They shouted in Spanish—some prayers, some curses, some promises. A cannon boomed from the rebel ridge. The royalists flinched as iron shot tore a furrow through the sage and sent men sprawling.

The Spanish colonel rode forward, voice hard as steel:

"¡Formen línea! ¡Fusileros al frente! ¡No dispare hasta que lo ordene!"

Form line! Fusiliers to the front! Do not fire until ordered!

Karl's unit scrambled into shaky formation. The Mercers found themselves shoulder to shoulder with Canary Islanders and mestizo militia, men with eyes as frightened as their own.

Caleb muttered, "If we survive this, I swear I'm done bein' captured by empires." Karl almost smiled.

The royalist drums beat tat-tat-tat-tat, and the line advanced into the valley. Musketry cracked from the hilltop in an irregular, frantic manner. The rebels shot poorly at range, but there were many of them. Balls kicked up dust, tore into men, smashed jawbones, burst lungs.

Karl fired on command, feeling the familiar recoil thud into his shoulder. Smoke swallowed the line. Screams blended with Spanish orders. Rebel lancers with rawhide shields surged suddenly from the left flank, shouting *"¡Viva la patria!"* (long live the homeland!) as they thundered downslope.

The royalist line buckled. Ephraim roared, "Square! Square formation!" Some of the Canary Islanders understood and shuffled into a crude square, bayonets outward. Horses smashed into scattered pockets of infantry, lances skewering men like hogs at slaughter. Caleb fired point-blank into a rider's chest. The horse crashed through men and canvas water skins, spraying dirt and blood.

Silas dragged a wounded mestizo behind a rock. "Stay with me, amigo! Stay with me!"

Karl reloaded by feel and fired again. The rebels drew back, regrouping on the ridge. The field was a churn of bodies and broken weapons.

The Spanish colonel, bloodied but mounted, bellowed: *"¡Adelante! ¡Bayonetas! ¡Adelante!"* (Advance! Fix bayonets! Advance!) The royalists surged forward, bayonets fixed, clambering up the rocky slope toward the insurgents. Karl, Caleb, Ephraim, and Silas were swept along with them. The climb was brutal, musket fire raining down. When the royalists reached the crest, the rebels were unprepared for cold steel. Lines broke. Men fought hand-to-hand—bayonets thrusting, clubbed muskets cracking skulls, knives flashing.

Karl locked with a rebel no older than sixteen, the boy's knife flashing with desperate fury. Karl knocked the blade aside, seized his collar, and shouted: *"¡Ríndete!"* — Surrender! The boy spat blood in his face. A royalist corporal drove a bayonet through the boy from behind. The blade burst through the boy's chest. Karl shoved the dying youth away, breath shaking with the recognition that the young man had been fighting for freedom. Caleb grabbed his arm. "Karl! Move! They're pullin' back!"

The rebels were retreating down the far slope, reorganizing for another push. But Karl saw something else. Dust clouds beyond the ridge where fresh rebel reinforcements were circling to flank. He pointed. "There! Cavalry! They'll cut us off!" The colonel saw it too. He blew two shrill whistles and ordered: *"¡Retirada al arroyo! ¡Mantengan la línea!"* Retreat to the creek! Hold the line!

The retreat collapsed into chaos. Royalists scrambled downslope under volley fire. Men stumbled. Officers shouted. The Spanish cannon roared blindly. Caleb grabbed Karl's shoulder mid-run. "Hear me. We ain't dyin' for Spain." Karl answered through gritted teeth, "I know." At the creek, they joined what remained of their battalion behind low embankments. Ephraim and Silas slid in beside them. Silas panted, "We holdin' here?"

Karl looked at the Spanish colonel who was bloodied and surrounded, but still barking orders as more rebels appeared from every ravine. "No," Karl said. "Spain is losing." The rebels advanced again. This time with coordination and discipline. The line shook under musket fire. A cannonball ripped through a pond bank, showering mud and limbs. Men began to break. First in ones and twos, then entire clusters. The colonel fired his pistol skyward, screaming, *"¡Mantengan! ¡Mantengan!"* Maintain. Maintain.

But the battle was already lost. Karl seized Caleb by the collar. "Now! Into the mesquite! Run!" Caleb didn't argue. They dove through the creek bed, using smoke as cover. Ephraim and Silas were a few yards behind when a cluster of rebels surged into the waterway. Silas shouted, "Caleb! Go!" Ephraim dragged Silas behind a boulder, firing wildly to buy seconds. Caleb froze, torn. "Silas!" Karl yanked him hard. "He said go!" More rebel muskets fired. Ephraim returned fire from behind the rock, then disappeared in a cloud of gunsmoke and screams. Karl didn't see if it was death or capture.

There was no time. He and Caleb crawled through thorns and brush until they reached a dry gully. From there they ran, bent low, hearts pounding, the battle fading behind them into smoke and echoing shouts. They didn't stop until the sun dipped behind the mountains. Only then did Caleb collapse to his knees.

"My brothers..." he rasped, voice breaking. Karl placed a hand on his

shoulder and said, "We will return for them. But not today. Not like this."
Caleb clenched his jaw, tears streaking dust and blood. "Where now?"

Karl looked north. The direction of the United States, of Louisiana, St. Louis, of places he knew and one he would like to find. But danger waited to the north. "West, for now," he said. "It's too dangerous to try to get back to Texas. Let's keep moving." Caleb nodded once, as men do when they have no choice but to survive. Behind them, the hills burned with the last of the gunfire. Mexico fought for its freedom. Spain bled into the dust.

Bone-weary, Karl and Caleb threaded through arroyos and mesquite draws, gulping from clay hollows and chewing uncertain berries. Every snap of twig or rustle of leaves made Karl's pulse leap, and each step carried him farther from St. Louis. He imagined Annabelle under the same pale moon, unaware he still drew breath in this harsh land, and the thought twisted in his chest like the heat and thirst that gnawed at his stomach. Beyond the ridge, a coyote howled, reminding him the wilderness did not forgive hesitation, nor the choices that had led him here.

By the third day the thunder of battle was a memory, replaced by the dry rattle of cicadas and the endless plains of northern Mexico. Heat shimmered over the plains during the day and every mile seemed to test their bodies and their courage. When they reached a great basin, they stopped beneath the shade of a twisted live oak. Caleb knelt to tighten his boots, hands shaking, lips tight.

"They'll be hunting strays," he said, voice low. "The royalists, the rebels, even the rurales. Two men make a pattern. Patterns get noticed." Karl's mind raced. He knew every sound could be the approach of soldiers eager to hang them or press them into service. His response was calm. "Then we unmake the pattern."

Caleb stood facing the horizon, his face set hard enough to ache. He looked as though he might keep standing there until the land itself answered him. At last, he turned. "I'm going back," he said. "I'll follow every trail they might have taken." His voice roughened. "I'll find Ephraim and Silas—or I'll find the truth."

Karl stepped forward without thinking. "I'm going with you."

Caleb shook his head at once. "No." He met Karl's eyes, holding them. "You're not."

The refusal landed heavy. "They're my brothers too," Karl said. Caleb looked at Karl intently. "You've earned that. And that's why you'll go on."

He gestured north, where the land lifted toward unseen rivers. "As your brother, I recognize that you've got a future pulling at you. St. Louis. A woman. A life that doesn't end with you riding in circles chasing wind." Karl looked him in the eye. "Leaving you doesn't feel like honor." Caleb stepped closer. "Nor does turning away from the life that is calling for you. Ephraim and Silas would insist that you go north."

For a long moment, neither moved. Somewhere a bird cried out and went unanswered. Then Caleb extended his arm. Karl took it, forearm to forearm, the grip solid and final, the kind men shared when there were no more words worth risking. Caleb leaned in, their brows nearly touching and said, "If I don't see you again, don't you waste what we bled for." Karl smiled. Caleb continued, "And give that girl in St. Looie a hug for me."

Caleb released him and turned away before anything softer could be said. He walked east, shoulders squared, a man carrying the weight of obligation. Karl watched until distance thinned him into the land. They parted as brothers, each grateful for the other, bound by what they had already survived together.

Karl turned north. Toward St. Louis. Toward a future that thrilled and frightened him in equal measure.

The terrain tested Karl immediately. He crossed dry washes and climbed pine ridges, his stomach gnawing relentlessly. He slept beneath mesquite trees, chewing parched beef until his jaw ached, filling his canteen from trickling springs that smelled of iron. Running had carried him across oceans. Perseverance would carry him through.

Once, the cries of two lean coyotes drew him into a desperate defense. He hurled stones with all his might, and unleashed a primordial roar from his throat that carried over the scrub. The coyotes fled.

He avoided the roads, moving through cedar scrub where Spanish patrols rarely ventured, listening to every crunch of footfall. The boots that had carried him from battle finally split at the seams. He muttered curses to himself, half to ward off frustration, half to prove he was still alive.

By the time he saw the first adobe roofs of Monclova, he was starved, trail-worn, and hollow-eyed. He followed the scent of beans and roasting meat to a cantina near the barracks square, hoping for warmth and a place to sell the knife that had kept him alive.

But luck, if the last weeks could be called luck, had finally run its course. He hadn't made three steps before men rose from the shadows, steel gleaming in the lantern light. Hands grabbed him, yanking him against the bar, forcing the air from his lungs. Shouts cut through the clatter of bayonets. Every movement meant to intimidate and punish.

A captain appeared, red-faced, smelling of sweat and power. He smiled thinly at Karl's silence. *"Soldado o esclavo,"* he demanded— soldier or slave. One choice meant marching in battle beneath a flag. The other choice meant being chained beneath the earth in a mine.

Karl's jaw set. Every lesson learned under Lafitte's eyes, every scrape with Spanish patrols and river bandits, every bruise and hunger pang led him here. His choices had led him here. This was not the kind of choice he envisioned when he decided years before that a man ought to choose.

A soldier would return to battle and likely die before the end of the week. The mines meant darkness, chains, and slow ruin. But the mines also meant time. And time meant survival.

Karl lifted his eyes to the captain.

"Las minas."

Chapter 26

The silver mines of Nueva Vizcaya were worlds ruled by darkness, violence, and greed. Karl learned that his first day. The Spanish overseers chained the new prisoners at night and marched them down before dawn into shafts lit only by resin torches, where heat and dust turned lungs to leather. Men broke quickly here. Some from exhaustion, some from despair, and some simply vanished—lost to collapses, floods, or the labyrinth of galleries that spidered through the mountains.

Karl didn't break. He swung the hammer with efficiency, each strike sending sparks into the shadows. He drilled powder-holes with iron rods, sweat streaking his face as the heat pressed on his lungs. Every shovel of ore fought collapse. Every breath was a balance of exhaustion and survival.

The tunnels were so narrow that his heartbeat echoed like hammer blows. He learned to read the creak of a roof, the tremor in a wall, the whisper of danger before it struck. What he lacked in experience he replaced with what the Spaniards called *disciplina germánica*—a cold German discipline that made survival almost predictable.

The Indians and Mestizos noticed first. *"El Alemán no muere,"* they whispered. The German does not die. They were right. When others collapsed from heat, dust, or despair, Karl hauled their loads. When a roof groaned and a ceiling panel threatened to fall, he felt the tremor before anyone else, dragging men clear of a collapse that would have buried them alive. Even the grizzled Spanish overseers took note of Karl's obedience.

His grasp of Spanish allowed him to joke, to bargain, to ask questions that others feared to voice. Questions mattered here. Rumors built fortunes as often as tunnels. Each day brought whispered tales of a vein running deeper than reason, of a hidden chamber where silver glittered like frozen lightning. Men died chasing such rumors, lost to tunnels that shifted and engulfed them without ceremony.

One morning, as the miners pushed deeper into a newly discovered shaft, Karl's instincts screamed before his eyes confirmed it. Timbers groaned like old bones, the rock overhead shifting with a subtle, dreadful rhythm. *"El techo...,"* whispered a Mestizo, finger trembling as it traced the roof's first cracks.

Dust particles froze in the lantern light, a warning in the air. Karl grabbed a nearby support beam, yanking two men back as a plank cracked and plunged into the darkness. The ceiling trembled, a living thing poised to crush them all. "Move!" Karl shouted, voice raw as he forced the others toward the exit. He led them back to the tunnel's mouth, counting the seconds as the timbers above hissed and shuddered.

A deafening roar followed. Rock, timber, and dust exploded behind them, filling the shaft with a choking cloud. Men coughed, stumbled, and cursed, scrambling toward daylight. Karl felt the heat of the collapse on his back and the vibration through the ground beneath his boots. Only by lunging for the narrowest part of the shaft did he avoid being buried.

He collapsed outside, coughing, covered in dust, his heart beating almost too fast to measure. The other miners looked at him, voices finally rising from whispers to awe: *"El Alemán no muere."*

Karl's chest heaved. He had survived again, narrowly, by instincts honed on the Gulf, under Lafitte's watch. Karl touched his chest lightly. He rose, brushing the dust from his jacket, and muttered to himself, half-laughing, half-grim: "If Lafitte saw this… he'd call it a warm-up."

He turned back into the mine, stepping carefully, the shadows swallowing him as he vanished into the earth once more. Karl kept moving, kept watching, kept calculating. Every day he emerged coated in dust and sweat, hands blistered and cracked. But with every passing hour, every near-collapse, every whispered warning from the Mestizos or the Indians, he became something more enduring. He was a survivor, a witness to the world's brutality, and learning to master it.

After six months, his chains were removed. After a year, he was promoted above the pit-gang to barrileros, where he hauled ore buckets by mule and tallied loads. It was a small freedom, but freedom in a mine was measured by breaths of clean air.

By 1820, Mexico's war for independence was surging into the northern territories. Royalist soldiers were now stretched thin, and Madrid's grip was failing. Mines that had once shipped silver by mule-train to Veracruz now suffered ambushes and embargoes. Spanish captains grew paranoid. Insurgents demanded tribute. Prices of mercury and gunpowder soared. Karl, now literate in Spanish accounting and mine ledgers, was unexpectedly useful.

Spanish Lieutenant Don Isidro Valdés, the mine administrator, summoned him one evening as rifles cracked in the distant hills. "Alemán, you keep good numbers," Valdés said. "The mules arrive, the ore leaves. You don't lie."

"I have no reason to," Karl replied. Valdés inclined his head. "That is why you will be topo mayor—chief foreman," he said. "On my authority."

To the Mexican miners, this was a shock. Foreigners did not rise. But Karl worked harder than any overseer. Miners began to follow him willingly.

By late 1820, the Spanish Crown made one last effort to crush the rebels. The mines were ordered to supply silver to pay troops. Production doubled overnight. Powder stores ran dry. Collapses became weekly.

Karl slept two hours a night, learned to judge ore yields by touch, and negotiated secretly with the Insurgent procurement bands who roamed the mountains. He ensured no one shot the mule trains. He ensured the miners had food. He ensured that, when the war finally ended, the mines would still have men to work them.

By spring of 1821, the war reached its climax. Agustín de Iturbide, a royalist officer who had hunted insurgents for years, abruptly changed sides, uniting both factions under the Plan of Iguala. The Spanish empire in Mexico collapsed almost without another battle. Spanish officers fled north.

Don Valdés called Karl into his office. The room was stripped bare of flags and portraits. "The war is finished, Alemán," Valdés said. "Spain has abandoned us. Veracruz… all lost." He opened a cedar chest, revealing silver ingots stamped with the Crown's seal. "I will not make it to San Blas. But you are respected here. You should stay."

"I am still a prisoner," Karl replied. Valdés barked a bitter laugh. "There are no prisoners now. There is only silver and men who want it. Take five bars. For your labor. For your loyalty. I trust you more than the rebels. My legacy lives on through you." Karl stared in stunned silence. "If I take them, I'll be hunted."

"If you don't, you'll be a beggar," Valdés answered. "Choose quickly. I leave before sunset." Karl took the bars, not for greed, but because he understood leverage, just like Jean had taught him. Silver opened doors.

When Valdés rode away with the last royalist escort, the miners gathered at the gate uncertain of the future. Karl ordered food and reopened the ledgers, not as a prisoner, but as a man with equity.

Months later, representatives of the new Mexican government rode in from Durango. They were mestizo officers wearing tricolor sashes, bearing legal papers instead of rifles. They demanded back taxes. They demanded mining concessions. They demanded proof of ownership from a Spanish Crown that no longer existed.

Karl listened without interruption, then opened a small iron box. Inside lay five silver bars, the original payment, as well as three months' payroll receipts, ledger books filled in his own hand, and, most critically, promissory notes bearing Valdés's signature.

"Señores, the Crown is gone, but business remains," Karl said. "I will purchase the mine. I will pay taxes. I will keep the men working so silver flows under the new Republic." The officers exchanged looks. Silver taxes meant revenue. Silent mines meant nothing.

One of the officers, younger than the others and wearing his tricolor sash too stiffly, stepped forward. "There is a matter not addressed," he said, his tone sharpened by youthful ideology. "You are Alemán. Not Spanish. Not Mexican. This republic has just freed itself from foreign masters. Why should we hand one of its richest mines to another foreigner?"

A few of the miners outside shifted uneasily. Karl did not answer at once. Instead, he opened the ledger and turned it toward them so they could view pages filled in a firm, disciplined hand detailing wages paid through famine and war as well as blasting schedules reduced to prevent deaths.

"Because," Karl said evenly, "I kept this mine alive when Spain fled and before your flag arrived. The silver does not speak German or Spanish. It speaks production. And production pays your army."

The older officer studied the numbers, then glanced toward the gate where two hundred miners stood waiting, not with rifles but with expectation. After a long moment, he gave a slow nod.

"We did not fight for empty hills," he said. "We fought for a nation that works." He took the stamp and pressed it into ink. "Let the Alemán work."

In a single unguarded moment, without a musket raised or saber drawn, Karl became owner of La Mina de San Toribio, a mine that had paid for half of Spain's military campaigns in the province.

The time of dust and ledgers passed as fortune suddenly bent his way. Within two years he owned shares in two more silver mines and a small gold placer outside Culiacán. Mule trains carried his metal to the mint in Mexico City. Smelters knew his face. Guards rode with him, not because he was noble, but because men with silver were worth killing. Locals called him Don Carlos, part in jest, part in respect. He was the foreigner who understood the earth better than the engineers Spain had sent.

Wealth trickled slowly, then cascaded all at once.

In the rare quiet hours, when ledgers were shut and the lamps burned low, Karl would hold a glass of mescal and stare out at the Sierra Madre, wondering if Annabelle ever reached St. Louis. He wondered if she still remembered the boy who once promised he'd wait for her.

Mexico had given him fortune, power, even a title of sorts. But it had not given him answers. Now twenty-eight, Karl had already lived more lives than most men. He had been a Prussian farm boy, a stowaway across the ocean, a privateer in the Gulf, a soldier, a prisoner, and finally a foreman in the mines of Mexico. His hands were calloused, his instincts sharp, and he refused to die where others were buried.

What Karl learned quickly was that mine ownership minted enemies as quickly as it minted coins. Silver did not lie. Every peso had to come from someone's sweat, someone's land, someone's grief. A profitable vein could turn partners into rivals, foremen into spies, and government officials into wolves who knocked politely before they devoured you.

Mexico's new republic was young enough that half its laws were still wet on paper and the other half written in pistols. Silver financed everything—governments, revolts, churches, and men who believed in none of them. Karl watched disputes turn to lawsuits, lawsuits turn to gunfights. In Durango a Cornish captain was found beaten in a drainage ditch, his mouth stuffed with ore. Owners walked with guards now. Assayers carried pistols. And rumors of new veins traveled faster than the mule trains that carried the silver.

By 1825, La Mina de San Toribio no longer smelled of chains and blasting powder. It smelled of mercury, minting, and money—a metallic sweetness that made men greedy and sick in equal measure. Indian boys carried mercury in goatskin bags, coughing blood into their handkerchiefs. Smelter chimneys belched smoke day and night.

Investors arrived in polished boots—Scottish speculators, German engineers, American merchants from New Orleans, and even a French noble "in exile." They spoke of shaft angles and drainage pumps, of Cornish whims and Chilean grinding stones. They built new shafts, erected stamp mills, and drilled deeper.

When the output increased, so did the predators. A former royalist colonel arrived with soldiers, claiming the mine owed taxes "dating from the days of His Majesty." A local bishop demanded a tithe on mercury sales for the Church. A bandit chief sent letters sealed with candle soot, promising to burn the mill unless paid in silver bars.

Other attempts came in the form of physical violence. One day, Karl was riding back from Santa Rosa at dusk, two guards trailing him at a polite distance, when a shot cracked from the scrub above the road. The bullet tore through his hat brim. His horse reared violently. A second shot struck the mule behind him, dropping the animal in a screaming heap.

"Ambush!" one guard shouted, already swinging his carbine upward. Karl did not freeze. He dropped from the saddle, rolling behind the fallen mule as splinters of stone burst around him. Smoke drifted from the ridge above. He saw the muzzle flash before the third report and fired blindly toward it.

One of the guards went down, clutching his shoulder. The other guard returned fire in steady rhythm. Karl crawled forward, ignoring the metallic tang in his mouth. He felt no panic, only a narrowing of focus. He recognized the pattern. Not bandits. Too disciplined.

Someone had paid for this. A figure shifted against the skyline. Karl steadied his breath and fired again. The shape tumbled from the rocks and vanished down the slope.

Silence followed. They waited several long minutes before

climbing the ridge. Two bodies lay among the stones. Neither carried identification. One wore boots too fine for a highway thief. In the man's pocket was a folded scrap of paper bearing nothing but a crude sketch: the outline of La Mina de San Toribio.

Karl stared at it without expression. They hadn't tried to rob him. They had tried to erase him.

That night, back at the house overlooking the valley, Karl removed the ruined hat and set it on the table. The bullet hole stared back at him like a second eye. In the street below, a dozen miners had gathered and were chanting, *"El Alemán no muere!"*

Karl didn't feel immortal. He felt marked. Every claim, every demand, funneled through one man—Karl—because the townspeople had learned that *"El Alemán"* could face priests, soldiers, or thieves and not falter. Survival was no longer instinct. It was expectation.

One night in the cantina at Santa Rosa, a Sonoran merchant drunkenly accused Karl of cheating the Indians on wages. Before the insult finished, Karl had the man by the collar and pressed against a support beam, his voice cold as forged steel: "Do not confuse discipline with cruelty. I buried enough men in that mountain to know the difference." The room fell silent. Karl was protecting reputation more than venting anger. The merchant later returned with an apology. And a bodyguard.

Enemies, Karl was discovering, did not always announce themselves. Some shook his hand. Some toasted his health. Some asked questions about payroll and delivery schedules as if they were merely curious. All circled the same glittering heart: silver—the fuel that fed the newborn republic, and the lure that had claimed more men than war or love ever had.

Karl's innovations—timed blasting, water pumps, and steam-driven hoists imported from New Orleans—multiplied production. Mexican officials in Durango sent letters instead of soldiers. Mule trains wound through the mountains laden with bullion. Guards with carbines rode beside them. Karl, once a prisoner, now signed contracts with American bankers and Mexican governors alike.

The more the riches accumulated, the less Karl slept. Some nights he did not undress at all, only loosening his collar and closing his eyes in the chair behind his desk. Ownership demanded vigilance. Every signature made a friend or an enemy. A foreman could curse the overseer and sleep soundly. A proprietor lay awake counting consequences.

What he missed most about his new life surprised him. He didn't miss the danger. Or the hunger. He missed the brotherhood.

He missed Jean's sideways grin and the way he could read a man's weakness before the man knew it himself. He missed Silas's reckless laughter and Caleb's steady, wordless loyalty. In those days, hardship had been shared. Now the fire burned in a hearth that felt too large for one man. Every argument now happened in his own head.

Being "Don Carlos" meant men stood when he entered. It meant they lowered their voices. It meant no one spoke plainly unless he invited it. Respect was useful. But it was not warm.

Yes, he possessed silver, mules, contracts, armed guards. But no clear road. How does a man leave an empire he has built? He could buy wagons and secure escorts, but could he abandon two hundred miners who trusted his judgment? Could he vanish again, as he had from Hamburg and New Orleans?

He bought a fancy house overlooking the valley. The house had stone terraces and an arcaded veranda as well as a French piano he never learned to play. Local miners called him Patrón Alemán. Newspapers in Mexico City whispered of "the mysterious German industrialist of the North."

Somewhere beyond the smell of smelter smoke was Annabelle. And maybe somewhere beyond the mines was the version of himself that had tasted true love. Karl rested his hands on the stone railing and realized that power had given him everything except direction.

Even the silver bars on his desk looked less like wealth and more like distance. In the bottom drawer, beneath contracts and stamped decrees, he kept a small cloth bundle no clerk was permitted to touch. Inside the cloth lay Mama's wooden swan.

He sometimes turned it in his hands while listening to disputes about ore shares or wage advances, feeling the quiet weight of a promise made before he understood what keeping promises required.

He had written to Annabelle twice.

The first letter was careful, almost formal, informing Annabelle of his safety. He never attempted to send it. The second letter he never finished. Ink had blotted where he tried to explain what he had become. A mine owner. A negotiator with priests and soldiers. A man who carried a pistol under his coat and signed contracts worth more than his uncle's farm would have seen in a lifetime. Deep down, he wasn't sure she would remember him.

Sometimes, after a long day of arbitration and threats, he would stand before the French piano he had bought with an optimistic promise to learn. He pressed a key. The note rang clear and fragile, shivering through the large room. He did not know how to make it sing. Refinement, he realized, could not be bought like the machines that churned below.

Other nights he would step onto the veranda and look north, past the dark shoulders of the Sierra Madre, imagining a line drawn from this stone house through desert and river and forest all the way to St. Louis. He had crossed oceans once with nothing. The world called him Don Carlos. In his heart, he knew he was still Karl, a young man who had once counted blessings on a dock at dawn and believed that survival meant reunion.

Now survival meant building something strong enough to leave behind so that he could travel north without shame. Toward St. Louis. Toward Annabelle.

Maybe even toward the man he wished he had been.

Chapter 27

Success attracts apprentices, invited or not. Karl had often searched for a young man to guide, as Jean once guided him. He recalled Jean saying repayment came not in coin, but in knowledge passed on.

Karl's sharpest understudy was a boy of seventeen named Mateo Castañeda—thin as a rail, sharp-eyed, and fearless in tunnels where older men crossed themselves. Mateo had shown up at the assay office with a sack of ore and questions no laborer should have known how to ask. Questions about sulfur ratios, vein angles, and water. The clerk found it amusing. Karl did not. He instructed the boy to come back the next morning.

Within a week, Mateo was following Karl through shafts at shift-change, listening more than he spoke. He learned how to test for gas with a candle, how to read the timber supports for strain, how to see not just rock, but the vein behind it. And Karl, to his own surprise, found himself explaining things he had learned by survival. Mateo absorbed everything. He kept a small notebook in his shirt and scribbled diagrams in the margins. The men teased him, calling him *"el profesor."* The name stuck.

Karl called him "Prof" more often than his given name.

One afternoon, after a near cave-in that Mateo helped avert by spotting a groaning beam, Karl caught the boy staring into the dark with quiet reverence. "What do you see?" Karl asked. Mateo frowned, searching for words. "Possibility," he said. "And danger. But mostly possibility."

It was what Jean might have said. What Jean had taught him to look for in chaos. For a moment Karl felt the ghost of a man who lived five seconds ahead of everyone else.

Jean mocked mentorship, yet had been one anyway. Karl wanted to be that kind of man. Wanted to shape someone the way Jean shaped him, but doubt lingered like dust. Jean had been brilliant, reckless, larger than life. Karl was… industrious. Practical. A survivor. Was that enough? Would guiding Mateo repay Jean?

That night, on the veranda overlooking his valley of silver, Karl watched Mateo crossing the courtyard with ore samples under his arm and wondered if he was guiding the boy forward or simply keeping him alive. Mama would have said the first duty of a teacher was to shield the young from folly. Jean would have said the opposite—that without folly a man never learns what he's made of. Karl stood between those teachings, uncertain which one would make Mateo whole.

The older miners grumbled, as older men do when a younger one changes things, but they also watched him with a kind of wary pride. *"Se parece al Patrón,"* they would whisper. He looks like the Boss. Not in the face, but in the habits. How he walked a tunnel before approving it. How he stood with his hands behind his back when thinking. How he drank coffee alone at dawn before the shift bell.

Karl recognized himself in those gestures—and Jean too. Sometimes, in the assay room after hours, Mateo would ask about New Orleans, about

Barataria, about Lafitte. Karl would tell pieces, never everything, about skiffs loaded with contraband, about moonlit runs through the bayous, about Jean laughing in the face of danger as if death were a drunk cousin he could outfox. Mateo listened the same way Karl once had – head tilted, eyes narrowing, already imagining himself in the story.

One evening, when a courier from Durango delivered a bundle of contracts and maps, Mateo laid them across the veranda table and said, "If we open a shaft on the south ridge, we will need a smelter and rail line. The government will try to tax both."

Karl raised an eyebrow. "What do you propose, Prof?"

"Make them partners," Mateo said. "Give them a stake, and they will protect it." Karl stared at him. That was exactly how Jean had handled governors and consuls. Offer them profit instead of threats. He felt a strange unease, like déjà vu twisted out of context.

"You learned that somewhere," Karl said.

Mateo shrugged. "From you."

Karl knew better. Lessons traveled across generations without permission. Jean had not meant to teach him the game. He had simply played it in front of him. Now Mateo watched Karl the same way, and the results were unmistakable. The boy negotiated mule contracts, settled water disputes, and snubbed officials with a politeness sharp enough to draw blood.

Karl watched all this from the edges, torn between pride and worry. Jean had been bold and sometimes reckless. Karl, shaped by survival and captivity, was cautious, strategic. Mateo was something different, a synthesis of both. Bold when needed, cautious when wise. He smiled like Jean and planned like Karl.

Mentorship brings its own collisions. For Karl and Mateo, the dispute began over timber. The new western shaft required deeper bracing. Mateo had drawn up a system using angled reinforcement beams instead of the heavier vertical supports Karl preferred. Mateo's design would save cost. It would speed expansion.

It would also risk collapse if miscalculated.

Mateo stood next to Karl in the open yard where miners gathered in a loose semicircle. Ledgers rested on a crate between them. Mateo did not lower his voice.

"The old design will slow production by a third," he said. "We will lose contracts. We will lose buyers."

Karl felt a shift, not in the numbers, but in the air. Miners watched him now not just as Don Carlos, but as the older man being questioned.

Karl folded his hands behind his back. "You are certain?" he asked quietly.

"I am," Mateo said. "You taught me to calculate risk. I have done so."

A murmur passed through the men. Karl recognized the moment. It was not about timber. It was about succession.

A year prior, Karl might have corrected Mateo publicly. Might have cited figures, named dangers, reminded the yard who signed wages. Instead, he remembered a different dock, a different crowd, and Jean standing unbothered while younger men tried to prove themselves sharper. Jean had never crushed them. He had invited them to hang themselves with their own certainty.

Karl stepped aside. "Then we will use Mateo's design," he said evenly. The yard fell silent. Even Mateo was caught off guard. Karl continued, voice calm. "You will supervise every brace personally. If it holds, the credit is yours." He paused. "If it fails, the dead will also be yours." No anger. No threat. Just arithmetic.

The weight of it settled visibly on Mateo's shoulders. Karl turned to the miners. "You will follow him. And you will report to him. I will not countermand his orders."

Then he looked back at Mateo — not as employer, but as something closer to equal. "Leadership," Karl added quietly enough for only him to hear, "is not proving you are right, Prof. It is living with the consequences when you are wrong."

For a long moment, Mateo held his gaze. Then he gave a quiet assent.

The bracing went up under Mateo's watchful eye. Every beam was measured twice. Every angle corrected. The shaft held.

Weeks later, when the first ore cart rose smoothly from the deeper vein, the miners cheered Mateo's name. Karl did not interrupt them. He merely stood at the edge of the yard, hands clasped behind his back, feeling something unexpected. Pride—and relinquishment.

As the mines grew, so did the world around Karl and Mateo. Investors from London came sniffing, diplomats crossed the country to see the northern operations, and newspapers began printing a new phrase: "the Castañeda System," referring to Mateo's innovations.

One night, after the men had gone to their quarters, Karl poured two glasses of mezcal and placed one beside Mateo's stack of maps. "You'll outgrow this place," Karl said quietly.

Mateo took a sip before responding. "What do you mean?"

"You think in straight lines now—prospects, rail lines, markets. This mine won't hold you forever." Mateo looked puzzled, then amused. "If you want me gone, just say." Karl shook his head. "No, Prof, it's not that. Jean once told me something similar. I didn't understand it until after he left."

"What was it?"

Karl hesitated, hearing Jean's voice not just in memory but in tone, amused and sharp all at once: *A man cannot captain the same ship forever.* He did not repeat it aloud. Instead he said, "A man must know when he is building for the present, and when he is building for what comes after him." Mateo studied him, brow furrowed. "And which am I?" Karl managed a tired smile. "Both."

After Mateo left for the night, Karl stared out over his silver-lit valley, feeling the weight of time settle around him. Jean had once been the storm. Karl had been the survivor. Mateo might be the future. The chain was never planned. It simply happened as if ordained by the universe. One man teaches another how to see possibility in danger. The next teaches someone else how to build from it. And somewhere in the pattern, Karl realized he had become the mentor he once doubted he could be.

It was the unbroken circle Jean would have laughed at, Mama would have prayed over, and Annabelle… Karl did not know. He only wished she could see it.

By 1833, Karl's holdings stretched from the tunnels at Valenciana to the smelting yards outside Marfil. Contracts were signed in his name, wagons loaded at his order, payroll dispersed by his hand. He was now thirty-eight, past the age when a wealthy man would settle in with a wife and build a family. With success came invitations—dinners behind iron gates, salons smelling of rose water and cigar smoke.

Success also caught the attention of Mariana Saldaña.

Mariana was the daughter of a Creole rancher, quick to laugh and quicker to argue. She was educated at a convent in Querétaro, yet unafraid of mine dust or politics. Mariana rode horses like a vaquero and debated priests on philosophy. When they first met at the Durango governor's ball in 1833, she greeted him with a mocking bow.

"So you are the ghost German who owns half the mountains?" Mariana asked, with a wry grin. Karl smiled back. "Only the silver ones," he said.

Mariana was everything Guanajuato admired: educated, fluent in French, quick-witted, and quietly confident in an old family name. She entered rooms as if light followed her. Miners bowed. Bankers stood a little straighter.

Mariana visited the mines once, escorted by her father and half a dozen retainers. The air was thick with sulfur, the shaft mouths ringing with hammers on stone. Mariana did not flinch. She asked questions—good ones—about yields, wages, and markets in Zacatecas. Her father listened with surprise. Karl noticed the way her gloves tightened when the hoist rattled, and how her gaze darted to him when the carts thundered past, seeking reassurance he could not articulate. He offered his arm and said, "Trust the timbers. They hold." She smiled, and for a moment the dust did not seem so heavy.

After that, Mariana began appearing with Karl with heightened regularity—at the refinería, at the plaza during market days, on balconies overlooking the callejóns where guitarists played late into the night. The city whispered that the German was courting her, or she him, which, for gossip, was the same thing.

Karl, for the first time since New Orleans, found himself uncertain about the possibility of reuniting with Annabelle. Maybe he had everything he ever needed here.

He admired Mariana's intelligence, her composure, the way she turned men's arrogance inside out with a single raised eyebrow. His challenge lay in quiet moments, when the day's ledgers were closed and the hacienda slept. That's when his mind still crossed the Gulf and the rivers and the prairies to St. Louis. He remembered Annabelle's hands, gentle with embroidery, soft from piano keys, trembling as she boarded the ferry. He remembered the way she looked back only once, as if any more might break her resolve. He wondered if she had forgiven him. Or forgotten him.

He had built a life. He had shouldered obligations. He had amassed a small fortune. These should have been proof enough of forward motion. Instead, they felt like arguments he rehearsed against a judge who never rendered a verdict. Annabelle's memory returned without mercy, not as comfort but as accusation. As if every choice since had been measured against a moment he could neither revisit nor release.

He told himself that God might have placed Annabelle in his thoughts as a sign. Perhaps his inability to escape the thoughts of her marked something essential—not merely who he had loved, but the moment his life had divided into before and after. Letting her go would feel like betrayal. The truly bothersome part, Karl realized, was that if his life were another shape, one where he had never met Annabelle, he would have loved Mariana with the fierceness a woman deserves.

For years, townsfolk assumed Karl and Mariana would marry. It was not a wild assumption. Five years of Sunday dinners beneath her mother's citrus trees, of business trips to Veracruz where they stayed in adjoining rooms to avoid gossip, of summers at her family's hacienda in Durango. All of it wove them together in a pattern people recognize. The kind of pattern that ends in a church, not a question mark.

Mariana loved him with a fierce, patient certainty. She admired his discipline, his quiet humor, the way he treated vaqueros and bankers with the same level-eyed respect. Her parents approved. Her brothers teased her. Even the local priest once rested a hand on Karl's shoulder and said, "Marriage is the refuge of strong men, Señor Steinheimer."

Mariana thought it was inevitable — not if, only when. And there were moments when she believed the *when* had finally arrived.

Once, on a moonlit veranda in Veracruz, Karl reached into his coat while speaking of futures and partnerships and ships. Mariana's breath caught. For a moment she saw her whole life unfolding—children with German cheekbones and Mexican eyes, a house in the high country, laughter at Christmas, his hand at the small of her back in church while the priest spoke their names. Karl drew something slowly from his coat.

It was Mama's wooden swan. The little carving caught the moonlight. He held it carefully, almost reverently, as though presenting something holy. Mariana laughed. Too quickly. "It is… very unusual," she said.

Karl smiled, not yet sensing her disappointment. "My mother kept it by our Bible," he explained. "Said it guarded the house. She believed it carried peace." He turned it in his palm. "I have carried it across oceans. Through war. Through everything."

Mariana looked at the swan, then looked away. "It is plain," she said. What she wanted to say was: it's not gold. Not promise. Not permanence.

"I thought…" She stopped herself. Karl waited. "I thought perhaps," she tried again, gentler now, "you were reaching for something else." The words were light. Almost playful. But they landed. He saw that she had expected a ring. That she was hoping for certainty.

Karl tried to recover. "This," he said quietly, placing the swan in her hands, "is the most important thing I own." Mariana turned it over politely, not reverently. "It is a memory," she said. "It is not the future." Karl dipped his head.

She handed it back quickly. "You keep it close," she said. "It clearly means much to you." Her tone carried distance. Karl slipped the swan back into his coat. His face did not change. His voice remained steady as he resumed speaking of investments and futures. But something inside him tightened. He had hoped for respect and received indifference.

Mariana leaned against the veranda rail. "I suppose," she said after a moment, almost to herself, "I had hoped for something meant for me." The words were quiet. Honest.

Karl did not answer immediately. He had meant the swan as an invitation into his history, into the part of him that had survived. He understood now that what she wanted was not his past. She wanted his future.

Another time, on the hacienda, when cicadas whirred like spinning coins in the heat, Karl rode in from the north with wildflowers and a bottle of mezcal. Mariana's mother pulled her aside, smiling. "He has that look. Prepare yourself." But when evening came, Karl spoke only of smelters and claims and the price of silver in London.

Karl never proposed. It was not cowardice, at least not the kind Mariana could accuse him of. It was something quieter, knotted deep. When conversation neared the edges of permanence, he would shift ever so slightly, as if the ground beneath him was uncertain. He had mastered the dance of evasion, a delicate step of half-truths and soft gestures that looked enough like affection to keep hope alive.

Mariana waited. And waited. And waited, because waiting is what women did when they loved fiercely and the world expected patience from them. What Mariana never saw was Karl lying awake on the other side of inevitability, staring at a ceiling he increasingly hated, thinking: *I should ask her. She deserves that. I could build a life here.* His hand would curl into a fist. *It would be easy. So easy. Too easy.*

Then, somewhere beneath the weight of Mexico's silver hills and the clamor of minted coins, another thought would slip in like unwanted correspondence—*What if ease is not my path? I have never known ease.* What if there was still a debt to the Mercer brothers, to Jean Lafitte, to Papa's ghost, to the restless part of him that refused to be domesticated by fiestas and haciendas and tidy futures? What if a girl in St. Louis still waited for him?

Five years into their companionship, Mariana finally asked what had been on her mind for years. "Mi amor," she said gently, "I have waited longer than most. Are you saving yourself for sainthood?"

Karl felt the old instinct rise. He should soften, divert, offer a gentler version of the truth. He studied her face in the low lamplight and wondered whether honesty would wound her more than silence. Some truths, once spoken, could not be gathered back.

He considered sparing her. He considered saying *not yet*, or *circumstance*, or any of the respectable evasions men had used for centuries. But the thought soured immediately. What kind of foundation was built on concealment? What kind of love survived a lie chosen for comfort?

Karl smiled, but it was a thin, brittle thing. The moment had come whether he welcomed it or not. He exhaled slowly, as if steadying himself before deep water.

"No," he said quietly. "For someone I lost."

Mariana met his gaze steadily. No flinch. No retreat. "A widow, then?" she asked carefully. He shook his head. "No. A girl from St. Louis."

The words landed between them. Karl felt strangely lighter for having spoken the truth, as it seemed to lose some of its power to haunt. Whatever followed, pain or understanding, at least it would be earned honestly.

Silence settled between them. Mariana studied him for a long time. The line of his jaw held firm as if that alone might keep the past from spilling into the room. "You will soon turn forty-three," she said at last, her voice stripped of cheer. "Shall you pine for a ghost?"

Karl did not answer. He only watched the lamplight on the glass. After a moment, he whispered, "Her name was Annabelle."

Mariana said nothing after that. She remained with him, believing as many women do that time is a faithful physician. In this case, with this patient, time merely taught her that some wounds choose their own pace to heal.

Or never heal at all.

Chapter 28

On a warm late summer evening in 1838, Karl sat in the local cantina with
Mateo and several American engineers. Men laughed, cards slapped
against the worn wood, and the scent of mezcal mingled with roasting
goat.

The cantina door swung open. Two overdressed travelers entered—
clearly Americans, a man and his wife—carrying the dust of a long
journey. They had Midwestern accents, sunburned faces, and the weary
politeness of travelers far from home.

The man approached the bar and spoke loudly: "We're from St.
Louis, Missouri. Looking for Señor Don Carlos, owner of the mines. We
bring papers regarding metal contracts."

Karl froze mid-sip. Mateo nudged him. "Patrón… they speak of you."

Karl stood and guided his visitors to a table near the courtyard where
the evening breeze softened the heat. Drinks were poured. Ledgers and
assay reports exchanged. Contracts discussed. Inevitably, small talk crept
in. The wife laughed politely at something her husband said, then turned to

Karl.

"Forgive me, Señor Steinheimer. You mentioned you once lived in Louisiana. Did you ever make it north to St. Louis? It is quite the city now, full of noise and ambition! Every year more Frenchmen, Spaniards, and even Protestants."

Karl kept his voice light. "I know the place, though I've never had the pleasure to visit. Do you… know many families there?"

"Oh yes!" she said, delighted to be useful. "We try to keep a wide circle, it's good for business. The Chouteaus, the Lacostes, and a wagon merchant Kelley are among our closest friends."

Before the lady could continue in detail, Karl interrupted. "Do you happen to know Annabelle Dixon? Her last name may have changed. She was Dixon when I knew her."

"Of course, I know Annabelle," the lady replied. "She's a fine woman, though life dealt her trials."

Karl felt the world pause around him, as though the cantina walls had leaned closer. He kept his voice steady. "She is married?"

The woman waved a hand. "No, no—she's a widow. Her husband died in the battle of New Orleans. A beauty once, I'm told, but raising a child alone leaves little time for flirtation. Still, she seems happy enough. Works at the Catholic church. Sings at Mass. Very polite, very private."

Karl set his glass down before his hand could betray him. Blood roared in his ears. Annabelle—unmarried. Alive. Living her life.

"And the child?" he asked, trying not to pounce on the question.

"Oh, she's grown now. Early twenties, I'd say. A charming girl. Quick tongue, clever eyes. Helps the parish with their bookkeeping, I think."

Karl raised his glass. "Her name?" he asked.

The wife replied as if discussing the weather.

"Karla," she said. "That's the girl's name."

She lifted her glass and took a polite sip.

Karl set his own glass down carefully.

Karla.

The cantina did not go silent, yet somehow he heard nothing. No laughter. No glasses clinking. Only the echo of a name he had never spoken and yet somehow belonged to him.

The woman continued, unaware. "Father Desruisseaux says both mother and daughter have strong wills. He once joked that God must have made them from the same mold and run out of patience halfway through."

Karl forced a polite nod and closed the ledger. Conversation continued, but Karl was lost in thought. When the ink dried on the contract and the couple departed into the lantern-lit courtyard, he remained seated.

Karla.

Alive. Grown. Utterly real.

The silver on the table caught the lamplight, throwing reflections across his hands. Hands that had mined, fought, smuggled, survived. Yet trembled now at a single spoken name.

Karla.

Often the moment a man's past tilts toward his future goes unnoticed. Mateo noticed. He leaned closer. "You're pale, Don Carlos. Who is Annabelle?"

"Someone I should have died for, Prof," Karl said, staring into the distance. He stood abruptly, called for the tab, and strode into the street. Stars burned above the plaza. Church bells tolled the hour.

Mariana found him pacing the veranda when she arrived, summoned by worried servants. "Did someone die?" she snapped. "No," Karl said.

"Then why do you look like a ghost?"

"She's alive, Mariana. She's in St. Louis."

The name required no explanation. Mariana's face hardened—not with surprise, but with old pain. "And?" she asked.

"I leave tomorrow."

Mariana inhaled sharply, struck by the words. "After five years… that's all you say? No thought for me? For the life we built?"

"I cannot stay. Not now. I have a daughter. Karla."

"You foolish, stubborn German!" she hissed. "Do you think she waited for you? Do you think she wants you now?"

"It does not matter what she wants," Karl said quietly. "It matters that I must see her. And see my daughter."

Mariana's eyes flooded. Karl had never spoken of a daughter. But she refused him the satisfaction of tears in the moonlight. "You built empires here but never built a home. And you won't build one in St. Louis. Go and chase your ghost. But when you return, and you will, you will find I have learned to live without you."

She walked away without looking back.

Karl began plans for the next day's departure. When word spread that Don Carlos was riding north, and word spread quickly, the town erupted into a low thunder of whispers. What was leaving the yard that morning could build a town, maybe an empire. Three hundred pounds of gold and five hundred pounds of silver, counted and double-counted under the watch of armed clerks. By modern reckoning, it amounted to nearly nine million dollars.

Everyone knew the dangers of the route. Rebels. Royalist deserters. Apaches. Opportunistic Americans. Comanches drifting down from the plains. Worst of all was the greed of one's own escorts.

Karl did not travel light, and he certainly did not travel unguarded. He had arranged passage under the protection of Manuel Flores and his company, a man whose very name could settle arguments or start them.

Flores had agreed, for a suffocating price, to steer Karl through the most uncertain and perilous leg of the entire journey: across the high country, then north into Texas, where the land belonged to no one and everyone at once.

While Karl checked the cinches on his saddle, Mateo strode across the courtyard with the swagger of a man who had already made up his mind. "If you think I'm letting you get yourself shot between here and God's country, you're half-cracked," Mateo said, thrusting a rifle scabbard into Karl's hands.

"It's a long way, Prof," Karl answered quietly. "I won't ask you to leave your home."

"You didn't ask," Mateo replied. "I'm telling you. And besides—" he leaned in, voice dropping— "I need to meet the woman who would make a man walk away from all you have." Karl didn't argue. It would've been useless, and he was too grateful for the trusted company to pretend otherwise.

Manuel Flores arrived shortly after, mounted on a dusty bay mare, carrying the uneven bearing of a man who had survived ambushes, cholera, Comanche raids, and three marriages (not all peaceful). His moustache curled like a hawk's wing, and his eyes never stopped measuring distance, wind, and threat. He was carrying dispatches from Chihuahua to the northern presidios.

Safety was in numbers, and Flores traveled with twenty riders: Tejanos, mestizos, and hired ranch hands from the Nueces Strip. Every one of them carried a carbine, a knife long enough to shame a kitchen sword, and the look of men who would live through hell even if it meant dragging others down with them. Flores eyed Karl's cargo as the last crate was lashed down. "You travel heavy, Don Carlos," he said.

"I travel prepared," Karl replied, "and I'm much lighter now that I've paid you." Flores grinned, revealing a gold tooth. "Prepared men die slower, that's all," he said. "But slower is better than fast." A few of his men laughed — not out of humor, but recognition.

The outer gates were unbarred. Dust plumed up as the column moved into formation. Wagons first, riders flanking, and Flores at the point like a spear tip.

Before riding out, Karl turned once toward the veranda above. Mariana stood there in a dark riding jacket, arms crossed hard over her chest, eyes like black stone. She did not wave. She did not speak. She had spent enough years waiting for promises that never materialized. Now she watched him leave. She held her chin high. Her stance was of a woman who had decided not to break. Mateo noticed. Of course he did.

Mateo murmured, "You want to—"

"No," Karl cut in.

Mateo smiled. "Good. She'd have thrown a pot at your head. Big one too — her mother keeps the good clay."

Flores snorted at that and kicked his mare forward with a click of his tongue. One by one the wagons rolled through the gate, guards scanning the junction of roads like hunters waiting for a sign.

By the time they hit the main trace heading north, the mine had vanished behind them in a haze of dust and heat. Inside that haze Karl left behind more than bullion. He left behind a woman who wanted a future. He left behind a version of himself who might have stayed to give it to her.

If he failed, he would not return as Don Carlos. He would return as a man who gambled an empire on a memory. Mariana's words, claiming he could not build a home, haunted him.

The road did not care. It demanded payment in sweat, and sometimes blood.

St. Louis was calling. Karl could hear it.

Chapter 29

The first leg toward South Texas took them through Mapimí and Monclova, where bureaucrats demanded stamps and signatures before releasing border permits and militia escorts. They forded the Rio Grande near a ragged cluster of dirt-floored huts that would one day be called Laredo. For now it was nothing but mud and men who watched from the shade with rifles laid across their knees.

Once across the river, the real danger began. The lawless emptiness between the Rio Grande and the San Antonio River was ruled by no flag, coveted by several, and patrolled by men who preferred plunder to politics.

That first night in Texas, they camped beneath mesquites as thick as wire brushes. The cook tossed thinly sliced beef on the iron. The scent of scorched fat hit Karl like a trapdoor opening under his feet—Mama at the iron stove frying pork scraps in lard for winter suppers. He could almost see her apron swaying.

Flores jabbed a stick at the fire, snapping him back. "From here to San Antonio, the only laws are cattle thieves, Lipan Apaches, and the Comanche cavalry," he said. "Sleep in shifts. Keep your powder dry. And if we pass cattle herds with no brands—don't ask questions."

Two days later, near the Nueces River, the brush ahead erupted with mounted riders. Vaqueros turned bandits cut in from the riverbank claiming they were tax collectors.

Flores didn't slow. "Tax collectors?" Karl muttered.

"As real as your grandmother's beard," Flores said. Then, louder —"Hands to rifles!" Gunfire cracked through the mesquite. Horses screamed. Two mules went down in the traces, a few silver bars sliding into the mud. Three bandits dropped in the crossfire, another tumbled into thornscrub, and the rest vanished into the brush.

When the smoke cleared, Mateo dragged a wounded rider, little more than a boy, to a wagon. "First blood," Mateo said, chest heaving. "And it's not even noon." Flores spat into the river. "Better bandits than Lipan. Bandits only want money. Lipan want scalps, not silver."

On the fourth night, rain drove them into a cluster of pecans along a dry arroyo. The men slept in shifts beneath canvas, while guards whistled to one another in the dark so no one's voice would carry. Karl lay with a saddle beneath his head, staring at lightning crawling silently inside distant clouds. Fatigue dragged him under. Sleep came cruel and vivid.

He dreamed of St. Catherine's church bells, of Mama praying at the kitchen table, not for blessings, but for him to stay put. In the dream he disobeyed again, as always, and the bells became cannon, and the kitchen table became a battlefield trench.

Then came Annabelle, so clear he could smell the roses pinned to her blouse. She spoke his name, not scolding, not beckoning, simply saying it, as though naming him made him real. When he reached for her, she stepped back into a river fog and disappeared. He woke with rainwater dripping from his hat brim and the drum of horse hooves moving at the perimeter.

Flores sat nearby, oiling his rifle. "You talk in your sleep, Alemán," Flores murmured.

Karl wiped his face and said nothing. Dreams could not change reality.

After weeks of heat and half-glimpsed riders in the mesquite, the stone walls of San Antonio de Béxar finally rose ahead. The town was a scatter of missions, adobe houses, open plazas, and the Alamo walls still blackened from '36.

In the plaza, American traders haggled beside Tejano ranchers and German settlers. Mexican officials watched from shaded awnings. Karl sold some of his silver and used the proceeds to buy fresh horses, wagon tools, and two guides who claimed to know every crossing and limestone ledge between Béxar and the upper country.

Flores arranged a meeting with the two guides to learn what dangers lay ahead. After the meeting, Flores told Karl, "The guides advise that we move through Seguin and Bastrop, then up past the high country toward Liberty Hill. I will take you as far as Nacogdoches. After that, you are on your own. It should be open range to the rivers and trails that lead to Missouri."

Karl could feel Annabelle drawing closer. Karla too.

They spent only two days in San Antonio. On the third morning, they turned east toward the little settlements that dotted the edge of Comanche country. No one rode easy. Not after what they'd seen on the prairie.

The second night out, camped among oak motts near Cibolo Creek, Karl noticed Mateo squinting into the moonlight. "What do you see?" Karl whispered. Mateo didn't answer at first. "Nothing I can name. But I think we're being followed."

Flores agreed. He ordered cold camps from that point on, no fires, no singing, no light that could betray their position. They rode by dawn, rested at noon, and pushed again at dusk, letting heat and shadows hide them. Once, crossing a dry arroyo, they found a pair of fresh hoofprints, unshod, pointing in the direction they were traveling. "Those are not Spanish horses," Flores said. "They're watching us. Waiting for a place they like better."

The trail forced them northeast, across tangled cedar breaks and limestone ridges where creeks sank and disappeared underground. By late week they reached the Balcones escarpment, the land opening into rolling savanna. Flores pointed with his chin. "East of here is a hamlet called Liberty Hill. Only a few cabins and corn patches, but if we reach it by tomorrow we can take water and news." Karl acknowledged Flores, though his eyes kept scanning. Every flutter of grass looked like horsehair. Every hawk's shadow felt like a scout.

That night they bedded down in a hollow between two limestone shelves, horses tied close, rifles within reach. Coyotes yipped in the distance. Once, past midnight, Karl swore he heard the soft, rhythmic thrum of hooves on distant dirt. He held his breath until the sound returned no more.

The convoy reached the outskirts of Liberty Hill late the next afternoon. Nothing moved in the settlement but dust. No dogs. No chimney smoke. No voices. Flores raised a fist. "Too quiet," he whispered. Before anyone could answer, a lone Comanche rider crested the ridge to the north. He was painted in scarlet and charcoal.

The ridge remained still. Too still. Then, without warning, a dozen riders poured down the slope, war whoops splitting the air. Feathers and lances flashed. Horses kicked up dust like wildfire.

"Circle the mules!" Flores roared—but the Comanche were already among them. Two riders split wide, drawing fire, while a third slashed behind the column and drove a lance into a mule's flank. The animal shrieked and collapsed, spilling part of the load.

Flores fired twice, dropping a rider and unhorsing another, before a spear tore through his coat and grazed his ribs. He barely stayed in the saddle. "Move the strongboxes!" he shouted to Karl. "North! Now!"

Karl understood instantly. There was no saving the wagons, only saving what they could carry. He, Mateo, and two of Flores' men—Santiago and Rojo—leapt into action. They hacked open the mule panniers, hauling out sealed iron-bound strongboxes, gold in one set, silver in another. "Take the lead mule!" Karl shouted.

Santiago seized a small, fast mule already half-rigged with loaded panniers. Mateo and Rojo grabbed additional saddle-bags stuffed with silver reale bars and slung them across fresh mounts. A Comanche swept in with a lance. Karl blasted him from the saddle with both barrels of his shotgun. "Go!" Karl barked. "Go now!"

Flores tried to wheel his horse to support them, but a volley of arrows came from the ridge and one struck deep beneath his arm. He stayed upright long enough to fire once more, dropping a rider, before a lance knocked him from the saddle.

"Flores!" Mateo screamed.

Flores struggled to one knee in the dust, one hand clamped to the arrow shaft. His eyes found Karl.

"Ride, Alemán," he rasped. "We'll buy you time."

Then he turned back toward the charging riders and fired.

Karl kicked his horse north, shouting, "To the creek! Head for the trees!" Santiago led with the mule, Mateo and Rojo flanking, rifles firing backward from the saddle. Arrows hissed through the mesquite. One lodged in Rojo's saddle but missed muscle. A pursuing rider threw a lariat. Santiago slashed it away just before it cinched a strongbox.

They reached a shallow creek and plunged down its embankment.

Rocks and mud flew. Horses slid. Strongboxes banged. They used the creek bed as a shield, hooves splashing and slipping as Comanche war cries echoed overhead. When the water deepened, Karl shouted, "Dismount!"

They hauled the boxes onto their shoulders, scrambling up the far bank under cover of the cottonwoods. The Comanche didn't try to follow into the tangle of brush. They circled instead, whooping, stripping the wagons, finishing the wounded. Flores and his men were still fighting, brief flashes of muzzle fire through dust, until the gunshots died out for good. The lone remaining sounds were the chirp of cicadas and the drip of creek water.

Rojo leaned against a tree, panting, black hair plastered to his forehead. "We have… what? Two strongboxes and saddlebags?"

"More than enough to die over," Santiago said bitterly.

Karl looked back toward the ridge. Smoke was rising. "Flores knew the odds," Karl said. "We honor him by not wasting his blood." No one argued.

They hefted the strongboxes onto the surviving mule and redistributed the saddlebags across two horses. The four men moved northeast along the creek in quiet disbelief, using the trees for cover. They stopped in silence. "Count what we have," Karl ordered, voice raw.

The four men tore open saddle boxes and packs, fingers slick with sweat and powder. Karl's hands were shaking as he lifted a chest to Mateo. He noticed blood on his sleeve that wasn't his. Two small chests of gold remained intact, and four torn silver sacks lay slumped against a fallen log, one ripped open from a lance strike, leaving bright coins scattered through the grass.

Mateo took the chest from Karl and placed it onto his knee. "Gold's all here in these two. Maybe two hundred and—" He paused, doing the numbers in his head. "Two hundred fifty pounds, give or take. We lost a box when the wagon went."

Karl let out a deep breath. "Silver?" Rojo shook his head. "Half the mules were hit. The crates split." They jammed the loose silver into saddlebags, weighed the sacks by hand, and came to the grim arithmetic. Maybe two hundred twenty pounds of silver, no more. Karl looked at Rojo and said, "We are lucky to have that."

The silence was eerie. They listened for more war cries that never came. Despite the quiet, the Comanche had not vanished. They were patient hunters. Karl could feel their eyes on the ridges, waiting for the heat to soften the intruders. He forced his mind forward. "We move north. We can't go back to San Antonio. Too many eyes. We cross through the timber to the three rivers country. Flores said there's a crossing by Holland."

"Long way," Santiago muttered.

"Better than a short burial," Mateo replied, cinching the silver tight against his saddle.

They mounted, each horse now sagging under bullion worth kingdoms. Karl looked once over his shoulder to where Flores had fallen. The grass already bent over him.

"Ride," Karl said, and they pushed into the oak motts, leaving wagon smoke curling into the Texas sky. They rode in silence at first, but as the sun dropped Karl allowed himself one hard, bitter calculation. Out of eight hundred pounds in Chihuahua, only four hundred seventy remained. It would still buy a nice life in St. Louis. Everything was now measured by St. Louis.

Karl's thoughts were interrupted by Mateo. "Holland," he said, pointing to the east. "Flores said the rivers meet there." Karl raised his hat and said, "We go at first light and find cover there. We bury what slows us. And we pray those riders don't track this far."

Behind them, faint and distant, a single Comanche whooped, a long, cold, mocking call. Karl didn't need Flores alive to understand the message. The sound was not fading. It was moving.

That night, Karl stared into the fire while coyotes yipped in the brush. Mateo nudged him with the toe of his boot, eyes narrowed as if trying to read Karl's mind. "Do you think Annabelle will want to see you?" he asked.

Karl looked toward the horizon. "I don't know," he said. Mateo exhaled through his teeth. "You've risked Mariana. The mines. This entire fortune."

Karl's voice remained steady. "A man can build an empire in Mexico, survive wars and prisons, and still be a coward in one thing."

"And what is that?" Mateo asked.

Karl's answer was almost a whisper. "Women."

Chapter 30

Karl, Mateo, Santiago, and Rojo reached the Three Rivers country by mid-morning, the land rolling toward the hidden meeting of three ribbons of water known as the Lampasas, Leon, and San Gabriel rivers. It was a lonely place, quiet except for water sliding against limestone and the distant call of birds. Flores had once called it "good country for hiding bad things," and now Karl understood. He halted the horses beneath a massive live oak whose limbs spread like the beams of a chapel. The tree trunk was thick enough that three men could not have wrapped it with linked arms. Lightning had scarred it once, long ago.

"Here," Karl said. His voice was flat, resolved. Mateo frowned. "So close to water?" Karl shook his head. "Close to something a man would remember even if he tried to forget." Santiago and Rojo said nothing. They were too tired, too hunted, and too afraid to argue with logic that smelled of both desperation and experience.

They unloaded the two chests, two hundred fifty pounds of gold, onto the sand. Karl paced out the ground from the great oak, counting under his breath in German. At forty paces he stopped, dragged his boot heel through the dirt as a marker, then returned to the tree. "Dig there," he said.

The ground was soft enough near the riverbank that they could work quickly. Knives, hatchets, fists, and scavenged shovels scraped and clawed until a waist-deep pit gaped open, dark at the bottom. When they lowered the chests in, the earth swallowed them without ceremony.

Karl stared at the pit for a moment longer than the others. He was not thinking of Indians or bandits now, but of Jean Lafitte grinning beneath a Gulf moon as privateers lowered doubloons into the earth. He wondered whether treasure ever slept without first tasting blood. They filled the pit with scattered soil and leaves, brushed away their bootprints with cedar branches, then dragged a deadfall halfway over the site to disguise the fresh earth.

Then Karl returned to the huge oak. From his saddlebag he drew an iron spike—a leftover from a wagon repair back near Monclova. He set the point into the bark and hammered it with the butt of his pistol until it bit deep, half-hidden by moss.

Santiago raised an eyebrow. "For what?"

Karl wiped sweat from his brow. "For when we return."

Mateo tapped the tree trunk. "Anyone else sees that, they'll ask questions."

Karl shook his head. "Not here. Not this tree. A hundred oaks between here and nowhere, but only one that watches three rivers meet." Karl looked once more at the oak and thought: *If I die, someone else will need to know where to look.*

They saddled up and rode out at a trot, leaving the oak in silence. Mateo waved once at the oak as if saluting a grave. Karl looked over his shoulder. The tree stood unmoving, the spike glinting faintly like a secret the earth had agreed to remember.

They had not gone five miles when Mateo stiffened in the saddle.

"Riders," he whispered.

Karl followed his gaze. A flicker along the ridge. Then nothing. The prairie lay too still. No birds lifted. Silence pressed against his ears.

Then the ridge broke open. Comanche riders poured over it in two sweeping lines, horses stretched long and low, faces striped in red and ash. The earth began to tremble. Lances dipped. Bows rose. The air filled with shrill cries that seemed less human than elemental.

"*¡Vámonos!*" Rojo shouted, firing behind him. The shot vanished into dust. Karl wheeled left with Mateo, driving hard for a shallow arroyo fifty yards away that cut the prairie like a scar. Santiago's horse screamed as an arrow buried in its neck. The animal collapsed mid-stride, flipping him forward. Karl saw Santiago's hand claw once at empty air before the riders swallowed him.

Karl and Mateo were almost to the arroyo when a single Comanche broke from the flank. He was young and lean with braids flying behind him. He did not shout. He did not rush. He rode straight at Karl.

Karl saw the bow lift. For a moment Karl believed the rider might spare him. Then the bowstring snapped forward. The noise of battle fell away. No hooves. No shouting.

Karl reached for his pistol. Too late. He felt the impact before he understood it. A punch of iron hammered high in his thigh, just below the hip. Heat exploded through him. The force twisted him sideways in the saddle. His leg went instantly weak, as if cut from his body.

He fell. The ground struck like stone. Dust filled his mouth. His horse thundered on without him. He lay stunned, staring at the shaft jutting from his leg. It looked unreal. It looked placed there, deliberate, as if someone had chosen the spot on his body and marked it.

Mateo's horse reared above him. "Karl!"

"Ride!" Karl said through clenched teeth. The prairie was already shifting as the Comanche peeled away with terrifying discipline, their work finished. Rojo was gone. Santiago lay twisted in the grass, a lance upright through his chest like a cruel banner.

Karl tried to stand. White fire shot up his side and dropped him back into the dust.

The young Comanche had reined in at a distance, watching. Not gloating. Not smiling. Only measuring whether Karl would live. Karl met his gaze across the field.

Then the rider turned and vanished with the others over the ridge, leaving Karl broken in the wash of limestone and thorn, the arrow still trembling in his flesh. He had just a few silver pieces in his pockets. He was thankful he had kept them.

At nightfall, Karl crawled beneath a slab of rock. He listened for hooves. Once he heard distant cries. Victory or mourning, he could not tell.

He thought of Mama's voice—*Follow God and you will live long*—and how poorly he had obeyed anything but his own road. He lay awake beneath stars thick as spilled salt. His thoughts drifted to Annabelle, her hair smelling faintly of soap, wondering if she ever thought of him or if God had long ago decided they were two lines that never crossed again. Sometime near dawn he whispered, "God, if You mean me to live, send a horse… or mercy."

Somewhere between the ache in his leg and the slow crawl of days, he felt Mateo was alive as well. He hoped the young man would find his way back to Mexico and engineer the mines to heights Karl himself would never see.

Two days after the ambush, two Anglo drovers encountered Karl delirious beneath a stand of hackberries. His leg was swollen and blackening, the arrow still lodged. They cut the shaft, drew the barbs as best they could, cleaned him with whiskey, and bound him in linen torn from a feed sack. Karl thanked them in a rasping mixture of Spanish, English, and German, and they stared at him like he was half ghost, half outlaw. When he told them he was headed north, they shrugged and made room in the wagon. They were en route to Chicago to reunite with family.

Their little party pushed on, slowly, toward the Mississippi River. The wound worsened at every mile, sickness creeping up his thigh like smoke rising up a chimney. Karl felt its progress intimately. The drovers argued about turning back, about finding a surgeon, about cutting the leg. Karl refused. "To cut the leg is to kill me faster," he rasped. And they believed him, or perhaps they simply feared the procedure themselves, so they pressed north and east toward the great river.

By the time they reached Nacogdoches, Karl knew rot had taken hold. Gangrene. No doctor needed to tell him. The stench was foul. The skin had split. Karl could no longer walk. They carried him into a cheap boarding house across from a German beer hall. The landlady, a widow named Frau Keller, took one look at his bandages and crossed herself.

The nights were the worst. Fever would take him, sweat soaking his shirt, teeth chattering under blankets that smelled of horse and mildew. In those hours he asked the sky questions. What is treasure? What is life? What is a man's purpose? He thought of Mama singing German hymns beneath the rafters, her voice thin but sure. He thought of Jean Lafitte—the swaggering pirate-philosopher—teaching him that gold was both anchor and curse. He thought of Annabelle in St. Louis, her eyes bright with promises that life might never allow to flower.

The drovers stayed two days. They were not family, not comrades, just men who had done what decency required. On the morning they prepared to leave for Chicago, Karl called one of them, Samuel, close to his cot. "St. Louis," Karl breathed. "There is a woman named Annabelle

Dixon. I know only that she works at the Catholic Church." He fumbled for his satchel, hands shaking, and produced folded sheets of paper he had been writing and rewriting for two nights. "Take this to her," he said. "Do not say more than you must." Samuel accepted the letter awkwardly, embarrassed by another man's private affairs. "There are things written in here," Karl whispered, "that only one person should ever see. You deliver it to Annabelle Dixon. No other eyes." Samuel tucked the letter inside his coat.

"Wait," Karl said, breath shaking. "There's one other thing." He turned his head slightly, searching the cluttered table, the travel-worn satchel, the dim corners of the boarding room. He wanted to include one more thing—his small wooden swan, Mama's swan, the only family heirloom he possessed. He thought Annabelle should have it. She might need peace. Now, scanning the room, he could not find it. The thought struck him with a peculiar hurt, as if a piece of his past had slipped away when he was no longer watching. He remembered having it the day they buried the gold.

"That's OK," he said to Samuel. "I can't find it. The letter will suffice." He closed his eyes. No matter, he thought. Annabelle probably wouldn't remember the swan. He wasn't certain that Annabelle would even remember him as more than rumor—some half-legend of a man who sailed with pirates, chased treasure through wilderness, and never kept a promise long enough to make it home.

The letter, his last letter, said to Annabelle what he never had the chance to speak. In a trembling hand, over two long nights, he had written:

This summer of our Lord, 1839, Nacogdoches, Texas
My dearest Annabelle,
If this letter finds you, then I do not. I spent a lifetime learning

that gold is loud, but regret is louder. I loved you from the first day I saw you in New Orleans. I have loved no one since.

After the war I parted from Jean Lafitte and the sea. I longed to make it to St. Louis but Mexico took me first in chains, then in blood, and at last in opportunity. I rose from a miner to a patron. Men called me Don Carlos. Governors shook my hand. I owned silver and gold enough to ransom small kingdoms. None of it quieted your name in my mind.

I learned from travelers that you never married. They told me that you have a daughter. Karla. When I heard her name, I wept like a child.

I trust she is mine. If so, tell her this: her father was not a great man, only a stubborn one. He fought at New Orleans. He carried powder for Lafitte's guns. He chased treasure across oceans and deserts. And in the end he learned that courage is not in conquest, but in staying.

I did not stay. For that I ask your forgiveness, though I have no right to it.

Two chests of gold lie buried near the meeting of three rivers in Texas—the Leon, the Lampasas, and the San Gabriel. Forty paces northeast from a great oak marked by an iron spike. I enclose a map drawn from memory. If Karla seeks it, let it be hers.

But hear me now: if you burn this letter and never look for the gold, you will be the wiser for it. Wealth is a restless companion. Love is the only thing that keeps its shape in the dark.

The wound in my leg has turned. The fever climbs. I feel time narrowing. I should have come back to you empty-handed and alive. Instead, I send paper and apology.

Tell Karla her father loved her without ever holding her. Tell her he loved her mother beyond all sense. That is the only fortune I possess at the end.

Yours, with a full heart at last,   *Karl*

Karl watched from the window as their wagon rattled up the street and vanished into the pouring rain. He felt no triumph, only an exhausted hollowing, as though he knew a letter, if it did indeed stay dry and make it to Annabelle, could never convey what he felt. He sagged back onto the cot and stared at the ceiling beams. His leg throbbed steadily now. The stink of infection filled the room despite the open window. He knew he was beyond curing. He knew he was dying.

He had chased gold, silver, and jewels across oceans and deep into the earth, through storms, wars, betrayal, and blood. He had known hunger, known fear, known the kind of violence that stripped a man down to bone and nerve. None of it had ever weighed on his heart the way Annabelle's touch had, nor Mama's songs, nor Jean's rare moments of kindness behind the bravado.

The pursuit of gold had carried him across oceans. Annabelle's memory had carried him farther. Maybe that was the lesson. Many men, he suspected, went to the grave clutching coin, never knowing what it had cost.

He wondered what Mama would have thought of the life he had chosen. Would she have grieved his stubbornness, or smiled at the man it had shaped? His throat tightened as he addressed her in his mind. *I should have listened better*, he told her. *I learned that you were right more often than I know how to admit.* Her words had never left him, and now, at last, he understood what she had been trying to teach him all along.

He said it aloud, softly, to the empty room: "It's love."

Karl closed his eyes and whispered a prayer for Karla, that she might choose differently than he had.

Outside, rain washed the Texas dust from the street. Miles away, beneath a lightning-scarred oak where three rivers meet, two chests of gold slept in darkness.

Chapter 31

Samuel Keller found no Dixon residence marked by a tidy sign. Instead an old grocer sweeping his stoop pointed him to St. Stephen's, a brick-front Catholic church on the north side of the city, where neighborhood widows and seamstresses sometimes rented rooms or worked among the parish ladies.

He arrived near dusk as the bells rang for evening prayers, and asked after a woman named Annabelle Dixon. The priest, a thin man with silver spectacles, gave a motion of quiet recognition and called down the hall.

She appeared in the doorway carrying a bundle of mended linens, hair tied back, sleeves rolled. There was no fanfare, no mystery. Just a woman fatigued by the day's labor. Samuel stared at her, feeling the strange weight of Karl's letter.

"Miss Dixon?" he asked.

"Yes?"

He removed his hat. "My name is Samuel Keller. I've come a long road with news from Karl Steinheimer."

Her face changed. First confusion, then a flicker of alarm, then something like hope colliding with dread. Samuel offered the folded letter with both hands. "He asked me to place this in yours. Only yours." Annabelle set the linens aside and took the envelope gingerly, as if it were hot iron. The priest excused himself with pastoral instinct, ushering Samuel to the front steps of the church and leaving Annabelle alone in the small side chapel where candles flickered.

Annabelle broke the seal with trembling fingers.

At first she scanned a few lines—her own name, the date—and a choked sound escaped her throat. Then she sank onto the nearest bench and read every word slowly, lips moving, tears gathering. She read of his love. She read of Karla—*her Karla*—and a sob escaped. She read of his regret, his longing, his understanding that he would never see them, and her shoulders began to shake.

When she reached the treasure—maps, directions, the spike in the oak —she froze, staring in disbelief. She read those lines twice, then three times, tears dripping onto the page. Finally she set the letter down and pressed her palms to her eyes, sobbing openly now, grief, anger and tenderness tangled together. She had imagined Karl dead in New Orleans, perhaps in the battle or maybe in a Lafitte raid gone wrong.

She whispered aloud, voice ragged: "Oh Karl… why didn't you come sooner?" There was no answer in the candlelit quiet. Only the rustle of her dress as she bent over the letter again, touching the lines as if they were the last warm remnant of him.

When she finally emerged from the chapel, eyes red, the pastor and Samuel both stood in respectful silence. "Did he suffer?" she asked. Samuel looked down. "He didn't scream. He spoke of God, and of you. He said he wished he had chosen love sooner." Annabelle closed her eyes, tears slipping free again. "Thank you for bringing his words," she said, voice frayed but steady. Samuel didn't know what else to do, so he tipped his hat and stepped back toward the door, leaving her holding the letter to her chest like a relic.

Once home, Annabelle folded the papers, laid them atop her chest, and closed her eyes. She pictured Karl as she last knew him—young, brilliant, stubborn—and now a man of wide scars and wider roads. That night, Annabelle knelt by her bed and prayed. Not for wealth, nor vengeance, but for clarity.

The next morning, Karla found her mother sitting at the kitchen table, the letter laid out in front of her like a relic from some earlier life. A single candle burned low, and Annabelle hadn't touched her breakfast.

"Ma?" Karla asked. She was twenty-four, built like Annabelle, with Karl's fair hair, a resolute sort of beauty born from work rather than fashion. "What's happened? Father Mark said you got a letter." Annabelle looked up, eyes red. She tried to smile but it faltered. "Sit, sweetheart." Karla sat, confused and alert.

Annabelle hesitated. For years she had kept the story simple: *Your father died in the Battle of New Orleans—a hero against the British.* It was noble, patriotic, and conveniently final. It made Karla proud, not longing. But as Annabelle touched the edge of Karl's letter, she felt the lie grow heavy. She slid the letter across the table. "Read it," she said.

Karla frowned. "What is it?"

Annabelle's voice barely held. "Your father."

Karla read in silence, eyes shining but still dry. She read the confession of love, the regret, the longing to meet her. When she reached her own name—Karla—she froze.

"He knew my name," she whispered, stunned. Annabelle forced an uneasy smile. "He learned it recently. From travelers. He was trying to come here to meet you. He never made it." Karla read on about the mines, about the meaning of treasure, and then about the treasure itself. The spike.

The map. The gold. She looked up slowly. "Mama… is this letter true?"

"He didn't have the ability to lie, at least not to me," Annabelle said softly. "And gold doesn't rot in the ground."

Karla folded the letter carefully, almost reverently. "We have to go," she said. Annabelle's head snapped up. "Go?" Her voice carried a steel Karla had never heard. "To Texas? Into Comanche country? Into border wars and lawless river bottoms?"

"He buried it there," Karla said. "He died there."

"Everyone dies in Texas," Annabelle shot back. "Rangers, farmers, traders. You think you will fare better because you have a map?"

Karla stiffened. "You said yourself gold doesn't rot in the ground."

"And neither do bones."

Silence tightened between them. "We wait," Annabelle said at last. "Ten years. Maybe more. When Texas is settled. When there are rail lines and courts and sheriffs. Not now."

Karla stared at her. "Ten years?"

"I am trying to keep you alive."

"You're trying to keep me small."

Annabelle flinched as if struck.

"That gold is his," Karla continued, voice shaking. "He buried it with his own hands. He marked the tree. He meant it for us."

"He meant for you to live," Annabelle snapped. "Not to chase ghosts across a battlefield he never escaped."

Karla stood so abruptly her chair scraped the floor. "It's not just the gold."

"Then what is it?" Annabelle demanded.

Karla's face trembled. "Roots."

Annabelle's expression softened for a fraction of a second, then hardened again. "You have roots. You have me."

"That's only half," Karla said, her voice breaking despite her effort to keep it steady. "Everyone else knows where they come from. They have stories and names and graves to visit. I have a lie about New Orleans and a folded letter."

Annabelle's breath caught.

"You told me he died a hero," Karla went on. "You let me stand in church and be proud of a story that wasn't mine. You stole the truth from me."

"I protected you!" Annabelle's voice rose for the first time. "You were born out of wedlock in a city that devours girls for less. I gave you a name that would not shame you."

"I never felt shame," Karla said quietly. "I feel robbed."

The word landed heavier than shouting.

Annabelle's hands began to shake. "You think I wasn't robbed?" she whispered. "I lost him once. I buried him in my mind because I had to survive. And now you want to walk into the same wilderness that took him from me?" Her composure cracked. "I cannot lose you too."

For a moment neither spoke. Karla's anger faltered at the sight of her mother's fear, but it did not disappear. "You didn't lose him to Texas," Karla said more gently. "You lost him because he never made it home."

Annabelle closed her eyes. The truth cut clean.

"He wrote that love is more important than gold," Karla continued, softer now. "He died believing it. If we find it, we'll prove him right. We'll use it for something good. Something that would have made him proud."

Annabelle shook her head slowly. "Understanding him will not bring him back."

"No," Karla said. "But it might make me whole."

The room went very still. Annabelle was not convinced. The thought of losing her daughter was too much. She reached for the map. Then, with sudden resolve, she carried it to the stove. Karla's eyes widened. "Mama —"

The corner of the map caught flame. Annabelle watched the paper curl into ash.

"Enough," she said hoarsely.

Karla stood frozen, fury and disbelief flooding her face. When the last ember died, Annabelle turned back, exhausted but unyielding. "I made a copy. It's locked away. And it will stay there until I am certain Texas will not swallow you."

Karla said nothing.

Later that night, after Annabelle's breathing had steadied in sleep, Karla rose silently. She retrieved her notebook from beneath her mattress and, by candlelight, began to redraw the rivers from memory. Leon. Lampasas. San Gabriel. She sketched the oak and marked it with a small iron spike. Her hand did not tremble.

If her mother meant to protect her, Karla would not fight that love. But she would not surrender her father a second time.

Months passed. Time marched at its usual indifferent pace, altered only by the expectations of those watching it. Karla was watching it, pleading with the stars that Texas would soon be safe.

In the meantime, the girl got busy gathering information.

Almost immediately, she was haunting the docks where keelboats and steamers arrived from the west. She asked flatboat men about Texas rivers, surveyors about boundary lines, traders about Comanche country. She listened twice as much as she spoke, learning that men loosened their tongues faster around a pretty woman who pretended ignorance.

Annabelle watched all this with tightening worry.

"Karla, child, Mexico and Texas are nothing like here," she cautioned as they crossed the market one morning. "Maps are unfinished. Trails vanish. Men vanish."

Karla folded her arms. "Then we learn how to avoid vanishing."

She bought an atlas of North America from a bookseller on Olive Street. She acquired a French map of the *Provincia de Texas* printed before the Revolution. She traced river systems with her finger at night: the Brazos, the Colorado, the Trinity, the San Gabriel. She compared Spanish names to American names. She searched for places where *three rivers meet*.

Annabelle hovered in the doorway some nights, pretending to sew. "You're sure it was Texas and not Louisiana?" she asked once—quiet, hopeful. "His letter mentioned three rivers," Karla replied without looking up. "The Leon, the Lampasas, and the San Gabriel. That puts them in the Texas frontier, not Louisiana." Annabelle sighed. Karla kept studying.

She began asking questions of anyone who would give her a moment: U.S. Army quartermasters who spoke of their years in the Mexican War as though describing a nightmare; Cherokee and Osage families pushed westward by the slow violence of expansion; and German immigrants who had relatives in New Braunfels.

Karla took it all in—scribbling notes, drawing rough maps—until the river landings of St. Louis felt like a crossroads of the Texas frontier. She kept a small notebook with dates, names, river crossings, and Comanche trails. Annabelle found it once on the table. It read: *San Gabriel River? ... Lipan + Comanche raids through the 1830s-40s ... Note: oak trees common in bottomland ... Ask about spike in trees—perhaps surveyors or scouts do this?* Annabelle closed the book slowly, feeling both pride and fear.

Slowly, Annabelle's opposition softened, though her concern remained. She still fretted when Karla spoke with hunters near the barracks, still scowled when she pored over Spanish land grants at the courthouse, still paced when she interviewed a former Texas Ranger passing through town.

But she no longer tried to stop her. One night, as Karla studied an atlas, Annabelle came to her and said, "When the time comes, we will go to Texas together. Something in my soul needs to see it too."

Karla closed the atlas, stepped outside, and looked up at the night sky over the Mississippi. The riverboats groaned against the current as night settled over St. Louis. Her father had left her no house, no land, no certainty. Only a letter, a map remembered, and a name to reclaim.

Karla decided it would have to be enough.

Chapter 32

Annabelle watched Karla study river charts and Spanish dictionaries late into the night. Karl had once crossed half a continent chasing fortune. Now their daughter was preparing to renew the chase in his name.

"It seems your father has given us a journey, even in death," Annabelle whispered to Karla one evening.

The years passed—not in idleness or forgetfulness, but in preparation. Texas did not become safer overnight. Safety was a process. A long process.

When Texas became the twenty-seventh state in 1845, the news reached St. Louis by steamer and rumor at the same time. In 1846, the United States marched south, and war bloomed along the Rio Grande. Steamboats on the Mississippi carried soldiers instead of cotton, and St. Louis spoke in anxious tones about places most had never seen—Matamoros, Monterrey, Buena Vista.

Karla and Annabelle waited. Karla continued to gather information. She read newspapers, interviewed veterans returning from the front, traced supply lines on hand-drawn charts.

The Mexican-American War dragged on. The frontier remained chaos. Comanche and Kiowa war parties roamed the plains while chains of forts rose along the Brazos and Colorado, uneasily biting into contested land. German settlers arrived in waves, founding New Braunfels and Fredericksburg, pushing the frontier west with stubborn optimism.

Another year passed. Then two more.

Annabelle never remarried. She had no interest. Karla had suitors—many of them—but none could compete with a ghost buried under an oak tree in Texas, so they were quietly turned aside.

By 1849, exactly ten years since Karl's letter arrived, Texas began to change. Rangers patrolled the central corridor. Stage routes connected San Antonio to the coast. Traders reported that the San Gabriel country, once Comanche heartland, was seeing farms, missions, and even surveying parties.

One chilly evening, Karla unrolled a new map on the dining table. The map had been printed in New York, fresh from the presses, showing county lines instead of blank wilderness. "Mama," she said, voice trembling with certainty, "the time has come." Annabelle stared a long while at the map, tracing with her eyes the rivers and the roads that did not exist ten years before. She then retrieved Karl's letter to pack with the maps.

Mother and daughter did not travel alone. Annabelle hired experienced river men to help navigate the lower Mississippi and a teamster to manage supplies. They boarded a steamer at the St. Louis levee, passing the cathedral where Karl's last letter had been delivered. Annabelle touched the rosary around her neck and whispered a prayer, not for treasure, but for answers. The steamer carried them south through Memphis, Vicksburg, Natchez. Karla stood at the rail each dawn watching fog lift from the riverbanks, wondering if Karl had done the same decades earlier as a young privateer on Lafitte's schooners.

In New Orleans, Annabelle's breath caught. Time folded over itself. The Governor's Hall, Jackson Square, the docks—it was all still there, only older, more American, less French. The memories felt like they belonged to another lifetime and yesterday all at once.

"Mama," Karla murmured, seeing her mother tremble, "we won't be here long."

"It's all right," Annabelle replied, steadying herself. "Ghosts cannot harm us."

From New Orleans they took a coastal schooner to Indianola, then hired wagons inland to San Antonio. The land was harsh but not lawless as it once had been. German farmers plowed fields where Comanche war camps once stood. Army forts dotted the frontier. Survey markers lined the roads.

Karla studied every river crossing. "The San Gabriel," she whispered when she finally saw the name on a stage route map. Annabelle closed her eyes. "We're close."

The search for gold lasted far longer than Karla had anticipated. At first there was a feverish optimism, sparked by new horses, new guides, new maps sketched from memory and rumor.

Soon enough, the reality of the passing of time emerged. Men in Holland recalled the old oak differently now. Some swore the tree stood near a bend of the creek. Others remembered a field whose boundaries had shifted with time and cultivation. Every detail contradicted another. Landmarks once obvious had long since fallen, burned, been fenced, or plowed under. The land itself had changed more than the stories that clung to it.

They found trees struck by lightning and trees bent by wind. They found cedars twisted like augers. They found elm and oak stripped by harsh winters. They never found an iron spike rusted into a tree trunk. They never found the tree.

With each passing week the search party grew thinner. Men who had joined for adventure or profit drifted home when enthusiasm gave way to sore backs, meager camp rations, and the creeping suspicion that perhaps none of it had ever existed except in the imagination of a desperate girl and her mother. By the third month, even Karla began to wonder.

One night beside a dying fire, after the others had withdrawn to bedrolls, she turned to her mother and said quietly, "What if it was all a sham? What if there was no gold, no arrow, no tree. Just a story to keep you chasing him forever?" Annabelle stared into the coals for a long moment before answering. "It wasn't a sham."

"How do you know?" Karla asked. Annabelle tipped her head back and looked at the clear, bright sky full of stars. The same stars Karl had once named for her in the courtyard at the convent before the war. When she spoke, her voice was steady. "Because Karl was many things— reckless, stubborn, sometimes foolish—but he did not lie to me. Not once. And because a man inventing a sham doesn't take an arrow to the leg and vanish into a life he never wanted. He would have come back boasting with gold in his pockets. Instead he left his heart with me and paid for it with sorrow." She turned back to Karla. "That is how I know."

Karla said nothing after that. But the next morning she saddled her horse without argument and they continued on. The results remained unchanged. They did not find the spike. Without the spike, there was no gold. As autumn bled across the prairie, weariness hardened into exasperation. The remaining men muttered openly now, about wasted weeks, false tales, and how fools' errands were for younger backs. Even Karla began to ride in silence, eyes searching more from stubbornness than hope.

On the final afternoon, as they prepared to break camp for the long journey back to St. Louis, Karla spotted something half-buried beneath a tangle of grass and leaf rot. It was small, weathered, and largely hidden. She pointed it out to her mother.

Annabelle dug on both knees through the hard Texas soil with the back of her sleeve. She paused, rubbing the dirt between her fingers, wondering, not for the first time, if happy memories had tricked her into chasing something that never meant to be found. St. Louis felt far away. So did youth. So did Karl.

She scraped again, slower now, as if giving destiny one last chance to make amends. Something began to emerge from the dirt, which was packed hard, as if someone long ago had knelt here. It was a hard shape smaller than her hand. Annabelle cleared around it until wood showed through the grime. Then wings. Then a curved neck.

A tiny wooden swan surfaced from the earth, crude in form yet unmistakably carved with care. The wood had darkened in the soil, the edges softened, but the swan endured. Annabelle froze. The world seemed to shrink around that small shape in her palm, its pale wings trembling like they remembered the chilly dockside dawn.

Mama's swan.

In an instant she was back in New Orleans. Karl was pressing it toward her, voice low, asking nothing except that she take this piece of him. She had left it behind. She had left *him* behind. And now here it was, risen from the dirt like a stubborn preacher reminding her that true love never dies.

For a long moment she simply stared, unable to move, unsure whether to laugh or cry. Her hand closed around it tightly, as if she feared that even now it might slip away. Joy burst through her. She realized she had found the treasure at last.

"Karla," she called, her voice unsteady. Karla turned her horse and rode closer, boots knocking against the stirrups. "What now? Another button?" she asked, clearly expecting nothing of value.

Annabelle opened her hand. Karla leaned forward, squinting. "That's it? A bird?" She frowned. "Looks homemade. And ugly too." Annabelle couldn't help but laugh, a wild little sound. "Yes," she said. "Ugly."

Karla rolled her eyes and tugged her reins. "Well, if that's treasure, may the prairie bless us with crates of it," she said, already losing interest as she nudged her horse ahead to rejoin the party.

Annabelle stayed where she was for a moment longer, holding the world in her palm. Ugly, yes. But it was Karl's. And it had waited. She slipped it inside her coat, close to her breast, so that the little swan could whisper its old truth. Love is the answer.

Annabelle and Karla retraced their path on the way home, spending two nights in New Orleans before heading north. The city greeted them with noise and color, music spilling from doorways and spice thick in the air. Annabelle discarded any unease she felt, focusing instead on creating new memories with her daughter.

On the second night, as they meandered in the Quarter near the riverfront, a commotion erupted in the street ahead. Voices rose as the crowd scattered. A flatboat crew had lost control of a loaded cart on the incline, barrels breaking loose and rolling toward the market stalls. Before she could react, a barrel struck Karla's hip and hurled her hard against the stones.

A man reached Karla before Annabelle could. He hauled the barrel aside with a curse, knelt, and caught Karla as she tried to rise too quickly. His grip was steady, practiced, as if he were used to damage. "Easy," he said. "You'll crack something if you stand too fast."

Their eyes met. And held. Annabelle saw it at once. Not attraction exactly. Admiration. The dangerous kind. The sort that rearranges the future without asking permission.

The gentleman insisted Karla be seen by a physician and escorted her there. The doctor declared Karla to be bruised but unbroken. As a precaution, the doctor recommended Karla stay in New Orleans. He would see her again in a week to determine if she was fit for travel.

Benjamin Renaud, Karla's rescuer, spoke with the soft authority of someone accustomed to docks and labor, to men who listened because they had to. He knew the city's edges, its safe alleys and its worst corners. He reminded Annabelle of someone, though she kept that thought to herself. By the third day, Benjamin had attached himself to the company of Karla and Annabelle with the quiet inevitability of someone meant to remain.

Within the week Karla and Benjamin were inseparable. They would slip away at dusk, sharing laughter that startled even themselves. Their bond carried urgency, sharpened by the knowledge that Karla's time in New Orleans was passing.

One evening, as the city cooled and the river smell crept back into the streets, Benjamin asked Karla about Texas. Not idly. Not as something to fill the quiet. He waited until Annabelle had stepped inside to speak with the innkeeper, then leaned against the low brick wall and said, "You came a long way," he said. "Most people don't do that without a reason."

Karla hesitated, then gave him the truth. Her father, the man she never met. The letter. The maps. The spike in the tree. The buried treasure. The hope, half foolish and half stubborn, that something of value had been left behind and might yet be claimed. She spoke of dust and distance, of men who believed just enough to keep going, and of how the hunt itself had become a kind of answer, even when the prize remained unclaimed.

Benjamin listened without interruption. He did not smile at the absurdity of it, nor ask the question she had come to expect—*Did you truly believe it was there?* He kept his eyes steady, as though treasure hunts were simply another way people tried to make sense of their lives.

"I've heard the same talk here," he said at last. "Buried gold down in Barataria. Spanish coin, old chests swallowed by mud and palmetto. Men spend their lives digging for it." He shrugged lightly. "I never went looking. Figured some things are worth more as stories."

Karla looked at him. She certainly had a story to tell.

Benjamin met her gaze and added, almost offhandedly, "Besides, maybe you found your treasure here, not in Texas." She laughed once, caught off guard. "And where is that treasure?"

Benjamin smiled, not in a teasing way, but with certainty. "Standing here, talking to you."

Karla laughed heartily but said nothing. Still, she recognized there was something about this man that had her thinking he may be right. Annabelle returned in time to catch Karla's laugh and saw the light in her daughter's face. Annabelle felt a familiar stirring, unsure whether Karla should be this comfortable with a man she just met.

A few days passed and the doctor cleared Karla for travel, despite the fact that secretly Karla was hoping for her stay to be extended.

Benjamin wanted to leave with them when they turned north. He could not. There was unfinished business in the city. Benjamin did not soften it with excuses. He did not dress it in romance or tragedy. He simply said there was work owed, an obligation entered into before he met her, and that walking away would not merely stain his reputation but invite consequences.

"What sort of consequences?" Annabelle asked, too quickly. Benjamin's gaze shifted to Annabelle. For the first time since they'd known him, something shuttered behind his expression. "The sort that follow a man," he replied evenly. "And sometimes reach those beside him."

Karla waved it off with a small shake of her head. "You make it sound like you've angered pirates." A faint smile tugged at his mouth, but it did not warm his eyes. "New Orleans has its own varieties." He explained only what he could. He had entered into an agreement that involved moving cargo. Names had been signed, but the venture had not yet settled its accounts. Until it did, he was bound. If he disappeared north without settling what was owed, men would notice. Men who did not forget.

Annabelle felt the air shift. As always, in New Orleans, debts were rarely simple. They tangled with river contracts, warehouse ledgers, gambling tables, and darker trades that never appeared on paper. Annabelle knew that "unfinished business" could mean anything from unpaid wages to something that required silence rather than settlement.

"And if it cannot be finished?" Annabelle pressed.

"It will be," he said, not boastfully, simply as fact.

He turned back to Karla then, and whatever steel had entered his voice dissolved. "St. Louis," he said, placing the name between them as if it were a promise written in ink. "As soon as I am free." Karla believed him instantly. She saw integrity in a man determined to settle his affairs rather than flee them. To her, it was proof of character.

Annabelle did not know what to believe. She saw uncertainty framed by risk. Benjamin appeared to be a man accustomed to walking near shadows without flinching. Yet, when he took Karla's hands in his, there was nothing counterfeit in the tenderness. That, perhaps, troubled Annabelle most of all. Devotion, she knew, did not always cancel danger. Sometimes it sharpened it. Karla was a grown woman, though the search for Karl's treasure had stunted her romantic life. Annabelle recognized, as all parents must, that her daughter was free to make her own choices.

Benjamin and Karla parted on the same pier where Annabelle had last seen Karl. Annabelle tried to hide in the shadows, uneasy with the promises made and the ache of interrupted love. She thought of Karl and the consequences of choices made too quickly and paid for too long. She pulled the wooden swan from her pocket and prayed for peace.

Winter was closing in by the time Annabelle and Karla reached St. Louis. Annabelle unpacked Karl's letter first to ensure it was returned to a safe place. She noticed that it had softened during the trip from handling.

The townsfolk who had whispered and scoffed at their departure now whispered differently, curious whether the women had returned wealthy or broken. They received their answer soon enough when Annabelle sold her remaining jewelry and Karla found work typing ledgers in a warehouse office near the riverfront.

For a time, Karla moved through the world as if half awake. She was resentful, embarrassed, occasionally bitter. Part of the embarrassment stemmed from the failed search, part from the thought that she had fallen for a man she may never see again. Karla would catch Annabelle studying the little wooden swan where she kept Karl's letter and turn away in frustration.

One evening, unable to hold back her disappointment any longer, Karla said, "You wanted to find the gold more than anyone. Why aren't you angry?" Annabelle set aside her mending and folded her hands in her lap. "Because I did find what I was looking for," she said.

Karla frowned. "We found nothing."

Annabelle reached for the swan on the table. The carving was crude, its wings uneven, its neck too thick. Karla thought the swan to be a worthless oddity, but she could not remember a time when her mother had not guarded it like something sacred. "This belonged to Karl," Annabelle said quietly. "It was his mother's before him. I know that he wanted me to have it. That he wanted you to have it. The swan proves he had a family once, and he loved them. When we found it in the prairie, do you know what that meant?"

Karla hesitated. "That he passed that way?"

"That he remembered," Annabelle corrected. "That he loved us and that he carried love through war and mountains and mines and fever. That a man can lose his country, his health, his fortune—yet still save a piece of his heart for someone else. Maybe this swan is not worth a single coin but it's worth life itself to me."

Karla's expression faltered. "We came back empty-handed."

"Empty pockets," Annabelle said, smoothing her daughter's hair. "But not empty-hearted. Karl thought gold might save him, but he was wrong. It's love that saves. Always."

Karla lowered her gaze. "Then why did we search at all?"

"Because you needed to know him," Annabelle answered. "Not as a legend or a letter, but as a man who left tokens of love in the world. This is your treasure, too, even if you don't see it yet. Your father called it an inheritance of the heart."

For years, Karla struggled to understand why the swan mattered. It had no value that could be spent or weighed. Perhaps the true inheritance had been the search itself. She didn't have him and she didn't have his treasure, but she had chased what he had left for her. In that manner, maybe she had not come home empty-handed. It was not the fairy-tale ending of which a girl dreams, but it was the only one the universe was willing to give.

Karla's consolation came with the thought that maybe her treasure would arrive in the form of Benjamin. He was real, not a wooden artifact from the past. At first, Benjamin's letters came regularly, written in a firm hand that steadied Karla each time she broke the seal. He spoke of progress, of contracts closing, of obligations nearly settled. Each letter ended the same way: *Soon.*

The letters thinned. Then they stopped. Weeks passed. Then another month. The river froze solid enough for wagons to dare its crossing. Karla began watching the post road in the mornings, pretending it was habit rather than hope. She defended him even though Annabelle never accused.

"He said he would come," Karla pronounced regularly. Annabelle said nothing. She too had once made a promise she was unable to keep. She knew circumstance could erode promises. People could disappear into new lives that held more convenience than the old ones.

By February, Karla stopped speaking of dates. By March, she stopped reading his old letters aloud. Spring came hesitantly, thawing the river inch by inch.

Finally, a figure of a man appeared on the north road. At first Karla did not recognize him. The set of the shoulders was wrong. His stride was slower, marked by a slight limp. The man she had known in New Orleans had carried himself like someone certain of his direction. This one walked as if each mile had been argued with.

Her breath caught. For one suspended instant, disbelief held her still. She had told everyone he would come. She had defended him when letters stopped. She had lain awake imagining excuses for him and then hating herself for inventing them.

The figure came closer. Stiff. Thinner. Weather-worn. Her heart shifted to terror. What if he had survived something that had changed him beyond recognition? What if she had loved a version of him that no longer existed? Karla tried not to think. She crossed the distance in a rush, boots slipping in the mud. When she reached him, Benjamin removed his hat. The scar on his temple caught the sunlight.

He whispered, "I said I would come."

She playfully struck his chest once with her fist before gripping his coat in both hands. "You stopped writing," she said. "I thought—" Her voice failed.

Benjamin caught her wrists gently, as though afraid she might shatter. Up close she could see the bruising beneath his eyes. She traced the thin white line at his temple with trembling fingers.

"What did they do to you?" she whispered.

"Nothing I didn't answer for," he said.

That frightened her more than if he had said nothing at all. She searched his face, not for romance, but for proof. Proof that he had not come north out of guilt. Proof that he had not fled something worse. Proof that she was not a pleasant detour on a longer road.

"I have been acting like a fool," she breathed. "I told them you would come. I told myself you would come."

His jaw tightened, regret in his eyes for the silence he had forced her to endure.

"I said I would come," he said again, not triumphant, simply steadfast.

The certainty in it released her emotions. She pressed her forehead against his chest and wept, weeks of doubt pouring out against the coarse fabric of his coat. Benjamin held her carefully at first, as though uncertain of his right to do so. Then his arms tightened.

Annabelle remained where she stood, watching. She saw the way Karla's body softened against him. The way her emotions dissolved into relief. Whatever he had endured in New Orleans had marked him, but he had come.

Between sobs, Karla said, "Thank you for being a man of your word. You were right. I found my treasure."

After the flood of joy had passed, Annabelle found Benjamin standing alone near the woodpile, testing his bandaged hand as though measuring what strength remained in it.

"You settled your affairs?" she asked. Benjamin understood her meaning. "Yes," he said.

"That scar on your forehead," she said quietly, more of an observation than a question. "A warehouse dispute," he answered. "Men disagreed about what was owed."

"And your hand?" she asked. Benjamin paused, just long enough. "I disagreed back."

Annabelle studied him. There was no boasting in his tone. No dramatics. Only the calm of someone who had stood his ground and paid for it.

"Was it legal business?" she pressed. His gaze held hers evenly. "In New Orleans," he answered, "legality depends on who writes the ledger."

That was not a direct answer. But it was honest. And it sounded like something Karl might say. She stepped closer. "If something follows you north—"

"It won't," he said. Not sharp. Not defensive. Certain.

"And if it does?"

His jaw tightened. "Then it will find me ready."

Annabelle let the silence stretch between them. The only man she had ever loved lived close to edges and believed his resolve could outpace consequence.

"Do you love her?" she asked at last.

Benjamin did not hesitate. "Yes."

"Enough to keep danger from her door?" The faintest shadow crossed his face, maybe it was the memory of what he had endured in the Quarter. "That is why I finished what I started."

Annabelle gave a small nod. She saw then what she hoped Karla saw.

Benjamin was not innocent. He had navigated murky waters and emerged bloodied but upright. Whatever had bound him in New Orleans—smuggling venture, dock syndicate, gambling credit—he had cut it loose. At a price.

"You understand," she said, "that if harm comes to her—"

"It won't," he repeated. This time, it sounded less like confidence and more like vow.

Annabelle held his gaze another moment, then gave the smallest inclination of her head. "Then when the time comes I will stand beside you at the altar." Benjamin exhaled—barely perceptible—but real.

Annabelle never learned precisely what Benjamin had endured to free himself from New Orleans and Karla never asked, but time would reveal that whatever debts had once held him there had been settled in full.

Benjamin and Karla were married before the year turned. As promised, Annabelle stood witness, hoping New Orleans had given her daughter the miracle it had once withheld from her.

Annabelle smiled as she watched them. True love had returned to her family at last.

Only time would tell if it would prove kinder than her experience.

Chapter 33

Marriage steadied Karla. She could finally imagine a future free of treasure maps. A year later, in 1852, she bore twin sons, Jacob and Elijah—clever, loud, and endlessly curious about locomotives, weapons, and the city's new wonders. They grew up in a house that smelled of starch and ink, where Benjamin's ledgers overlapped with Karla sorting family papers at the dining table late into the evenings.

Karl's maps remained tucked inside the old family Bible, a vault for the family's most fragile hopes. Between its pages lay the weathered maps, Karl's fading letter, and a pressed sprig of prairie sage Annabelle had plucked on their last day in Texas—"for remembrance," she'd said. The wooden swan was kept near the Bible.

Karla spoke little of the journey after her sons were born. The failure lingered in family lore. The humiliation still stung when relatives whispered or when Annabelle's eyes clouded at the mention of Karl's name.

Jacob and Elijah, overhearing fragments of adult conversations, learned only that "the Texas hunt" had cost their mother much. The maps held no allure for them. If anything, the maps seemed cursed. They preferred the certainty of city streets and printed timetables to rumors of buried gold and trees that vanished into history.

The Bible stayed shut on its shelf except for Sundays and funerals. When Annabelle died in 1858, Karla placed a photograph of her between the psalms and returned the book to its place.

Years passed. Jacob and Elijah grew, enlisted, married, and had children of their own. St. Louis changed around them, now bustling with electric streetcars, telephones, towering stone churches, and a skyline that crept upward as the century marched toward the inevitable wars of men and machines.

The Bible endured all of it. As did the swan.

In the early years of the new century—1908 to be exact—one of Jacob's sons, Frederick Renaud, found himself drawn to the faded maps almost by chance. Frederick was recording the birth of his eldest son Charles when he uncovered a ribboned envelope of family records. He pulled out and held in his hands a fragile paper with spidery lines tracing creeks and hills and compass points, as well as strange notes about "the spike" and "the three rivers." All of it captured his imagination, stirring a curiosity his father and uncle had never shown.

Frederick didn't speak of it at first. He simply returned to the Bible on quiet evenings, studying the maps with a seriousness that would have startled all known relatives. Frederick sensed the maps held more than treasure. They spoke of ancestral mystery, and he had a mind that favored such things.

He treated the Bible documents like a constellation chart. The map was a star. The rivers formed a line toward some forgotten purpose. He traced the routes onto onion-skin paper, listening for echoes across the years. The swan came with the Bible as part of the inheritance. He admired the wooden figurine, not for meaning, but because he sensed it held the breath of those who carved it. The significance of the swan largely had been lost in family lore.

Frederick often wondered aloud whether younger minds might take up the search someday, not for wealth but for the solving of an old family riddle. His oldest son, Charles Renaud, took that idea to heart. Charles was not a dreamer like his father. He was methodical, analytical, and fascinated by the physical world.

When Charles enrolled at Saint Louis University in 1926, he declared geology as his course of study, an unusual choice for a city boy whose family kept books and managed warehouses. Charles could read land the way other men read language. He spoke of strata, erosion patterns, floodplains, and glacial remnants as if they were characters in a novel. When asked once by Frederick about the maps, Charles only shrugged and said: "If I ever do return to Texas, and I might, better to know how to tell a river's age from its banks than chase fairy tales blindly." Frederick smiled at that.

The old dream, the one that had challenged Annabelle and haunted Karla, did not die. It merely went to rest, waiting through wars and generations until curiosity replaced shame and science replaced rumor.

The gold, Charles Renaud was certain, still slept in Texas soil. The family no longer chased it with desperation. Now, they would approach it with scholarship. Which, perhaps, was progress of a kind.

Charles graduated from Saint Louis University in the spring of 1930 with a mind tuned to the rhythms of the earth. The world was tilting into depression, and geology, especially petroleum geology, was one of the few sciences for which companies still paid good salaries. Within a few months Charles received an offer from Standard Oil, based in Houston. By autumn, he was riding a Pullman car south, treasure maps lay pressed flat inside his satchel, like contraband waiting to be discovered.

Texas treated him well. Oil companies prized his meticulous surveys, his habit of spending evenings hunched over topographic charts, and his talent for reading landforms with only a compass and notebook. Promotion came slowly during the lean years, but steadily enough that by the late 1930s Charles had built a modest nest egg. He thought often of the maps in the Bible. He thought of Karl, of buried treasure, of his great-grandmother Karla returning to St. Louis brokenhearted. He let the thought simmer for a decade.

By 1941, Charles had saved enough to risk a venture of his own. He requested a leave of absence, packed instruments and provisions, and drove northwest, reaching the prairie near the little town of Holland, a town few beyond Bell County had heard of. What he found there startled him.

Where the confluence of the three rivers once sprawled wild and unclaimed, there now stood a large white-frame house with a deep porch and manicured lawn. A flag snapped in the wind. A polished brass sign by the gate read: Judge A.B. Lanford

Charles introduced himself, removed his hat, and chose his words with care. He did not mention pirates or arrows or maps hidden in family bibles. He said only that his people had once lived and traveled through this part of Texas, that an ancestor had left a record of valuables buried near the meeting of three rivers, and that those records had passed quietly from parent to child for generations.

He stressed that he was an engineer, not a fortune hunter, that his interest was genealogical as much as anything else. He had no intention of damaging property or making a spectacle of the matter. The judge listened without interrupting. His expression gave nothing away, save for a slight narrowing of the eyes behind wire spectacles as Charles spoke of inherited notes and old boundary descriptions.

When Charles finally reached the request, which was to excavate a modest area on the north side of the property, the judge folded his hands, considered for a moment, and then shook his head.

"Son," he said, "I will not have my property torn up over some old yarn. I've heard tales of buried Yankee gold, Spanish gold, Comanche gold. Everyone's gold but mine. If I've built atop a fortune, well, it'll just stay there. But I've no objection to you exploring the grounds so long as you don't bring in dynamite or backhoes."

It was better than nothing. Charles thought he might be able to find the old oak tree. He accepted the terms and spent a week measuring sightlines, pacing off distances, and interviewing locals. According to his great-great-grandfather's notes, the gold lay forty paces from a massive oak with a spike in it, near the confluence. But the rivers had shifted over the years, floods had rerouted channels, and the great oak, if it ever existed, was nowhere in sight.

Nevertheless, Charles's activity drew attention soon enough. Farmers idled their tractors along the fence line to stare. Children gawked from a distance. A young reporter from the *Temple Telegraph* arrived one morning with a notebook and more enthusiasm than good sense. The headline a few days later read:

ST. LOUIS GEOLOGIST IN SEARCH OF "BURIED TREASURE" ON JUDGE LANFORD'S PROPERTY

The article did nothing to help Charles's dignity, but it accomplished one unexpected thing. It stirred memories. A few days after publication, a stooped old man appeared at the judge's gate. He carried something wrapped in burlap and asked to speak with "the treasure man." The judge waved him onto the porch, and Charles followed.

The old man introduced himself as Asa Boone. He untied the burlap and revealed a single metal spike, old and blackened by heat. "Read that piece in the paper," he said. "Got to thinking about a winter back in '93. Cold one. Had to burn up a lot of seasoned oak from a clearing near here. After the logs burned, this spike was sittin' in the ash pan like some leftover bone. Odd thing was, the oak had grown around it clean. The iron must've been buried deep in the trunk. Too stout to toss, so I've been using it as a doorstop ever since."

Charles examined it. The iron was hand-forged, long and square-shanked, more akin to early 19th-century spikes than railroad spikes of later manufacture. It fit the family lore uncannily well. "I'd like to buy it," Charles said as he pulled a ten-dollar bill from his wallet. Charles thought he was overpaying for an iron spike that doubled as a doorstop.

Asa's eyebrows rose. "Ten dollars? Son, I've used that spike to keep out the northerly drafts for near fifty years. I reckon it's worth at least twenty dollars to me—if I'm to part with it at all."

Twenty dollars in 1941 was no small sum, even for an oil geologist. But treasure hunts demanded their own strange economies. "Very well," Charles said, handing Asa a twenty dollar bill.

The exchange caused another stir in town. The *Telegraph* printed a follow-up column detailing the sale of the iron spike. Young boys speculated in the streets about buried pirate gold and gunfights. Charles ignored them and returned to his surveying with renewed seriousness. The spike proved the tree had existed, and the maps gained new weight as evidence.

Now all Charles needed was time. Time to locate where the oak once stood, time to account for shifts in the rivers, time to determine whether Judge Lanford's house sat atop a forgotten fortune.

Time, as Charles would soon learn, was a complicated commodity.

For a few weeks Charles lived with the spike wrapped in oilcloth, poring over geological surveys and old military maps of Bell County. He traced meanders of the rivers as they had been in the 1840s, charted their shifts after floods, and marked likely ground where an oak of considerable age might have stood. By his calculations, the oak had stood no more than one hundred feet from the judge's porch. He sensed he was making progress.

He had begun to plot in earnest when the world shifted beneath him. December 7, 1941 arrived like a hammer blow. Pearl Harbor.

Within weeks the oil companies were contracting directly with the government. Exploration shifted to wartime priorities, and field geologists like Charles were suddenly indispensable, but not for treasure hunts. Charles locked the spike in a steamer trunk, folded his surveys away, and reported east for work tied to pipeline routing. The judge's porch and Asa Boone passed into memory.

After the war Charles returned not to Texas, but to St. Louis. His father's health was failing, jobs were steady there, and a neighbor introduced him to a bright, skeptical schoolteacher named Margaret Wilson. Charles married Margaret in '48. Charles kept his oil maps, his field journal, and the family Bible tucked into the bottom of an old cedar chest. Margaret called it "the relic box" with an indulgent smile. She never believed a word of the story.

To her, Karl was a romantic fabrication. Annabelle and Karla were tragic figures inflated by family myth. The gold was an old German tale that had crossed oceans and centuries until it found a new nest in Texas. She loved Charles, but she did not appreciate the family myth making.

Charles spoke of returning to Texas one day, especially after he heard that Judge Lanford's property was for sale. He even wrote a proposal to the Missouri Historical Society, arguing that the Karl/Annabelle maps represented a notable migration story of Germans into Mexico and Texas and warranted proper exploration. The proposal was politely declined.

Time passed. Their two children grew. Bills mounted, priorities shifted, and the cedar chest stayed shut.

On a gray April morning in 1969, just after his sixty-first birthday, Charles died quietly in his sleep. Margaret arranged the funeral beneath a bright sky and a tent trimmed with bunting, surrounded by family and friends who spoke of Charles's laugh and the stubborn vitality that had carried him through so many years. It was, by all accounts, a celebration of life. Laughter broke through the hymns. Stories were shared.

At the graveside, as the breeze tossed the canvas overhead and the pastor spoke of heavenly rest and journeys completed, Margaret made decisions that no one there could have foreseen.

When the casket lay open, she stepped forward alone. Into its dark interior she placed Asa Boone's square-shanked oak spike, an artifact of obsession and endurance alike. To the pastor she said, in a voice only he could hear, "No one else should chase echoes."

Then she reached into her coat pocket for the wooden swan. She intended to lay it next to the spike before placing the Bible in Charles's hands. In a single gesture, she hoped to end the long inheritance of rumor and restless searching. To seal the myths away with Charles and let the earth finish what time had begun.

The swan lay heavy in her palm, weighted with a century of memories. Her fingers would not open. For a moment, she felt the swan resist the earth, as if it belonged somewhere above ground, still carrying its message. A gentle pressure grew in her hand, and within her soul, as if the swan were guiding her. Margaret shuddered as a whisper brushed her ear, soft as breath against skin: *It's an inheritance of the heart.* She felt it stir in her chest as if the swan had spoken. No one else heard the whisper.

Later, Margaret would claim she had simply moved too slowly to include the swan and the Bible in the casket. Her grief had thickened in the moment, and the lid had closed while her thoughts wandered. It was an explanation people accepted, because it asked nothing of them.

In truth, Margaret knew better. Her hand had not failed her. Her hand had been restrained. Something, or someone, had held her hand as gently and decisively as a promise. For an instant, it felt as though another hand lay folded over hers, unseen yet undeniable, warming her skin through the thin leather of her glove.

Margaret tried not to think about it. She came to accept that some things were meant to remain above ground in the living world. Some things were meant to be an inheritance of the heart. A wise person accepts what is meant to be.

For the rest of her life, the memory of those few seconds would return without warning, sending a tremor through her body as vivid and alive as the swan in her hand that day.

The earth took Charles. And it took the spike, one tangible thread of a century-old search.

God willing, the Bible remains in the Steinheimer family. As does the swan, still carrying the tender inheritance of the heart.

Somewhere beneath the dust of history and Texas soil, the gold still waits.

Epilogue

Today, in Texas, the three rivers still meet.

No one racing down Interstate 35 at eighty miles an hour feels the heat rising off the asphalt or sees the glints of water beyond the guardrails. No one sees the old roots, gnarled and knotted, buried deep beneath the ground, where oaks once stood and men once swore promises they meant to keep.

The humming road silences history.

The Texas Department of Transportation reports that more than one hundred thousand cars pass each day within a handful of miles of where Karl buried his treasure.

Legend says the treasure remains hidden. The gold sits, patient and unclaimed.

Drivers hurry past, chasing fortunes of their own.

Thankfully, somewhere between Hamburg and Hispaniola, New Orleans and Mexico, Texas and St. Louis—between history recorded and history lost to time—truth survives.

The opportunity to choose endures.

The courage to act persists.

Love worth all risk lives on.